# THE BODY AT ST EDMUND'S

KATE HARDY

Storm

ALSO BY KATE HARDY

**A Georgina Drake Mystery**

*The Body at Rookery Barn*

*The Body in the Ice House*

*The Body Under the Stage*

*The Body in the Lighthouse*

*The Body at the Roman Baths*

*The Body at the Vineyard*

*The Body at the Windmill*

*For Gerard, who enjoys pottering around ancient churches as much as I do, and with special thanks to Phil.*

ONE

'Thanks for having Bert, Sybbie. I shouldn't be too long,' Georgina promised, smiling at her friend. 'I'm meeting the new vicar, taking a few background photos of the church, and doing some headshots of Liam Jacobs, the expert from a Norwich firm who's going to repair the stained glass. Then, hopefully, I can take some shots of the glass roundels themselves once he's taken them down.'

'No problem. You know Max and Jet love playing with him,' Sybbie said, making a fuss of Georgina's liver-and-white springer spaniel.

Georgina was grateful that her friend was kind enough not to mention the real reason she didn't want to leave Bert unsupervised: during a recent murder case, her dog had accidentally eaten some poisoned food. The vet had stepped in and saved him, but the incident had left Georgina a touch anxious about her dog when he wasn't by her side.

'I'll see you soon, Bert,' she promised. 'You can't come with me today because I'm not sure how welcome you'd be in the church.'

'Get Walter and Kathleen Reeves on your side, and you'll be fine – Walter's the one who manages the church, but Kathleen's the one who manages Walter,' Sybbie advised.

'Walter and Kathleen Reeves?' Georgina asked.

'Walter is the senior churchwarden – has been for decades – and he's a very big part of the Parochial Church Council as he's also the treasurer,' Sybbie explained. 'His wife, Kathleen, sorts the coffee and tea after services, and does the rota for the flower arrangers. They've just celebrated their golden wedding anniversary.'

Of course Sybbie Walters – Lady Wyatt of Little Wenborough Manor – knew exactly who was who in the village. Georgina had only moved here a few years ago, so although she was making friends in the area, she was grateful for Sybbie's insider knowledge. 'Bernard's on the PCC as well,' Sybbie added. Bernard was Sybbie's husband. 'And Kathleen sometimes asks if she can raid my garden for the church flowers.'

The gardens at Little Wenborough Manor were open every Sunday during spring and summer, including Sybbie's famed National Collection of azaleas. Georgina wasn't surprised that the church flower arrangers asked for flowers from Sybbie's garden.

'Thanks again, Sybbie,' Georgina said. 'I owe you lunch.'

'No, you don't – it's what friends are for. But I agree, we should have a lunch date, maybe in Holt,' Sybbie said with a wicked grin.

Holt was a beautiful Georgian town about half an hour's drive away; Sybbie loved the place for the antique shops, particularly if she had the chance to add to her collection of vintage Staffordshire pottery spaniels, and Georgina couldn't resist the art galleries. Both of them enjoyed the tea shops. 'Bernard will murder me if I let you loose in a certain shop,' Georgina warned.

'Don't worry. I'll buy him a map or something to distract him,' Sybbie said airily.

Georgina chuckled. 'Check your diary for good dates, and I'll see you soon,' she promised.

After making a last fuss of Bert, she headed for the village's thirteenth-century flint-built church, where she was due to meet stained-glass restorer Liam Jacobs. He was removing two of the medieval panels from the church windows for restoration. One was a roundel depicting the martyrdom of St Edmund, the saint to whom the church was dedicated, and the other was a slightly later piece depicting a centaur playing a viol with a dog running round his feet. Some of the leadwork around the glass had started to crumble, and Liam was going to remove the leading, clean the glass, restore any damaged sections and then replace the leading to make the window watertight again.

Georgina had been asked by a specialist heritage magazine to take photographs and do a profile of him; apparently Liam was a rising star in the world of glass restoration, and she was looking forward both to her task and to the chance to learn more about the glass in the church.

The weather was a perfect spring day, with a bright blue sky; new leaves were sprouting from the trees, and spring bulbs were blooming in the village gardens. The churchyard was full of daffodils, their heads nodding in the breeze.

Before her meeting in the church, Georgina went to visit Doris Beauchamp's grave – the eighteen-year-old girl who'd died more than half a century before at Rookery Farm, Georgina's home, after falling down the stairs. Doris's younger brother, Jack, kept the grave looking bright with pink silk roses; her former boyfriend, Harrison, had paid the local florist to place fresh pink carnations, Doris's favourites, on the fourteenth of every month. Since Harrison's death, Georgina had taken fresh flowers to Doris's grave. Today it was the first of the pink tulips from her garden.

'I love that you bring me flowers. And those tulips are gorgeous. Thank you,' Doris said in her ear.

Georgina had got used to the ghost in her house talking to her through her hearing aids, since the very first day they'd 'met' when she'd discovered a dead body in her holiday cottage. They'd become friends, and Doris had helped her solve several mysteries from the past, bringing peace to those who couldn't rest. She'd comforted Doris when things were difficult for her, and Doris had helped Georgina through some tough times, too. It was an unlikely friendship, and it had put a bit of a strain on her relationship with her partner, DI Colin Bradshaw – a staunch disbeliever in ghosts – but it was one that Georgina had come to treasure. And at least at Doris's grave she could talk openly to her friend without people questioning her sanity. 'My pleasure,' Georgina said softly.

'It's a perfect Monday morning. The churchyard looks lovely right now. Very Wordsworth,' Doris commented.

'I loathe that poem,' Georgina said. 'Apart from anything else, the credit ought to go to his sister. Give me Shakespeare any day. That bit from *The Winter's Tale* where Perdita talks about flowers to Florizel – "Daffodils,/That come before the swallow dares, and take/The winds of March with beauty…".'

'That's lovelier than Wordsworth,' Doris agreed. 'Though I really don't like that play. I still don't get how Hermione could forgive Leontes for what he did.'

'Love conquers all, I guess,' Georgina said. 'Though I'm with you on Leontes. I can't warm to that play. I'm glad that Stephen never played him. But some of the imagery, especially in Bohemia, is gorgeous.' She finished arranging the tulips, thinking about her late husband. He had been a noted Shakespearean actor and direc-tor, and it was the pain of missing him so much in London after he'd died from a heart attack that had persuaded Georgina to move to Norfolk three years ago.

'I'd better let you get to your meeting,' Doris said.

'Speak soon,' Georgina said, and pressed her fingertips against the gravestone.

She walked down the gravel path to the south porch. The floor was made from alternating square red and black tiles, laid on the diagonal to look like diamonds, and there was a wooden bench on each side with their ends carved into 'poppyheads'. A noticeboard giving services' times and dates was pinned to it, along with other notices about Sunday school, coffee mornings and how to contact the vicar. The oak door had ancient iron strap hinges shaped like the boughs of an oak tree, with smaller branches and oak leaves coming off it – representing the oak tree that St Edmund, the church's patron saint, had allegedly been tied to by Danish raiders before they shot him with arrows – and the door handle had a circular ring plate made from oak leaves.

Georgina turned the handle and stepped inside. The church itself was beautifully light, with whitewashed walls, open benches with carved ends, and a glorious hammer beam roof complete with angels and the most beautiful fan vaulting. But most striking of all was the atmosphere; the emotional blend of warmth, love and stillness that she associated with medieval churches. One of her secret pleasures was visiting ancient churches on quiet afternoons and photographing the glass, the carvings or the wall paintings. Although the only church services she attended were weddings, christenings and funerals and she wasn't part of the congregation here, she loved the architecture.

There was a large, sturdy stepladder standing next to one of the windows – the one with the panels of glass that were going to be removed and restored – and an equally sturdy table was placed next to it, with what looked like packaging materials set out ready to protect the glass in transit. Georgina could hear the hum of a conversation. Although her hearing aids were good, she sometimes still had trouble working out the direction of sound. A quick glance showed her that there was an open doorway at the back of the church. She discovered that it led to a covered walkway going to the church hall, a modern room that also contained a small kitchen area. Tables and chairs were stacked neatly at one end, and there was a bookcase and a toy box. Four people were congregated around the countertop by the kettle: a man in his late thirties wearing a black shirt with a white circular collar who was obviously the vicar, a slender, dark-haired man who looked to be in his late twenties and whom Georgina assumed was the glass specialist, and two people who looked to be in their early seventies whom she assumed were Walter and Kathleen Reeves.

'Hello! You must be Mrs Drake,' the vicar said, extending a hand to shake hers. 'Welcome to St Edmund's. I'm Craig Phillipson, the vicar. Let me introduce you.' His next words confirmed her assumptions. 'Walter and Kathleen Reeves – our churchwarden and the lady in charge of the flower arrangers and refreshments – and Liam Jacobs, the glass specialist.'

'Nice to meet you,' Georgina said, shaking everyone's hand.

'The kettle's only just boiled,' Kathleen said. 'Can I get you tea or coffee?'

'Coffee would be lovely, thanks. Just milk for me, please,' Georgina said.

'I was just saying to Walter, we need to increase security in the church,' Craig told her earnestly. 'People have been seen trying the locked doors at night. It's all to do with these rumours flying around about lost treasure.'

'We do need to increase security,' Walter said, 'but it's nothing to do with lost treasure. That's just a fairy story that's never had any truth in it.'

'But, Walter, it's on the *internet*. Lots of people listen to the TreasureChest podcast. Everyone has dreams of finding lost treasure,' Craig said. 'And Russell Dawson has a solid reputation as a local historian. I had a very interesting conversation with him about the treasure.'

Walter rolled his eyes. 'People might come out here to have a look, but as soon as they realise there's nowhere to hide any treasure in the church, the word will soon spread and all the visits will die down. It's just a *story*, Craig.' His lips thinned. 'Though you're right that we need to improve our security. There's been a spate of people stealing lead from the roofs of other churches in the area.' He folded his arms. 'St Edmund's is struggling enough for funds as it is. The last thing we need is to risk having our lead stolen – there'll be a huge excess on the claim, and the insurance company will hike our premiums at the next renewal.'

'I'm sure it won't come to that, Walter,' Craig soothed.

Georgina remembered Sybbie telling her that Walter had been the PCC treasurer for years. He probably had a better grasp of the financial situation than the relatively new vicar did.

'I'm going to finish off that survey I was doing outside the church. Moss,' Walter added. 'Which will cause a great deal of expensive damage to the fabric of the building if we let it get hold. And then I'll be at home or at the allotment, if anybody needs me. Excuse me.' He banged his mug down on the table.

'Walter! You haven't finished your coffee,' Kathleen pleaded. 'And I was about to cut the cake.'

'Thank you, but I don't need cake. I need to look at that moss,' Walter said, looking cross, and stomped off.

Kathleen bit her lip. 'Sorry. He's a bit worked up today.'

'He'll calm down, Kathleen. He always does,' Craig said blithely.

The vicar probably meant well, but he came across to Georgina as a mansplainer. According to Sybbie, Kathleen and Walter had just celebrated their fiftieth wedding anniversary; Kathleen would obviously know her husband's moods rather better than anyone else did. Not wanting to make the tension worse, Georgina just gave an awkward smile.

'But I'd be delighted to have some of that cake, please. It's your famous banana bread, isn't it?' Craig asked brightly.

Did vicars not get a social skills module as part of their training? Georgina wondered. She was starting to sympathise with Walter; the vicar was definitely setting her teeth on edge.

'Yes, it is,' Kathleen said, with a patient smile that told Georgina just how often the older woman had to deal with this kind of attitude. 'Liam, can I offer you some cake?'

'That's very kind of you, Mrs Reeves,' Liam said. 'But can I check that there's no coconut in it? I'm allergic to it, unfortunately,' he explained.

'No, there's no coconut in it – no other kinds of nuts, either,' Kathleen reassured him. 'Just bananas, flour, baking powder, sunflower oil, a bit of brown sugar and some flaxseed.'

'Then thank you, I'd love some. But could I be terribly rude and eat mine later?' Liam asked. 'The builder's due here soon to make the window watertight. Mrs Drake also needs to take some photographs, and I'm running a bit behind schedule.'

'Of course,' Kathleen said. 'I'll wrap it in greaseproof for you, so it doesn't go dry.'

'And I need to get on with some admin. No rest for the wicked, haha!' Craig said jovially. 'I'll let you all get on.' He accepted his cake from Kathleen, and left the church hall.

'I'll be in the church, working on the window,' Liam said, following suit.

'Let me cut you some cake, Mrs Drake,' Kathleen said.

'Georgie, please.'

'And I'm Kathleen.' The older woman smiled.

'My friend Sybbie tells me you sometimes use her flowers. The display by the lectern is really lovely,' Georgina said.

'Thank you.' Kathleen looked pleased.

'Yes. My dog's currently playing with her two,' Georgina said with a smile, 'because I wasn't sure if he'd be allowed in the church.'

'Oh, he'd be allowed,' Kathleen said. 'I'd give you permission on Walter's behalf. We're meant to love all of God's creatures, aren't we?' The expression on her face told Georgina that maybe not everyone involved with St Edmund's would agree. 'I'm sorry that Walter was so grumpy just now. He's not usually this – well, *crusty*. His bark really is worse than his bite. Please don't take any notice.'

Georgina wondered how often Kathleen had to apologise for her husband. 'I won't. But he sounded quite upset about the roof.'

Kathleen sighed. 'He is. And it doesn't help that the church was left some money last year. He thinks the bequest should've been spent on repairing the roof, because it's leaking and causing some problems with damp and flaking plaster. But the money was left by an artist who lived in the village, who wanted the bequest to be used to restore the glass. The roundel of St Edmund is one of the oldest bits of figurative glass in the county, so it's important.' She bit her lip. 'I used to teach art, before I retired, and I dabble a bit in modern stained glass so I know how to do the leading, but obviously when something's seven centuries old, it needs looking after by an expert rather than an amateur.'

Georgina was pretty sure that Kathleen Reeves would be just as meticulous with the leadwork as someone who'd trained officially in restoration. And maybe then the money could've gone to fix something else in the church that couldn't be handled by a parishioner. But sometimes things had to be seen to be done. She took a bite of the banana bread. 'Oh, this is gorgeous, Kathleen. Could I ask you for the recipe, please?'

'Of course.' Kathleen smiled and dug in her handbag before withdrawing an A7-sized card. 'Here we are. People are always asking for the recipe for this and my choc-chip cookies, so I printed off a few and keep them with me.' She rolled her eyes. 'I really ought to be more modern and put it in my phone so I can just message or email it to people.'

'I have a box of my favourite recipes on this size of card,' Georgina said. 'This will slot in perfectly. Thank you, Kathleen.'

She walked with Kathleen back into the church. Liam was up the stepladder, starting to remove the panel from the stonework.

'Would it be OK to take some pictures of you as you're working?' she called up.

'Of course,' he said.

'And then maybe once the panels are down, I can take some close-ups, and perhaps some of you later in the week in your workshop, while you're actually working on it?' she suggested.

'That's fine,' Liam said. 'When I get down from the stepladder, we can set up an appointment. Would you like me to talk you through the process?'

'Yes, please,' Georgina said.

'Do you mind if I stay and listen?' Kathleen asked. 'I used to teach art, and I really love that centaur roundel. It's based on a design from the Ormesby Psalter, you know – named after Robert of Ormesby, who was the subprior of Norwich Cathedral in the 1330s.'

'And who owned the psalter,' Liam said. 'I looked up the history.'

Kathleen looked approving.

'I love it, too. Though I think my favourite piece of glass here is the Angel Gabriel at the top of the window to my right,' Liam continued, gesturing to the window. 'I just can't resist fifteenth-century angels. Especially when they're wearing feathery trousers like that one.'

Georgina looked at the glass. 'He's dressed just like the costume one of the players would have worn while acting in the Mystery Plays on a cart,' she said. 'I love the fact some of the feathers are gold.'

'That's from silver staining,' Liam said. 'I think it's his blue wings I like most. And all that wild curly hair. He reminds me a bit of Dominic, my partner.'

It reminded Georgina of Colin's hair when it started getting long, too; though Colin was more noted for his resemblance to Colin Firth as Mr Darcy. 'It's lovely,' she said, and took a shot of the angel. 'Can you talk me through the restoration process, so I can make some notes for the article?'

'Sure,' Liam said. 'The two roundels contain less complex shapes than some of the other glass panels here. Basically, I need to take the crumbling lead off and replace it, but I need to know how it's going to fit back in the space, so I'll do several rubbings of the glass first – a bit like a brass rubbing, putting paper on top of the glass and rubbing a crayon over it. Then I'll put tracing paper over that and draw it in pencil, so I can see exactly where the lead is. And then I'll do a line drawing showing where every individual piece of glass is cut.'

'If I was still teaching, I'd be begging you to come and talk to my A level class,' Kathleen said. 'I think they'd find that really enlightening, seeing all the stages of glass from rubbing through to the cartoon and finally the glass itself.'

'I enjoy talking to students,' Liam said. 'I've been thinking about doing some mini videos so I can show students how I do things. It'd be easier for them to see close up and also would save everyone worrying that they might accidentally knock a piece of ancient glass off the bench.' He smiled at Georgina. 'Once I've done the prep work, I remove the glass from the lead matrix. Obviously the glass is thin and fragile, so you have to be careful – but you also need to protect yourself when you remove the cement. If you're working with something that was restored in Victorian times, the cement's likely to contain red lead, which is toxic, so it's a good idea to use a mask, keep your workspace clean, and vacuum up all the dust as you go.'

'I develop my own photographs when I use an analogue camera,' Georgina said, 'and that means using toxic chemicals.' Colin had grilled her about the contents of her darkroom when she'd first met him and he'd been investigating the death of Roland Garnett. 'But I had no idea that glass restoration involved toxic chemicals, too.'

'Oh, yes. Arsenic in particular,' Liam said. 'As well as giving you white colour for the glass, it takes out the bubbles from the glass. That's one of the ways you can tell old glass from newer. The new stuff will have bubbles in it.'

Georgina felt a shiver run down her spine. The last cold case she and Doris had worked on had involved arsenic.

'Once I've got the glass out of the lead and cleaned, I might need to cut a new piece of glass to replace anything damaged,' Liam continued. 'Sometimes glass decomposes.'

'Decomposes?' Kathleen asked. 'Do you mean green glass disease?'

'Yes, but it affects other colours as well, particularly purple. I've only actually seen it myself once,' Liam said. 'The glass develops a network of fractures and it literally crumbles – the glass loses all its transparency, so no light gets through. It's sometimes called "crizzling" and it's basically caused when the glass has too much alkali and not enough calcium oxide.'

'Calcium oxide is also known as quicklime. You need it to stabilise the glass,' Kathleen said to Georgina. 'Glass is an amorphous solid. It's basically made from sand, soda ash and limestone, heated together.'

'You add metals to colour the glass,' Liam said. 'Then it's cooled to below melting point, formed into a bubble and then a cylinder, then finally cut and formed into sheets.'

'This is fascinating,' Georgina said, meaning it. 'And you two are quite a double act.'

'It's so nice talking to someone who understands what I do,' Liam said, smiling at Kathleen, who beamed at him.

'If you're interested in modern glass, you're welcome to come and have a play in my studio, Georgie,' Kathleen said. 'Obviously I don't work with old glass, like Liam, but the principle's the same. You mix the paints, add water to make it a soft paste, then add gum arabic as a binding agent, which helps the paint flow from the brush and stick to the glass.'

'Then, when you've finished painting, you fire the glass in a kiln,' Liam said. 'When it's cooled, you assemble it on a light panel to check the coloration works, particularly if you're trying to match a piece. Once you're happy, you put the lead back round the glass to clip it together. It's the same technique that's been used for centuries, using hand tools, glass and lead. You bend and manipulate the lead so it goes round the shapes.'

'Add the tallow flux, which binds the solder to the lead, and rub it over the joints,' Kathleen said. 'Then you solder the joints – though obviously nowadays we can use an electric soldering iron to melt the solder. And you definitely need to use a mask, because the fumes are toxic.'

'Finally, you put on the leaded light cement – it's a mixture of linseed oil, calcium carbonate and a blackening agent, plus some chemicals to help it dry,' Liam said. 'You brush it onto the glass panel, and it squeezes the cement between the lead cane and the painted glass, which strengthens and weatherproofs the window. Add a bit of powdered chalk to take up the excess grease and oil, leave it to cure for a day, then clean the excess cement off. Once you've done that, you can give the window a final clean and put it back in the stonework, secure it in place with lime mortar, and use copper ties to tie the window to the supporting saddle-bars here.'

'I think I've followed what you told me,' Georgina said, 'but it's all very complicated. I think I'll stick to photography!' Though it was wonderful to see two people so passionate about their craft. 'I definitely want to take some photographs during the restoration process,' she added, 'if you don't mind me coming to the studio.'

'And I'd love to see it, too,' Kathleen said.

'You're both very welcome to come to the studio,' Liam said. 'But if I can be horribly rude now, I'd like to concentrate on getting these two panels out safely.'

'We'll leave you to it,' Georgina promised. 'When can I come back to do the close-up pictures of the roundel?'

'In about an hour?' Liam suggested. 'They should be safely down by then – well, they have to be, as the builder's due to block up the window.'

'Lovely. I'll do that.' Georgina smiled. 'I can take some pictures of the outside of the church in the meantime. I won't get in your way.'

'I'll go and tidy up in the kitchen, then make a few calls in the church hall to check everyone's happy with the new flower rota,' Kathleen said. 'Give me a shout if you need anything, Liam.'

'Can I give you a hand in the kitchen, Kathleen?' Georgina asked.

'Thanks for the offer, but it's fine,' the older woman said with a smile. 'You go and take your photographs. Walter should be about in the churchyard somewhere, if you have any questions about the building. He's very good on the history.'

'All right. Thank you,' Georgina said, and left the church, closing the heavy oak door behind her.

She took some shots of the ironwork and the bench-ends in the porch, then headed out to the churchyard. Walter was nowhere in sight, so she assumed maybe he'd finished his survey and had gone home. In the meantime, she took a few shots of the church exterior.

'I'm glad you're on your own, Georgie,' Doris said, and Georgie started because she hadn't expected her friend to suddenly start speaking to her through her hearing aids. 'Because we need to talk...'

TWO

Whenever Doris wanted a chat, it usually meant that someone had contacted her, asking for help to find out what had happened to them when they died. Given that they were standing in a churchyard, there were no doubt a few people around who might be candidates for help, Georgina thought wryly.

'OK. Who are we talking about?' Georgina asked.

'Martha Plowright,' Doris said. 'Her grave's over here, on the south side of the church.'

Georgina walked through the graveyard under Doris's direction until she found the grave. Bending down, she read the inscription in the sandstone slab. 'In loving memory of Martha Plowright, beloved wife and mother, who died 15 May 1871, aged 25 years. And also of her husband Harvey Plowright, dearly loved by his family and his patients, who died 19 November 1920, aged 79 years. Reunited.' There was a carving of two hands clasped together. As with many of the older graves, there was no vase for flowers.

'She was young,' Georgina said.

'Not just Martha. Three places to the left, there's Abraham Locke,' Doris told her. 'Bram was Martha's older brother. He was the vicar here at St Edmund's until he died.'

Georgina found the grave. 'In loving memory of Abraham Locke, vicar of this parish, beloved son and brother and a friend to all who needed him, who died 13 March 1871, aged 30 years.' She paused. 'That's so sad. Only a couple of months before Martha. So who are we investigating, Bram or Martha?'

'Both, really,' Doris said. 'Though Bram first, I guess. I've been speaking to Martha. Harvey, her husband, was the local doctor, and he was also Bram's best friend. There was an outbreak of typhoid fever in the village in 1871,' she added. 'Harvey treated as many cases as he could, though obviously there weren't antibiotics back then and mortality was high. Bram, as the vicar, was duty bound to help his parishioners. He visited with food and did his best to comfort the sick.'

'And he caught typhoid and died?'

'That was what everyone thought,' Doris said. 'Except Martha. The thing is, as I said, Harvey was a doctor. He'd been studying papers and corresponding with various doctors across the country. He believed that good hygiene would help you avoid catching typhoid.'

'Which has a strong basis in fact,' Georgina agreed.

'Exactly. Despite all the patients he treated, Harvey didn't catch typhoid,' Doris confirmed. 'He told Bram how to keep himself safe when visiting typhoid victims, and Bram was meticulous about following Harvey's instructions, washing his hands with carbolic soap and being careful what he ate or drank. He should have been safe. Martha thinks there was something fishy about his death. She thought someone had poisoned him, using something that caused symptoms that would look similar to those of typhoid.'

Georgina remembered what she'd learned a few months ago about arsenic from her son, Will, who was a scientist; the symptoms of arsenic poisoning were nausea, stomach pain and watery diarrhoea, which were very similar to the symptoms of cholera and gastroenteritis. It was thought that many cases of arsenic poisoning went undetected in the early nineteenth century because the deaths were blamed on cholera or food poisoning. Was this the case here, too? But who would want to poison the vicar, and why? 'What did Harvey think?'

Doris sighed. 'Martha had recently had their first child. Obviously she wasn't getting much sleep, and Harvey thought she was just being over-fanciful because she was overtired. He believed that Bram died from typhoid.'

'This doesn't quite add up, though,' Georgina said. 'Why did Martha think that Bram had been poisoned?'

'There's this story about St Edmund's – I remember hearing it when I was at school,' Doris said. 'Apparently there used to be a tunnel running from the church to where the priory used to be. Just before Dissolution, the prior hid some of the church's treasure in the tunnel.'

Georgina's skin prickled. 'The vicar was saying earlier there's a rumour about lost treasure in St Edmund's. Apparently, there was a recent podcast episode about it. People have been seen trying the locked doors at night – obviously people who want to find the treasure.' She frowned. 'But Walter, the churchwarden, thinks it's all just a fairy story.' She paused. 'Could there be some truth in it?'

'The same rumours went around when I was a child, though nobody ever found a tunnel under the church,' Doris said. 'But Martha says Bram had been reading the diary of a former vicar and believed he'd found some clues to the location of the tunnel. She thought Bram might have been close to finding the treasure, and perhaps he'd talked to someone about it. Her theory is that someone decided they wanted the treasure for themselves and killed Bram before he could find it.'

'So it was murder disguised as death by natural causes.' Georgina paused. 'And that's why Martha can't settle and she's contacting you now? Because nobody listened to her?'

'She was hunting for her brother's killer and asking questions. She had a suspect in mind and was on her way to talk to him when she had a riding accident and died.' Doris paused. 'This is where I wish you could see me as well as hear me, because I'd do those finger quotes around the word "accident".'

'Do you think Martha was murdered, too? And by the same person who killed Bram?' Georgina asked.

'I wouldn't be surprised,' Doris said. 'Martha has unfinished business. She can't remember who it was she wanted to talk to, but I'm assuming it must have been someone who was close to Bram. I mean, you wouldn't tell just *anyone* about being hot on the trail of hidden treasure, would you?'

'Martha's husband was a doctor, so he would know about poisons and which ones caused the same symptoms as certain diseases,' Georgina said slowly. 'And he was Bram's best friend, which makes him one of the most likely people Bram would have confided in. But surely Bram's brother-in-law couldn't have been the murderer?'

'Colin always says that most murder victims know their murderers,' Doris reminded her. 'But if we're thinking Harvey might have been the murderer, that theory has a few holes. For a start, Martha wouldn't have needed to ride somewhere to talk to her husband. She could have tackled him at home. Besides, would a doctor kill a man who was his best friend and his brother-in-law over money, even if it was a substantial amount? And would he then kill his own wife, too?'

'There are cases of doctors who were serial killers, so being a medic isn't a guarantee of innocence,' Georgina said. 'We can't rule him out completely.'

'Where do we start ruling people out – or in?' Doris asked.

'We need some documentary evidence,' Georgina said. 'Obviously Bram couldn't have written anything about his own death in the parish register, and Martha died after him so he couldn't have written about her, either, but whoever took over from Bram might have written something in the margins. Some of the people who filled in the parish registers could be very chatty.'

'Where are the registers for Little Wenborough?' Doris asked.

'The older ones might be at the Records Office, and with any luck they might have been digitised. There also might be an obituary in the local paper to give us a lead. Because the deaths happened in the village, there might be something in the Manor's archives, too, so I'll ask Sybbie if she can check for us. I remember her telling me a couple of years back that the priory was supposed to have been sited on the land at Little Wenborough Manor, so there might be something in one of Bernard's maps.'

'And there's Billy the butcher. He might have something in the village history archives,' Doris said.

'I'll ask them after I've finished here,' Georgina promised. 'I'll look up that podcast, too, and see what it has to say about this alleged tunnel and the treasure. And then we can look at the evidence and see if there's anything you can use to jog Martha's memory.'

'Back on the case again. The Wenborough Detectives,' Doris said. 'Sybbie will enjoy this. Cesca, too.'

'In other words, you want an excuse to see the baby,' Georgina said with a grin. 'I'll arrange it.'

'Thank you. But it looks as if there are visitors,' Doris said. 'You'll be needed, so I'm going. We'll talk later.'

A man emerged from the white van which had just parked in the church car park, and brought out a ladder from the back. Georgina walked over to him. 'Good morning. Would I be right in guessing you're the builder who's come to help Liam with the window?'

'Yes. Alfie Payne,' he said, holding his hand out to shake hers.

'Georgina Drake. I'm a photographer,' she said, gesturing to the camera slung round her neck. 'I'm doing a piece for a heritage magazine about Liam and his current project. Would it be all right if I take some shots of you as you're blocking up the window, for background?'

'Sure,' he said with a smile. 'I'll just touch base with Liam, first.' He walked with her to the church and propped his ladder against the church porch.

But when they went inside the church, Liam wasn't on the stepladder where Georgina had expected to see him. He wasn't standing by the table he'd set up earlier, either. There was a gap in the window where presumably he'd removed the two panels, but the restorer was absent.

'Liam?' Georgina called.

There was no answer.

Frowning, she walked over towards the area where he'd been working. And then she saw him, collapsed on the floor – and he didn't appear to be breathing.

Memories hurtled through her head: the day she'd returned from a photo shoot to find her husband, Stephen, on the living room floor of their London home, his body still and lifeless. She'd been too late to save him from the heart attack. And it had taken her years to build her life back, without him.

She shook herself. That wasn't helping Liam.

It looked as if Liam had been sitting on one of the pews, eating Kathleen's banana bread, after he'd taken the stained-glass panels out safely and put them on his table. Some of the cake, still in the greaseproof paper, had dropped onto the floor. Had Liam fallen ill unexpectedly and collapsed before he could call out for help? Or – a feeling of unease prickled down her spine – was it something more sinister?

'Call nine-nine-nine,' she said urgently to Alfie, who immediately took his mobile phone from his pocket and began dialling the emergency services.

This didn't *look* like a crime scene. With a silent apology to Colin in case she was wrong and it turned out to be one, but also knowing that the preservation of life had to come first, Georgina went over to Liam, put her camera bag down by the pews and knelt beside him. He wasn't breathing, but touching his face told her that his body was still warm. His collapse had obviously been very recent, and there was a chance she could save him.

She shook his shoulder gently. 'Liam? Are you OK?'

There was no response.

Georgina remembered that when you were unconscious, your muscles relaxed and your tongue could block your airway. She tipped his head back, hoping that the movement would shift his tongue and open his airways again, but he still wasn't breathing.

She could hear Alfie in the background, clearly talking to the emergency services. 'No… hang on. Georgina, is he breathing?' he asked.

'No,' she said. 'But he's still warm, so I'm going to start CPR.' Two pushes per second, five to six centimetres deep, she remembered from the training she'd done years back, using the same rhythm as The Bee Gees's 'Stayin' Alive'. She started compressions, humming the song in her head. It would keep oxygen-rich blood flowing to vital organs until his heart started again.

Please let him respond.

*Please.*

'Hello? Who's there?' Kathleen called from the other end of the church. 'What's happened?'

'It's me, Georgina, and Alfie, the builder. Liam's collapsed. We just came in and found him lying on the floor. Alfie's on the phone to the emergency services,' Georgina explained, still pushing down hard on Liam's chest.

'I was one of the First Aiders at school before I retired,' Kathleen said, hurrying over to join them. 'Let me help. Oh, dear God, the poor young man.' She knelt down. 'Have you done any breaths, yet?'

'No,' Georgina said.

'Then I'll do it. Keep counting the compressions and we'll swap over after two minutes,' Kathleen said.

Between them, they focused on trying to resuscitate Liam.

'The ambulance is on its way. What can I do?' Alfie asked.

'Maybe see if you can get a defibrillator?' Georgina suggested. 'Is there one in the church hall, Kathleen?'

'No, but the Red Lion has one,' Kathleen said. 'It's just down the road. The white building with the thatched roof.'

'I'm on it,' Alfie said, and rushed out of the church.

Swapping over from the compressions every two minutes – by which time Georgina's wrists ached from the exertion – she and

Kathleen continued to administer CPR. It could only have been a few minutes, but it felt like hours. And still Liam wasn't breathing. It was beginning to feel hopeless.

The church door opened with a bang, and the paramedics hurried in.

'There's still no response,' Georgina said, anguished. She hadn't been in time to save Stephen, but surely she'd been in time to save Liam?

'What happened?' the lead paramedic asked, taking over the compressions while his colleague set up the defibrillator.

'I have no idea,' Georgina said. 'I came in with Alfie, the builder – he's gone to get a defibrillator from the pub down the road – and we found Liam lying on the floor.' A hazy memory swam through her head. Hadn't he said he was allergic to coconut? And Kathleen had reassured him there wasn't any coconut in the cake.

The cake Liam had clearly been eating when he'd fallen ill…

Alfie came running in with the defibrillator.

'Cheers, mate, but we're already sorted,' the paramedic said. 'All stand back, please.'

The defibrillator delivered the shock, but Liam's heart didn't fall back into its natural rhythm.

A second shock didn't work, either. Or a third.

'He said earlier that he was allergic to coconut,' Georgina said.

'So it might be anaphylaxis? Does he have an EpiPen?' the lead paramedic asked.

'Sorry, I have no idea,' Georgina said. 'But if he does, he'd keep it somewhere close, wouldn't he?'

A quick search of Liam's clothes and his work bag revealed nothing.

'Maybe it wasn't a really severe allergy, then,' the paramedic said. 'Because if you needed an EpiPen, you'd always keep it with you.'

The paramedics gave him an injection of epinephrine and

continued with CPR and shocks, but Liam's heart simply wouldn't restart.

'I'm so sorry,' the paramedic said. 'His circulation's been down for too long. I think we need to call it.' He sighed. 'I'm sorry to say that I'm confirming extinction of life.'

'It's a sudden, unexpected death, so we need to call the police,' Georgina said. At the surprised looks from Alfie and Kathleen, she added, 'My partner's a policeman, so I kind of know the drill.' And they didn't need to know that she'd been in this position several times before. 'Actually, it would make sense for me to call him now.' She took her phone from her pocket, stepped away from the others and dialled Colin's number.

'Georgie, I'm sorry but I'll have to call you back. I'm about to go into a meeting,' Colin said.

'Perhaps you can send Mo or Larissa out, then,' she said. 'I'm at St Edmund's church in Little Wenborough. There's been an unexpected death.'

'Right,' Colin said, and his tone changed completely. 'I'll get Mo to do the meeting for me. I'm on my way.'

'Thank you,' she said.

'I'll call you from the car and perhaps you can fill me in,' he said. 'When you say unexpected, are you telling me it's suspicious?'

'I'm not sure,' Georgina said carefully.

'I'll be there as soon as I can. We'll need to collect evidence if it's a crime scene. Even if it isn't suspicious, we'd still need to collect evidence for the coroner.'

'I think we might have already contaminated the area,' Georgina said quietly. 'When we tried to resuscitate him.'

'Which is completely understandable. Ask everyone to stay at the church for now, please, and we'll take statements when we get there,' Colin said. 'I'll be with you soon.' He paused. 'Are you OK, Georgie?'

He knew what had happened to Stephen, and was no doubt thinking about that now. 'Yes,' she said. 'But it's just so terribly sad.

He was so young. He was still warm when I found him.' Unlike her husband. 'I hoped I could...' Her voice broke.

'You *tried*, Georgie. And I know you. You did the best anyone could have done,' he said, his voice warm and reassuring. 'Don't blame yourself.'

'No.' Though that was easier to say and much harder to do. She felt so guilty for failing Liam. For not being able to save him. And in a church, of all places; somehow that made the death feel worse. It seemed like only a few minutes ago that Liam had been talking to her about glass and how he did his job. And now... it was all over.

'I'll see you soon,' Colin promised.

She ended the call, and texted Sybbie to let her know she'd be late picking up Bert. *Very sad incident at church. Stained glass repairer died suddenly. Couldn't save him. Colin on way. Will let you know when I'm en route.*

Sybbie's reply was almost immediate. *Sorry to hear news. Are you all right? No rush to collect Bert. I'm in all day and he's no trouble.*

Georgina texted back, *Thank you x*

'Colin – my partner – is on his way,' Georgina said, returning to Kathleen, Alfie and the paramedics. 'And although this isn't a crime scene, it *is* an unexpected death, so the coroner will be involved. We need to...' How could she put this tactfully? 'Not disturb things, as much as we can.'

'We can at least cover him up,' Kathleen said. 'And if you all come next door to the church hall, I'll make us all a cup of tea while we wait for the police. And I need to let the vicar know what's happened.' She bit her lip. 'Oh, that poor young man...'

# THREE

Colin parked next to the ambulance in the church car park at Little Wenborough, and turned to his constable, Larissa Foulkes. 'This all sounds fairly straightforward, from what Georgie told us on the way here. The stained-glass restorer collapsed unexpectedly and died. Any evidence we can gather for the coroner might be a bit compromised, but that can't be helped – trying to save a life has to come first.'

'So now we take statements, take photographs and collect any evidence,' Larissa said.

'Yes,' Colin confirmed. 'And you said Sammy Granger' – the pathologist – 'is on her way?'

Larissa nodded.

'Good.' Colin locked the car and they walked down the gravel path to the pretty flint church.

'This is a lovely spot. Especially with all those daffodils,' Larissa said.

'Yes, it is,' Colin said. He sighed. 'I just wish Georgie hadn't been involved in this.'

'It never gets any easier, finding a dead body,' Larissa agreed.

Colin twisted the heavy iron door handle, and the latch tipped up so he could open the door. There was a loud creak as the door opened.

Inside, the building was light and airy. There was a stepladder next to an open space in the window frame, where the restorer had obviously taken out a stained-glass panel.

Georgina came through a door at the opposite side of the church. 'Everyone's waiting in the church hall,' she said.

She'd obviously thought to keep everyone away from the remaining evidence, as much as possible. 'Thank you,' Colin said.

'Kathleen's suggestion,' she said. 'The vicar's here, too. Kathleen rang him to let him know what happened, and he came straight away and said a prayer over Liam's body. We covered him over out of respect, using a blanket from the ambulance.'

'All right,' Colin said. He and Larissa followed Georgina through the covered porch into the church hall. There were a couple of tables set up and the people sitting round them were all furnished with a mug of what he presumed was tea.

Georgina introduced him and Larissa to the others. The two paramedics; Alfie Payne, the builder, a muscular man with thinning hair in his early thirties; Craig Phillipson, the vicar, a slender and slightly fussy-looking man in his late thirties with a trendy haircut and a dog collar advertising his profession; and Kathleen Reeves, the volunteer in charge of the flower arrangers, a woman who looked to be in her seventies with pale grey hair tied back in a neat bun.

'Can I get you both some tea?' Kathleen asked.

'That's kind,' Colin said. 'Thank you. Just milk for both of us, and we'll take the tea however it comes.'

'Right you are,' she said, and bustled over to the kitchen area.

'We'll need to take statements from you all,' Colin said. 'If we can start with the paramedics, then we can release you back to the ambulance station. The pathologist is on her way, and she's arranged transport to the mortuary.'

The paramedics both gave identical accounts: they'd been called to a patient who'd collapsed and was unresponsive.

Georgina and Kathleen had been giving CPR to Liam when they'd arrived at the church, but he hadn't responded to it or to the shocks they'd administered with a defibrillator. 'Mrs Drake seemed to think that he was allergic to coconut, though he didn't have an EpiPen with him,' the lead paramedic said.

Georgina had mentioned that to him, too, Colin remembered. He'd double-check that. 'Do people routinely carry EpiPens if they have allergies?' he asked.

'If the allergy's severe enough to potentially give them an anaphylactic reaction, they do,' the paramedic said. 'But not all allergies are that severe.'

'Do you have any idea of the cause of death?' Colin asked.

'The most likely cause is a cardiac arrest,' the other paramedic said. 'You'd need to check with his GP to see if there were any underlying medical issues. The pathologist will have a better idea after they've done the PM.'

'Thank you both for your help,' he said. 'I'll let you go very shortly, but if you think of anything later that might be useful, however small, please get in touch.' He gave them one of his cards. 'I'll just write this up, and then if you could check it, correct any errors and sign it for me, please?'

The builder was next. Alfie confirmed that he and Georgina had walked into the church together; they'd seen the gap in the window and the stepladder where Liam had been working, but there was no sign of him until they drew closer and saw him collapsed on the floor. She'd started CPR while he rang the emergency services, and then Kathleen had come from the church hall to help with the CPR. He'd gone to fetch the defibrillator from the Red Lion, but the paramedics were already there by the time he returned.

'Do you work for the same company as Liam Jacobs?' Colin asked.

'No. I'm self-employed,' Alfie said. 'But they know my work at the studio, so I'm one of their regulars.'

'Has anyone contacted Liam's boss, do you know?'

'I haven't,' Alfie said. 'I assumed the police would be the ones to contact his work and his family.'

'That's fair,' Colin said. 'Did you know Liam well?'

'I worked with him on half a dozen jobs in the last few months, yeah,' Alfie said. 'He was a nice bloke. Always friendly and polite – one or two of them at that studio think they're a bit special because they've got a degree, you know? But not him. He'd go for a pint with you at the end of a job. Very down to earth for someone arty.'

'Do you know anything about him being allergic to anything?'

'Yeah – coconut,' Alfie said. 'He couldn't eat Thai food, because it made him ill. You know, with the coconut milk and what have you. But, weirdly, he could eat peanuts and they didn't affect him.'

'Did his colleagues know about the allergy?' Colin checked.

'Yes. If they brought a packed lunch to the studio, they knew they couldn't bring anything with coconut in it – just like my kids can't bring peanut butter sandwiches to school in their packed lunch if someone in their class is allergic to peanuts,' Alfie confirmed. 'Have you got the studio's details?'

'No,' Colin said. 'Would you have a contact name and number?'

'Bridget's the receptionist. She's all right. She'll help you.' Alfie took his phone out of his pocket and brought up the number for Colin, who scribbled it down.

'Thank you for your help,' Colin said. 'If you think of anything else that might help, however small, please get in touch.' He gave Alfie his card.

'Can I make that window watertight, now?' Alfie asked.

'Could you please hold off for another half an hour, until my constable's finished gathering evidence?' Colin asked. 'And I'll need you to read your statement, correct it if necessary and sign it, please.'

Once Alfie's statement was done, Colin called over his next witness.

Craig, the vicar, was of very little help. 'I'm afraid I wasn't here when it happened,' he said, looking around vaguely. Colin had to stop himself telling the man to pull himself together and focus. 'I met Liam here first thing this morning, of course, because he was here as soon as we'd unlocked the church, ready to start work on the window. I stayed for a cup of tea, but then I went back to the vicarage, to catch up on my admin. Kathleen called me to let me know what happened. I can't believe it. The poor man! Was it a heart attack or something?'

'I'm afraid we can't say what the cause of death was, at the moment,' Colin said. 'We're waiting for the pathologist.'

'I see.' Craig looked away. 'I don't really know what else to say. I'm still finding my feet here, you know? I've only been in the role for six weeks.'

Colin knew he ought to be sympathetic. He'd been in that position himself, not so very long ago. But he really hoped he hadn't been quite as feeble as Craig seemed to be. 'I know,' he said with what he hoped was a kind smile, because he knew if Georgina was sitting at this table, she'd nudge him and mouth at him to be nice. But he gave his standard statement-signing spiel, gave Craig his card, and got the statement signed.

Kathleen seemed to be the most useful of the witnesses. 'I met Liam here at the church this morning at quarter to nine with Walter, my husband, and Reverend Phillipson.'

'Is Walter here now?' Colin asked.

'No. He didn't stay. He went to check on the moss – there's a damp patch on the outside of the church he's worried about, and as the churchwarden he's responsible for the upkeep of the building – and he said he was going home or to his allotment afterwards. I stayed to tidy up the kitchen here and sort out the rota for the flower arrangers, plus I was hoping for a proper look at the roundels – the medieval glass Liam was taking down for restoration. I taught art, before I retired,' she explained, 'and I do a little modern stained glass.'

'Had you met Liam before?' he asked.

'The last time he came, when he did the initial survey. He

seemed a nice young man.' She blew out a breath. 'His poor family. They'll be devastated.'

'Do you know his family?' Colin asked.

'I'm afraid not,' Kathleen said. 'But I know how I'd feel if this happened to someone in my own family. Walter and I don't have children, just my nephew Aaron,' she said.

'Can you talk me through what happened, in your own words?' he asked.

'I made us all a cup of tea, and then Georgina arrived to take the photographs. We all had some banana bread with our cups of tea – well, Liam said he'd eat his later, because he wanted to get the panels down and packed safely for transport – and Georgina took photographs and talked to him about the glass.'

Colin had seen Georgina at work before and could imagine the scene. She was good at drawing people out.

'I tidied up in the kitchen and sat there working out the rotas for the church flowers until Liam was ready for us to come and see the glass. The door was open between the church hall and the church, and I didn't hear anything untoward until the main door opened – the door creaks and makes quite a racket,' she added. 'And then I heard Georgina yell out, "Call nine-nine-nine." Obviously something was wrong, so I hurried in to see if I could help.'

Kathleen confirmed everything that Alfie and the paramedics had already told him. 'Georgina was marvellous,' she added. 'And I'm not just saying that because I know she's your partner. No fuss, no bother, just got on with the CPR and did her best to save him.'

'That's Georgie,' he agreed.

'But we couldn't resuscitate him, and neither could the paramedics. That poor young man,' she said again. She paused. 'Then Georgie called you and I called the vicar. I also called the head of the glass studio, to let him know what had happened. He's sending someone out to package up the stained glass and take it back to the studio, and he'll ring Georgina to arrange a time for her to finish taking the photographs for her article.'

'The builder gave me the studio's number and suggested I

should talk to Bridget, the receptionist,' Colin said. 'Hopefully she'll be able to give me the contact details of Liam's next of kin. I'll need to see them, too.'

'I've spoken to her a couple of times and she was very helpful,' Kathleen said.

'I'm very sorry to ask,' he said, 'but I believe Liam was allergic to coconut. Is there a possibility that there was any form of coconut in your banana bread?'

She put a hand to her mouth, looking shocked. 'Oh, dear God. Is that what you think killed him? But it *couldn't* have been. He said he couldn't eat anything with coconut in, and I reassured him the banana bread was perfectly safe. I gave Georgina the recipe.' She shook her head, looking anguished. 'I don't use nuts of any kind in the cakes I make here, as a rule, because you never know if someone might be allergic. The last thing you need is the church cake stall making people ill.'

'It's a line of questioning, Mrs Reeves,' Colin said gently. 'I need to be thorough and check everything.'

'I...' She sagged back in her seat. 'There definitely wasn't any coconut in my banana bread. But if you want to take the rest of it with you, and get it tested in the lab, then I'll go and get it for you.'

'Thank you, Mrs Reeves. That might be helpful for the pathologist,' he said. But he knew from experience that food could be interfered with between the making and the eating. 'May I ask, did anyone help you make the cake?'

'No. Walter's the most terrible cook. He leaves me to it when I'm baking – well, until it's out of the oven, and then he volunteers to taste it for me.' She gave the kind of fond smile that Colin had a nasty feeling Georgina shared when she was talking about his own lack of culinary expertise.

'Thank you, Mrs Reeves,' he said again. He gave her one of his cards and said the same as he'd said to the others; she checked the statement, signed it, then fetched the tin of banana bread.

'I'll make sure you get the tin back,' he promised.

And finally he interviewed Georgina.

'Are you OK?' he asked, knowing about the tragedy that had brought her to Norfolk from London.

She nodded. 'Obviously it brought back some memories, but I'm OK.' A muscle worked in her cheek, telling him that she was far from OK but she wasn't going to make a fuss about it. 'I just wish I'd been able to do something to help poor Liam. Maybe if we'd gone into the church a couple of minutes earlier...'

'It probably wouldn't have made any difference. Right now we don't know what killed him. Sammy needs to do a PM,' he said. 'Did you eat any of the banana bread?'

'Yes. We all did – except Liam, who checked first that there wasn't any coconut in it because he's allergic to it. Kathleen gave me the recipe, and coconut isn't listed as one of the ingredients. I certainly didn't taste any coconut in it,' she said.

'You already talked me through what happened,' he said, 'but you know the drill.'

'You need a proper signed statement. OK. I'll run through everything.' She did so, waited for him to write it up, checked it, and signed the statement. 'What happens now?' she asked.

'We wait for Sammy to take Liam to the mortuary and do the PM. And I need to break the news to his family and his colleagues. Well, I gather Mrs Reeves has already done the latter.'

'She's efficient, Kathleen,' Georgina said. 'And she's kind. I like her.'

'I'm afraid I upset her, asking her if there was a possibility that there could have been any coconut in that banana bread,' Colin said. 'She was horrified to think it might have been the cause of his death, though she was adamant there wasn't any form of coconut in it.'

'I'll give her a lift home,' Georgina said, 'and reassure her that she hasn't done anything wrong.'

'She even gave me the rest of the banana bread so it can be tested in the lab to prove it didn't kill Liam,' Colin said. 'And it was her suggestion – I didn't ask.' He sighed. 'I have a feeling this was simply a tragic accident. Maybe Liam had some other medical condition that he didn't even know about.'

'Hmm,' Georgina said.

Colin frowned. 'Is there something you're not telling me?'

'Not about that poor young man. Let's just say I have a new cold case,' Georgina said. 'Which involves a tragic accident that might not have been an accident, and a case of typhoid that might not have been a case of typhoid.'

'And you think it might be linked to this?'

'Not exactly,' she said. 'It's to do with treasure from the priory that was hidden just before Dissolution, in a tunnel that allegedly led to the church. Apparently the story gains traction every so often, and just recently it was retold by a podcaster. People have been seen trying the church doors at night. Walter – Kathleen's husband – thinks that if enough people turn up here hoping to find untold riches, they'll realise there isn't a tunnel and the fuss will all die down again. The vicar, on the other hand, is fussing about it and thinks that the church needs extra security.'

'Hmm,' Colin echoed. The expression on Georgina's face told him that she shared his opinion of the vicar. 'I can't see an immediate link between treasure that may or may not exist, and a stained-glass expert who died unexpectedly.'

'I was planning to talk to Bernard and see if he has anything on one of his maps,' Georgina said.

Colin brightened. 'Well, if you need a hand, there, you know where I am.'

She patted his hand. 'I do. I'll see you later. I'm sorry you're going to have a rubbish rest of the day, having to break bad news to Liam's family.'

'It's part of the job,' Colin said with a sigh. 'I'll see you later.'

# FOUR

Georgina went in search of Kathleen, who was wiping down the tables in the church hall and looking as if she was on the verge of tears. Craig, the vicar, was sitting at one of the tables, looking helplessly at his phone and scrolling aimlessly through the screen. Oh, for pity's sake. Did the man not know how to wash up a few cups? And why wasn't he trying to comfort Kathleen instead of using his phone as a barrier to any kind of conversation? Kathleen had just tried very hard to save a man's life and failed. Of course she was distraught, which was why she'd just wiped the same table down again. She needed a hug and a chance to talk. The vicar, who obviously knew her from her role as a volunteer, shouldn't have needed any prompts from a stranger. He was about as much use as a chocolate teapot, Georgina thought crossly.

'That looks clean enough, Kathleen,' she said. 'You've had a nasty shock and you really ought to head for home. Have you called Walter to let him know what happened?'

'The allotment's in a bit of a dead zone,' Kathleen said. 'I left him a message, but he won't get it until he's back in an area with a decent signal.' Georgina knew from experience that there were pockets in Norfolk where the mobile phone reception was too poor to connect to anyone's phone.

'Let me give you a lift home,' she said.

'I can't leave – there's still all the clearing up to do,' Kathleen said, gesturing to the cups stacked by the sink. 'And the pathologist is yet to arrive, and Liam's colleague who needs to pack up the glass – I need to be here for them.'

No, she didn't. 'I'll help you with the tidying.' Georgina turned her brightest smile on the vicar. If he was too clueless to realise that he needed to step up, then she'd give him a prod. 'And I'm quite sure that Reverend Phillipson here can help the pathologist and the glass studio people,' she said.

He looked taken aback. Before he could protest, Georgina channelled her inner Sybbie. 'After all, although he has a lot of help from volunteers – which I'm quite sure he appreciates – at the end of the day he's the vicar, which means he's the one responsible for St Edmund's.' She widened her eyes at him, encouraging him to agree. 'And I'm sure he's quite capable of making a cup of tea for visitors and then washing everything up and putting it away afterwards.'

'I, um – yes, yes,' he said, with a rather sickly smile.

Georgina hadn't had much to do with the previous vicar, but she remembered him being rather more dynamic than Craig and actually mucking in with everyone else instead of drifting around aimlessly and expecting everyone else to get on with things. Maybe what Craig needed was to be thrown in at the deep end, she thought. 'Good,' she said. 'Kathleen, I'll wash, you wipe, and meanwhile Craig can stack the tables and chairs.'

'All right,' Kathleen said, biting her lip.

Once the church hall had been put back to its usual clean, orderly state, Georgina ushered Kathleen out through the church and walked her firmly towards her car. 'If you're not quite ready to go home,' she said, 'I'd be happy to make you a cup of tea in my kitchen. I would offer you a cuddle with Bert, my spaniel, but he's currently at Sybbie's. He was rather ill back in January, and I still don't like to leave him on his own.'

'I know you said earlier that you weren't sure if he'd be

welcome,' Kathleen said. 'I like dogs. There wouldn't have been a problem.' She gave a wry smile. 'Well, Walter would've asked you to please make sure he didn't mark his territory.'

'Bert's a good boy. Very well behaved,' Georgina said with a smile. 'Though he can't resist sausages.'

'I remember hearing about that whole class being laid low after eating the sausage rolls, and poor Billy's shop had to close until the investigation was done,' Kathleen said. 'And someone said your poor dog was ill because of it, too. It must have been such a worry for you.'

'It was,' Georgina admitted. 'Would you like to come and have a cup of tea with me?'

'That's terribly kind of you to offer,' Kathleen said, 'and please don't be offended, but I think I'd rather go home.'

'Of course,' Georgina said.

She followed Kathleen's directions to one of the pretty flint-and-brick cottages in the oldest part of the village, and parked outside.

'May I offer *you* a cup of tea?' Kathleen asked.

Although Georgina badly wanted to check on Bert and to talk to Sybbie about Martha Plowright, she also didn't want to abandon Kathleen. 'Thank you. That'd be lovely,' she said.

She followed Kathleen to the back door, which was locked.

'Walter's obviously gone to the allotment rather than coming straight home,' Kathleen remarked, and Georgina wasn't sure whether the other woman was more relieved or upset. Walter had seemed quite crusty, this morning, but maybe he was different with his wife. Or maybe he'd just lost patience with the vicar, which Georgina could understand because that was how she felt, too.

The kitchen-diner in the cottage was warm and cosy; the flooring was the traditional red pamment tiles found in many of the older buildings in the village, and the Shaker-style cupboards were a pale cream. There was a red jug of daffodils on the windowsill, alongside pots of herbs, and framed botanical watercolours, which Georgina guessed were by Kathleen, hung on the walls.

Kathleen made tea, and they sat down together at the scrubbed pine table.

'That poor lad. I can't get his face out of my head,' Kathleen said. 'He was far too young to die. And your partner asked me if there was any coconut in my cake.' She shook her head. 'I'll never forgive myself if my cake was responsible. But I don't see how it can be, when there wasn't any coconut in the cake. I used sunflower oil, too, not coconut oil.'

'The pathologist will have a better idea of what happened,' Georgina said. 'But I agree with you. If you didn't use coconut in the cake, how could it have affected him? I think it's more likely that Liam had some kind of medical condition that nobody knew about, including possibly himself.'

'It's been a difficult few weeks,' Kathleen said. 'My nephew, Aaron, wanted to lead the restoration project – he works at the same place as Liam, and obviously he knows the church because of Walter and me. But Liam was the new kid on the block, the star who'd been brought in from Oxford, so the project went to him and Aaron took it rather badly.' She sighed. 'Aaron's a bit... well, troubled. My younger sister Lainey – his mum – died from breast cancer, five years ago. He struggled with the last year of his degree, knowing that his mum might not live to see him graduate, and when she died he rather went off the rails. I've been trying to support him ever since.' She wrinkled her nose. 'I know I probably seem a bit old to have a nephew only in his mid-twenties, but Lainey was ten years younger than me, and she didn't have him until she was in her late thirties.'

'I'm sorry for your loss,' Georgina said.

'Lainey was lovely. She was one of those women who are like sunshine and make the world a better place just by being in it, you know?' Kathleen said. 'Her husband... well, men of my generation aren't good at emotional stuff, are they? We always said we'd do better than our parents, but we didn't. He shut himself off, and I had to step in to help poor Aaron, for Lainey's sake. It didn't help when his father decided to move away from

Norfolk because he couldn't handle all the memories in that house.'

Georgina knew how that felt. *The look of a room on returning thence*: that line from a Thomas Hardy poem had weighed heavily on her heart. Walking into a room, expecting to see Stephen there and feeling the loss all over again when he wasn't there... She'd talked things over with her children, though, before she'd put the house on the market and moved to Little Wenborough. And they'd been supportive; Will lived in Salisbury anyway, and Bea had stayed in Camden when she'd finished drama school, so neither of them had felt that their mum was ripping their home away. Clearly it hadn't been like that for poor Aaron.

'Aaron lost his mum, then he lost his home,' Kathleen said. 'His dad moved to Suffolk last year, and it's just too far for Aaron to commute to Norwich every day. He's got a house-share in the city, but I don't think he's very happy there. He's not eating properly and he's too thin.' Worry pinched her face. 'I think the only time he has a proper dinner is when he has Sunday lunch with us.'

'At least he has you to support him,' Georgina said.

'I try,' Kathleen said. 'I spoke to him about the situation the weekend before last. I said I'd try to make friends with Liam – after all, we have a love of stained glass in common. I suggested baking the banana bread to welcome Liam to St Edmund's, and I was hoping that he'd chat to me and I could persuade him to let Aaron work on the project with him. That cheered the poor boy up a bit.' She shook her head. 'And I *liked* Liam. I was pretty sure he'd listen to me. But that's not going to happen now, is it?'

'No, it's not,' Georgina said. 'It's a difficult situation all round.'

'It's just been one thing after another, lately,' Kathleen said. 'I'm worried about Walter, too. The church has felt like a big burden on him over the last few months because of the finances – it's set off his angina to the point where he's actually needed to use his GTN spray, which he only has to do if it's really bad. And the new vicar, bless him, seems utterly clueless. He's been here six weeks and still hasn't found his feet.' She bit her lip. 'Walter goes to the allotment because he says gardening keeps him sane. I worry that he's going to overdo things and keel over, and I won't know until it's too late. But I can't keep fussing over him because that'll only make him feel worse.'

Georgina thought about Colin and his blood sugar. 'Plus asking him to slow down might make him more stubborn,' she said. 'Middle-aged men can be so awkward about their health. I think it's because they don't like to feel vulnerable.'

'Your partner's like that, too?' Kathleen asked.

'Oh, yes. When he's busy at work, he doesn't eat properly,' Georgina said.

'Men,' Kathleen said, rolling her eyes. 'Walter's the same.'

'I was going to ask you,' Georgina said. 'What was that the vicar was saying about the lost treasure?'

'It's an old, old story,' Kathleen said. 'The rumours have floated about for decades – no, make that centuries. Every so often, the story gets brought up and retold. Over the years, people have looked everywhere for the tunnel between the church and the priory. It's where the prior supposedly hid his treasure just before Dissolution. The latest retelling is on a podcast, and people have been coming to the church to have a look round and see if they can find the treasure. We've tried to make all visitors welcome, but we also need to let them down gently because they're really *not* going to find something that'll make them rich beyond their wildest dreams. If it ever existed in the first place, it would've been found by now.' She looked thoughtful. 'My great-great-great uncle was the vicar here, back in Victorian times. Apparently, he was a bit of a scholar, one of these enquiring minds who's interested in everything. If anyone could have found the treasure, I think it would have been him, but he died quite young.'

'Your great-great-great uncle?' Georgina asked.

'Abraham Locke – known to everyone as Bram,' Kathleen said.

A tingle went down Georgina's spine. This might be her chance to find out more about Bram and Martha. 'You said he died young. What happened?'

'There were a few cases of typhoid in the village, back in the 1870s,' Kathleen said. 'As the vicar, Bram did his Christian duty to look after his flock, and took food and medicine to the sick. Sadly, he caught typhoid from them and died.'

Exactly what Martha had told Doris. But had Martha's suspicions about the real cause of Bram's death been passed on to the rest of the family? Georgina wondered. 'So your family's had a connection with the village for a long time?' she asked.

'I suppose so. My great-great-grandmother was Bram's little sister, Martha. She married the village doctor, Bram's best friend,' Kathleen said. 'Sadly, she died in a riding accident when my great-grandmother, Grace, was still a babe in arms. I think Martha was trying to carry on doing what Bram had tried to do, looking after the villagers, and the accident happened while she was taking food to people who weren't well enough to cook for themselves.'

'How sad,' Georgina said.

'Harvey – Martha's husband – never remarried,' Kathleen said. 'He said nobody could match up to her, so instead he hired a housekeeper and a nanny to help him bring up Grace. Our family stayed in the village, and although I went away to college – where I met Walter – we settled back here after we married. Little Wenborough is our home.'

'Walter's not originally from Norfolk, then?' Georgina asked.

'His family comes from south London,' Kathleen said. 'But he knew I wanted to come back to Little Wenborough when I finished my teacher training. He managed to get a training contract as an accountant in Norwich, and spent his whole career there, while I worked at the local high school.' She smiled. 'I know he can come across as a grumpy old man, but he's thoughtful and he always does the right thing. Well. Almost always,' she admitted. 'When that podcast about the supposed hidden treasure blew up recently, he started combing through Bram's diaries and correspondence, just in case there was anything about it in Bram's files – I'm the custodian of the family archives, you see,' she explained. 'He also borrowed some other paperwork from the vicarage, though he did that a couple of weeks before Craig was appointed and I don't think he's actually told Craig what he's borrowed. Obviously he'll return everything when he's finished studying them, but...' She winced. 'Once we'd met the new vicar, I think Walter was worried that Craig might get overexcited about the possibility of finding treasure and start blurting things out in the press. Things that really wouldn't be helpful.'

Georgina could well imagine that. 'I can understand that,' she said. 'I know you said Walter thinks it's a fairy story, but does he suspect there might be a grain of truth somewhere in the rumours?'

'That's why he's been combing through the papers, to satisfy his own curiosity,' Kathleen said. 'If the treasure does exist, it would belong to the church. It could be sold, and the money could be used to pay for the repairs to the building.'

So Walter was hedging his bets? Interesting, Georgina thought. But she didn't want to show her hand yet. She wanted to talk to Sybbie and Bernard, first, and see if there was anything about Bram Locke in the archives at the Manor. And then, once she knew a bit more, she might be able to ask Kathleen and Walter for help in looking through the Locke and Plowright family papers to find the truth about what happened to Bram and Martha.

'I'd better not keep you any longer,' Kathleen said. 'Here I am, running on about a lot of ole squit, as they say in this part of the world.'

'Kathleen, you've had a horrible morning. Of course I wasn't going to drop you off and leave you feeling miserable. Besides, it's been so interesting talking to you,' Georgina said, meaning it.

'Daft old woman, that's me,' Kathleen said.

Georgina rather thought Kathleen was nothing of the kind. She was sharp as a tack. Maybe she was used to being self-deprecating because of the men around her.

'I'll give you my card,' she said. 'My hearing aids connect to my mobile, so it's easy to get hold of me. Just leave a message if I don't answer – that usually means I'm in my darkroom and I can't have my phone in there with me, lighting up the room and spoiling the prints.'

'Oh, of course,' Kathleen said. 'I dabbled a bit with photography when I was younger, and I loved doing cyanotypes with my students. I never had a darkroom of my own, mind.'

'You're welcome to come and have a nosey at mine, any time you like,' Georgina said.

'I might well take you up on that,' Kathleen said. 'And how great that your phone connects to your hearing aids. I wish Walter would get his hearing aids updated. Half the time, he doesn't even wear them, and he can't hear a thing without them.' She rolled her eyes. 'He says it's so he doesn't have to listen to people running on about nothing.'

'There has to be an upside to not being able to hear,' Georgina said with a smile. 'I get what he means. Switching my aids off means I can read a book in peace on a train, instead of having to put up with people having loud and very dull conversations on their mobile phones.'

'There is that,' Kathleen agreed. 'Thank you for the lift, Georgie. And do give my best to Sybbie when you see her.'

'I will,' Georgina promised.

## FIVE

When she left Kathleen's, Georgina drove to Little Wenborough Manor to collect Bert.

Sybbie greeted her with a hug, and Bert turned round and round in excited circles, wagging his tail madly as if she'd been away from him for weeks rather than a handful of hours.

'Good to see you, dear girl. What an awful morning you've had,' Sybbie said. 'Are you all right? Because I'm guessing what happened to that poor young man brought back some difficult memories for you.'

Georgina had confided in her friend some months ago that she'd found Stephen, her husband, dead from a heart attack in their living room on her return from a photography assignment. 'It did,' she admitted.

'Was it a heart attack?' Sybbie asked.

'We don't really know,' Georgina said, crouching down to make a fuss of Bert. 'Kathleen was busy tidying up in the church hall, and I was outside the church taking photographs while Liam was removing the stained-glass panel. Neither of us heard a thing; but when the builder turned up and I took him into the church to see Liam, we discovered the poor man unconscious on the floor. Kathleen and I started CPR while the builder went to get a defibrillator, and the ambulance arrived very quickly, but unfortunately between us we couldn't save him.'

'How terrible,' Sybbie said, her face full of sympathy.

'It was an unexpected death, so I rang Colin. He came to sort out the witness statements and the paperwork. The pathologist will have to determine the cause of death,' Georgina said. 'And obviously Liam won't be restoring the stained glass now, but no doubt someone else at the studio will be able to take over the project.'

'How did you get on with Kathleen and Walter?' Sybbie asked.

'Very well. I gave Kathleen a lift home, and she sends her best. I liked her very much,' Georgina said. 'Walter seemed a bit impatient, before he left to look at some moss. But I think if I had to work with the new vicar, I'd be impatient, too,' she admitted wryly.

'He's a bit of a drip, I hear,' Sybbie said. 'Bernard isn't impressed with him at all.'

'Let's just say he needs a few prompts where his social skills are concerned,' Georgina said. 'I'm afraid I was rather bossy with him.'

Sybbie grinned. 'That's obviously rubbed off from me. Coffee?'

'Thank you, but no – I've just had a cup of tea with Kathleen,' Georgina said. 'But I would rather like to pick your brains.'

'Ooh.' Sybbie's eyes gleamed. 'Are you about to tell me we have a new case from Doris?'

Georgina nodded. 'She's not here with me right now, and I need some background on the village before I tell you more about it. I was wondering if Bernard might be around today? If he can spare the time, I'd like to talk to him about the history of this house and his maps.'

'I'm sure he'd be delighted to hear that. You know what he's like about his maps,' Sybbie said. 'I'll go and dig him out of his office. Max, Jet, stay with Georgie,' she commanded the Labradors.

She came back to the kitchen a couple of minutes later with her husband in tow.

'I'm sorry to hear you've had such a difficult morning, Georgie,' Bernard said, patting her arm sympathetically.

'It's much more difficult for that poor young man's family,' Georgina said. 'And I wasn't the only one at the church. Kathleen Reeves helped me give CPR. She's very upset that we couldn't save Liam.'

'I'll give her and Walter a call, later,' Bernard said, and Georgina remembered Sybbie telling her that Bernard was on the PCC with Walter.

'Sybbie says you'd like to talk about the manor and maps,' Bernard said, his face becoming more animated.

'I would,' Georgina said. 'I remember Sybbie telling me that there used to be a priory on the site of the manor.'

'So the story goes,' Bernard said. 'There's nothing left of it now apart from some stonework that was reused in the east wing.'

'Today I learned there's a story about a secret tunnel running between the priory and the church, and apparently just before Dissolution the abbot hid some treasure in the tunnel,' Georgina said. 'I was wondering how much truth there might be in the legend.'

'Not a great deal, I'm afraid,' Bernard said. 'I heard those same stories when I was growing up, and I spent ages combing the house and gardens for the entrance to the tunnel when I was a boy, but I never found a trace of it. I don't think anyone's ever discovered anything of this alleged tunnel at the church end, either. There are cellars here, but I believe they were used to store the wine and the beer brewed on the site, back in the day. You're very welcome to have a look yourself, if you want to.'

'I wouldn't be surprised if some of the stone and bricks in the cellars came from the old priory,' Sybbie said. 'But there aren't any secret entrances. This wasn't a Catholic house, so there aren't any priest holes or anything remotely resembling a tunnel in the house itself.'

'There are a lot of folk tales in the county about tunnels,' Bernard said thoughtfully. 'If you looked at them, you'd conclude that every single village in Norfolk had a secret tunnel running either from its church to one of the pubs, or if there was a priory from that to the big house. Whereas in truth these "tunnels", if they existed in the first place, were likely to be undercrofts.'

'What are undercrofts?' Georgina asked.

'Cellars or storage rooms, often lined with brick and sometimes with vaulted ceilings,' Bernard explained. 'Actually, Norwich has more medieval undercrofts than any other city in England, and some of them are open to the public during Heritage Week. The ones underneath the Guildhall were used as a prison up until the seventeenth century, and there are others underneath the Assembly House, Strangers' Hall and the Bridewell.'

'And I imagine at least one of them is meant to lead to either the cathedral or Norwich Castle?' Georgina asked.

'There's a tale about a pig being lost in a tunnel leading from Norwich Castle to Carrow Priory,' Bernard said. 'A man called William Gerish collected a lot of folk tales in the early 1900s. There's a collection of his unpublished work in the county archives. Several of the Norfolk tales involve someone playing a fiddle as they walk into the tunnel with their dog, and then the music stops and they're never seen again. And there are plenty of stories about hidden treasure in the county: everything from King John's treasure being stolen before it was "lost" in the Wash near Swineshead in October 1216' – he mimed speech marks with his fingers around the word 'lost' – 'through to a priory's treasure being hidden just before Dissolution. Often the treasure is described as a pair of golden gates or some silver bells, but there's not a great deal of truth in any of the stories.' He looked intrigued. 'Why are you asking?'

'The vicar mentioned it this morning,' Georgina said. 'Apparently the Little Wenborough story has been featured on a podcast, and people have been coming to the church to look for treasure.'

Bernard nodded sagely. 'I know the podcast you mean. TreasureChest. It's quite entertaining and the guy's very persuasive, but in this case I'm afraid it's just a story with no real evidence.'

'Does this have anything to do with the new case?' Sybbie asked.

'New case?' Bernard echoed.

'Actually, it does,' Georgina said. 'There was a vicar here in the 1870s called Abraham Locke. According to his younger sister, Martha, he was searching for the tunnel and thought that he might have found it. But then there were some cases of typhoid in the village. When Bram delivered food and medicines to the sick, he caught typhoid and died.'

'But obviously there's more to it than that, or Doris wouldn't be involved,' Sybbie said.

'Martha thinks he was poisoned in a way to make it look as if he caught typhoid,' Georgina said.

Sybbie's eyes widened. 'You mean like the arsenic poisonings Will told us about, earlier in the year, that were misdiagnosed as cholera in Victorian times?'

'Exactly that,' Georgina said. 'Martha started asking questions. And she died in a riding accident before she could find out more.'

'And I suppose Doris doesn't think it was an accident?' Bernard asked. 'So we have two suspicious deaths. Are there any suspects?'

'Not at the moment,' Georgina said. 'But this is where it gets interesting. Martha was Kathleen's great-great-grandmother. Kathleen has Bram's papers – and Walter has been working his way through them.'

'Which sounds to me as if Walter thinks Bram might have been onto something,' Bernard said. 'Walter's very level-headed. He'll keep things to himself until he finishes investigating thoroughly.'

'The 1870s,' Sybbie said thoughtfully.

'1871, to be precise,' Georgina added.

'That was the year your great-grandfather William was born, Bernard. Amelia was still alive then, wasn't she?' Amelia was Bernard's great-great-great-grandmother, whose diary and commonplace book had helped Georgina and Sybbie to solve previous local cold cases.

'She was,' Bernard confirmed. 'As was my great-great-great-uncle Frederick, her oldest son. He didn't die until 1879, which was when my great-great-grandfather Robert inherited the title and the estate.'

'So we need to have a look in Amelia's commonplace book and diary, and also see if there's anything in your great-great-grand-mother Caroline's diary and letters,' Sybbie said.

'Caroline was Robert's wife, wasn't she?' Georgina asked.

Bernard nodded.

'OK. And we need to check the newspaper reports, to see what they can tell us about the typhoid outbreak and whether there's an obituary for Bram,' Georgina said. 'Plus the parish records, in case there was a chatty vicar who made little side notes in the registers.'

'Meanwhile I,' Bernard said, 'will dig out all the maps and see if there's any hint of a tunnel leading in the direction of St Edmund's. I'm pretty sure there isn't, but it's worth double-checking.'

'Thank you,' Georgina said. 'Then, once I've got the information together, I can talk to Kathleen and Walter and ask if I can borrow Bram's papers.'

'Walter can be a bit – well, *rigid* in his outlook,' Bernard said. 'But he's worked with me on the PCC, so if you need me to have a quiet word with him, just let me know.' He grimaced. 'And that isn't meant to be any nonsense about the old boy network, or how men are superior.'

Georgina grinned. 'You're married to Sybbie. Of course you're not going to buy in to any of that nonsense! And you have a point. It might be easier for him to trust me, as a complete stranger, if he knows that I'm friends with you. Kathleen was certainly warmer after I mentioned my connection to Sybbie.'

'That's settled, then,' Bernard said. 'I feel rather privileged to have a small involvement in the new case.'

'Lunch, now, I think,' Sybbie said. 'I'll ring Cesca and ask her to join us, in case Doris comes back to you while you're here – I know she'd love to see the baby. And then perhaps we can make a start on the documents. You can borrow my laptop, Georgie, to save you going home to collect yours.'

'Thank you,' Georgina said. How lucky she'd been to make such warm, wonderful friends, people who included her so readily and treated her as if she were part of their family. And it warmed her that both Sybbie and Bernard, despite being so very down to earth, completely accepted Doris, too.

SIX

Colin called Sammy Granger, the pathologist, from his desk at Norwich police station. 'Liam's partner, Dominic McGowan, is prepared to ID the body for us officially, this afternoon,' he said. 'Is that convenient for you?'

'Give me until three, and I'll make sure Liam looks tidy,' Sammy said.

'Thank you.' He paused. 'I know it's early days, but can you tell me anything, yet? Was it a heart attack that killed him?'

'Possibly not. There are mucus plugs in the lungs, and evidence of pulmonary hyperexpansion,' Sammy said.

'Can you repeat that in layman's terms, please?' Colin asked.

'Phlegm is the mucus secreted by glands in the lungs. It traps and removes inhaled particles, cellular debris and dead cells, keeping the lungs healthy,' Sammy explained. 'But it can accumulate and plug up the airways, reducing the airflow. In the upper airways, where these are, mucus plugs lead to shortness of breath, shallow or rapid breathing, wheezing and coughing.'

'That sounds like asthma,' Colin said.

'Yes. As for the pulmonary hyperexpansion – that means air gets trapped in your lungs when you breathe out. It takes up space, so you find it hard to get fresh air into the lungs, and your lungs get bigger to make room for the new air. They get stiff and less stretchy, so it's harder to catch your breath.'

'What does that tell us about how Liam died?' Colin asked.

'There's swelling in his upper airways, too, which indicates a fatal asthma attack,' Sammy said. 'But there's also myocardial ischaemia – in other words, not enough blood flow got to his heart. That, together with the lung issues, would indicate anaphylactic shock rather than asthma.'

'Anaphylaxis. A potentially fatal allergic reaction?' Colin asked.

'That's my working theory, so I've stored samples and I'm working with fatal allergy protocols,' Sammy said. 'I've sent some femoral blood off for mast cell analysis – that means the lab will check for an allergic reaction. Can you check with Liam's GP or his next of kin about any known allergies?'

'Actually, I can tell you that one already,' Colin said. 'Georgie was there this morning when Liam was offered some banana bread. He checked if it contained any coconut, because he's allergic to it. Kathleen Reeves made the cake, though, and said it didn't contain coconut or any other kind of nuts. Apparently Liam ate some of the cake before he died, and Kathleen gave me the rest of the cake for you to test. That points more towards her innocence than guilt. If there *is* any coconut in that cake, it's unlikely that it was added by her.'

'I'll check the cake,' Sammy said, 'but I still need official confirmation of the allergy from Liam's GP or next of kin, including how serious it was – would it cause say just a rash or a bit of a stomach upset, or was it full-blown swelling of the tongue and throat?'

'I'll sort that,' Colin said. 'And if you can check his stomach contents for traces of coconut, that might be helpful. How quickly does an allergic reaction happen?'

'It varies,' Sammy said. 'I'll sort things in the lab, and I'll see you and Mr McGowan at about three.'

'Thanks, Sammy,' Colin said.

'She gets more and more gorgeous every day, Cesca,' Georgina said, looking at the sleeping baby. 'And that's from Doris as well as me,' she added, as Doris had come to join them.

'She's gorgeous when she's asleep,' Francesca said. 'But you see that red cheek?'

'Yes. Would I be right in guessing that's the first tooth on its way?' Georgina asked.

Francesca nodded. 'I keep teething rings in the fridge, and I've got the stuff you rub on their gums. But when she's wailing, she's inconsolable.'

'And sometimes you just need five minutes' peace,' Sybbie said. 'That's when you bring her over to Grannie. I'll sing to her and jiggle her about and take her mind off it.'

'Dearest ma-in-law,' Francesca said fondly. 'There are many reasons why I love you. I think you've just given me another one.'

Sybbie chuckled. 'And thank you for bringing the lemon cake. It's appreciated.'

'I'm sorry I'm being rude and refusing cake,' Georgina said, 'but I've already had some of Kathleen Reeves's banana bread today.'

'Now that's the stuff of legend,' Francesca said. 'When Sybbie asked me to come over for lunch, she told me what happened at the church today. I'm sorry you had such a tough morning. And that poor man. Do you know what – well, killed him?'

'No. The pathologist is doing the PM, so Colin will have a better idea after the report,' Georgina said.

'But we do have a new case to look into,' Sybbie said, and filled Cesca in on the details of Martha Plowright and Bram Locke.

'If you need a hand investigating,' Francesca said, 'I'd love to help.'

'We'd love to have you,' Georgina said with a smile. 'You get first pick of what to investigate: the newspapers, the parish records or the Manor's archives?'

'Ooh, I think the Manor's archives,' Francesca said.

'I'll help you, Cesca,' Sybbie said, 'as that's the biggest amount of documents to go through. Let me top up our hot drinks, and then we can get started.'

'Dining room?' Georgie asked. It was where they tended to do their research in Sybbie's house, because the dining table was enormous and had plenty of space for them to spread out documents.

'Dining room,' Sybbie confirmed with a smile.

'I'll grab the archive files. We're looking at 1871, right, Georgie?' Sybbie asked.

Georgina checked the photographs she'd taken at the churchyard. 'Abraham Locke died on 13 March 1871, aged thirty. Martha Plowright died on 15 May 1871, aged twenty-five. Harvey Plowright died on 19 November 1920, but he was seventy-nine at the time – which is a respectable age, and Doris didn't give any indication that his death was suspicious.'

'Bram was diagnosed with typhoid but might have been poisoned, and Martha died from a riding accident while she was asking questions about her brother's death,' Sybbie said.

'Put like that, it sounds suspicious,' Francesca said. 'But we know what we're looking for. Any mention of Abraham, Martha, Harvey and a typhoid outbreak, from around February 1871 onwards.'

'Do you want to do Amelia's diary while I work through the correspondence, Cesca?' Sybbie asked.

'Fine by me,' Francesca said. 'I'll keep working until Lizzie wakes up.'


The man who opened the door to Colin looked absolutely devastated. His eyes were swollen and bloodshot, and his dark curly hair stuck out in all directions, as if he'd repeatedly raked his fingers through it.

Colin showed him his warrant card. 'I'm very sorry for your loss, Mr McGowan. Are you sure you're up to identifying the body? Can I call anyone to accompany you?'

'No. I'll do it,' Dominic said hoarsely. 'It's the only thing I can do for him now.'

'All right,' Colin said gently. 'I'll drive you to the mortuary, and we can take as much time as you need.'

'Thank you.'

'Any questions you have, I'll do my best to answer,' Colin said. 'And I can arrange for a family liaison officer to support you.'

'I don't need any support. I just need...' Dominic's voice broke. 'Well, I can't have him back, can I?'

'I know this is going to be tough for you,' Colin said, 'and I'm sorry for that. I wouldn't ask if it wasn't necessary.'

'No,' Dominic said, and allowed Colin to usher him to the car.

Dominic was silent for most of the journey, and Colin didn't want to bother him with small talk. Though there was one issue he needed to sort out before they went into the mortuary. 'I'm sorry to ask,' he said, when they were a couple of miles from the mortuary, 'but I do need some information from you for the pathologist, before we go in. I believe Liam had an allergy?'

'Coconut,' Dominic said. 'He couldn't use any toiletries made with coconut, or eat anything made with it.'

'Was it severe enough for him to need an EpiPen?' Colin asked.

'Yes,' Dominic confirmed.

Yet the paramedics had said there was no sign of an EpiPen within Dominic's belongings. If you were that severely allergic to something, surely you carried adrenalin with you?

'Is that what killed him?' Dominic demanded. 'Coconut?'

'At the moment, the pathologist is still doing her report,' Colin said. 'I can't say anything for definite.'

'I *knew* it.' Dominic's face turned puce. 'Bloody Aaron Flint. He was the one behind this!'

'Who is Aaron Flint?' Colin asked. It was the first time the name had been mentioned to him – and the first suggestion that someone might not have liked Liam Jacobs.

'He's one of Liam's colleagues at the glass studio. He's always been jealous of Liam. He wanted the job at St Edmund's because of some family connection to the village, but Liam was the one who got it because he was by far the better craftsman,' Dominic said. 'Everyone in the studio knew Liam was allergic to coconut. Aaron must have found some way to get it into Liam's system.'

Colin decided not to mention the banana bread. Until Sammy had checked it out, they had no proof that it contained any coconut – or, if there *were* traces of coconut, who might have added them to the cake.

'I wish we'd never come to Norfolk in the first place,' Dominic burst out. 'But Liam saw the ad for the job at the glass workshop and it was his dream job. I'm on a year's sabbatical because I'm writing a book, so I agreed to move here with him for six months.' He shook his head angrily. 'I wish we'd stayed in Oxford. Then at least Liam would still be alive. And it's all bloody Aaron's fault. I'll kill him!'

'Mr McGowan, there's no proof that anyone killed Liam,' Colin said quietly. 'With any unexpected death, the coroner needs to investigate. The paramedics thought that Mr Jacobs might have had a heart attack.'

'How? Liam was only twenty-eight! He took care of himself. He ate well, he went for a run every day, he didn't smoke, and he barely drank. Of *course* it wasn't a heart attack.' Dominic gave him a look of sheer contempt.

Colin damped down his irritation. The man had just lost his partner and probably didn't intend to be rude.

'And you asked me about his allergy,' Dominic continued. 'You wouldn't have asked if it had nothing to do with his death.'

'Actually, I would,' Colin said. 'It's a line of enquiry and it helps us to rule things out. We need to be thorough.'

'I *know* Aaron's behind it,' Dominic muttered darkly.

Dominic had mentioned writing a book. Maybe talking about

that would help to distract him a bit and calm him down, Colin thought. 'What's your book about?'

'Folklore. I teach ancient history and folklore at the University of Oxford,' Dominic explained. 'That's how I met Liam. He was working on some glass, and I was teaching my students the legends behind it.'

'That sounds interesting,' Colin said.

'It's fascinating. There are so many tales that sprang up across different parts of the country but cover the same ground. There's one about a fiddler who explored a tunnel with his dog, playing his violin so people could follow him above ground. The music stopped abruptly and he was never seen again, though his dog reappeared a while later, shivering and shaking.'

A fairy story, Colin thought. 'Are there any stories like that about Little Wenborough?' he asked.

'Not about a fiddler – those tales are connected to Binham and Blakeney – but there's a story about the abbot's treasure, hidden in a tunnel between the old priory and St Edmund's church just before Dissolution,' Dominic said. 'Of course, there's a tale involving a tunnel about virtually every place in the country that had a priory. The tunnel led either to the church or the local big house.'

Georgina had mentioned the story and said that it had been retold recently by a podcaster. The result was an influx of visitors to the church, hoping for a lucky find. Was Dominic involved with the podcast? Colin wondered. 'Is this the story that was told on a podcast recently?' he asked casually.

'You mean the one by Russell Dawson of TreasureChest.' Dominic curled his lip. 'He's not a proper historian.'

Academic snobbery didn't sit well with Colin. 'Enthusiasts can often fire people's imaginations,' he said mildly.

'Dawson's an idiot,' Dominic said.

Colin had to remind himself yet again to be patient: the man had just been bereaved and might not usually behave like this.

Though he had a nasty feeling that Dominic might be like this all the time.

'OK,' he said mildly. 'So you don't think there's anything in the story?'

'I doubt it,' Dominic said. 'But Liam was so thrilled about restoring the glass. I said I'd check the church out for my book.'

Thankfully, they reached the mortuary. But before Colin had even opened the car door, Dominic said, 'You're going to arrest Aaron, right?'

'I need concrete evidence of a crime before I can arrest anyone,' Colin said. As Dominic's cheeks started to turn puce again, he said, 'But I will talk to him, because it's a line of investigation and my job is to be thorough, accurate and fair.'

'Thank you.' Dominic paused. 'Can I have Liam's things? At least his phone – it'll have photographs on it. Photographs I can't bear the thought of losing.' His colour heightened. 'And messages. Private ones.'

There might also be something on that phone that shed light on Liam's death, Colin thought. 'I'm afraid it could contain evidence for the coroner,' he said.

All the fight went out of Dominic. 'I just... It's the last thing I have of him. Photos. And if they get accidentally wiped...'

Yeah. Colin could understand that. 'We could take a copy of the phone's contents,' he said. 'And then I can let you have it back.'

'Thank you. I appreciate that.'


'Let's have a recap on what we've got so far,' Sybbie said when they'd been working for an hour.

'The newspapers report several typhoid outbreaks in the county throughout the year,' Georgina said. 'The Prince of Wales caught typhoid in November 1870 while at a house party near Scarborough, and he was laid up for weeks at Sandringham. The queen came to visit him and there were several bulletins a day. The outbreak at Little Wenborough was in February and March 1871, and four people died – an elderly woman, two very small children, and Bram Locke.'

'It makes sense that the very young and very old, the ones who are more likely to be vulnerable, succumbed to the fevers,' Sybbie said. 'But not a man who was in the prime of his life, had a relatively decent standard of living and was taking precautions not to catch typhoid. How old was Bram, again?'

'Thirty,' Georgina said. 'Not much older than the young man who died at the church today. Not that there's a connection between them.' At least, not one that she knew about. 'But it feels a bit close to home.'

'I agree,' Francesca said. 'Was there an obituary?'

'Yes. This one's in *The Bury and Norwich Post.* "We regret to observe in our obituary an announcement of the sudden death of the Rev. A. Locke, vicar of St Edmund's in Little Wenborough, aged thirty years, who expired on Monday afternoon from typhoid. He fell ill after ministering to a stricken family in the village and was greatly esteemed by all classes of the community,",' Georgina quoted. '"He was wont to bring help and sympathy to those in trouble, need and sickness, and a kind word and good counsel to those enjoying strength and health."'

'Amelia certainly rated him,' Francesca said. 'Her diary says she was deeply shocked and saddened to hear the news that Bram Locke had died, how he truly ministered to the sick and the poor and was a good man.'

'And Caroline's diary says she was very sad because Bram conducted her marriage to Robert, the previous year, and they were looking forward to him baptising the baby later in the year,' Sybbie added.

'It looks as if the curate from St Mary's in Great Wenborough came to help run the parish until the new vicar was brought in,' Georgina said.

'I'm not surprised,' Sybbie said. 'That's what happened when our previous vicar left.'

'Not all of the parish registers have been digitised, but the

Victorian ones were. It seems Bram was the one who buried Victoria Stebbings and her grandchildren John and Henry, who died from typhoid the week before he died; but George Saunders was the one who signed the register for Bram's burial. George wrote a note in the register at St Mary's that helped us find that unmarked grave, last summer,' she said to Francesca. 'He wrote in the burials register of St Edmund's that the whole village would mourn Bram.'

'But if the whole village liked him,' Francesca said, 'why did Martha think that someone had poisoned him? And who?'

'Her husband was the village doctor, who said Bram died from typhoid. He was also Bram's best friend, so I can't see any reason why he would be behind Bram's death,' Georgina said. 'It might be that she was distraught about losing her brother and couldn't accept that he really had died from typhoid, so she convinced herself that someone wanted to kill Bram – though I have no idea who. And perhaps the riding accident really *was* an accident.'

'But in that case, why would she have contacted Doris?' Sybbie countered.

'Unless,' Francesca said, 'what we have to prove is that there wasn't any kind of conspiracy. Did Bram keep a diary? Or Martha?'

'Kathleen told me she had the family papers,' Georgina said. 'I was going to ask her if we could have a look at them, but I was hoping we might find something that would help Doris jog Martha's memory, first.'

'Let's keep going,' Sybbie said.


Dominic made a formal identification of Liam's body, then confirmed the coconut allergy to Sammy.

'Was Liam allergic to any other kind of nuts?' Sammy asked.

'Just coconut,' Dominic said. 'I thought it was strange – I mean, nuts are nuts.'

'Coconut has a different protein profile to other nuts, so it's possible to be allergic to coconut but not tree nuts or groundnuts,' Sammy said. 'I'm sorry to ask, but did you ever know him to have an allergic reaction?'

'Once – he'd used some handwash that he'd been told was hypoallergenic, but it turned out to have coconut oil in it. He came up in a rash and then his lips started tingling. But he used his adrenalin pen and he was fine,' Dominic said.

'Thank you, Mr McGowan. That's very helpful,' Sammy said.

Dominic turned to Colin. 'Find whoever did this to Liam,' he demanded. 'Find them, lock them up and throw away the key.'

# SEVEN

Colin drove Dominic home and again offered him support from a family liaison officer; Dominic refused a second time and again insisted that Aaron Flint was behind Liam's death and Colin should arrest him.

'We're investigating this thoroughly, Mr McGowan,' Colin assured him. 'I'll be in touch with any news, and you can contact me and my team if you think of anything else that might be helpful.' Though, until the lab results came back, he had very little to go on.

At the station, he arranged to have the contents of Liam's phone copied, then for one of the junior constables to contact Dominic so he could collect the phone. And then it was a matter of going through the evidence he did have while he waited for the pathology report.

Later that afternoon, Sammy rang Colin. 'I'm still waiting to hear back from the lab about the mast cells, but I'm pretty sure it's going to be positive. I've done some tests on the cake you sent me earlier, and it's the same banana bread that was the last thing Liam ate.'

Colin went cold. 'Are you going to tell me it contains coconut?'

'Coconut oil,' Sammy said.

'Kathleen – the person who made the cake – told me it definitely didn't contain any form of coconut,' Colin said.

'Either she was lying,' Sammy said, 'or someone managed to add it to the cake without her knowing.'

'Agreed,' Colin said grimly. 'I have a few more questions to ask. Thanks for letting me know, Sammy.'

He called in to see Georgina on the way to Kathleen Reeves. Just giving her a hug and making a fuss of Bert made him feel more grounded.

'Rough afternoon?' she asked.

He nodded. 'Formal ID at the mortuary.'

'It must've been very difficult for Liam's partner,' Georgina said.

'Uh-huh.'

'What aren't you telling me?' she asked.

'I didn't like him,' Colin said. 'And then I felt guilty for not liking him. If you had been there, you would have reminded me that grief sometimes makes people act out of character. So I tried to remember that.'

'And?'

How well she knew him. And she always got straight to the point. 'Sammy rang. This banana bread... you ate some and you've been absolutely fine?'

'Yes. It was gorgeous. I asked Kathleen for the recipe because I planned to make some for you to take into work.' Colour leached out of her face. 'Oh. The fact you're asking – does that mean it really was the banana bread that killed Liam?'

'I'm afraid so,' he said. 'The lab tests showed it contained coconut oil.'

'But how?' Georgina asked. 'I've spent the afternoon with Sybbie and Cesca. Cesca says Kathleen's banana bread is legendary – everyone loves it and asks for the recipe.'

'Like Cesca's own lemon cake,' Colin said.

Georgina nodded. 'Exactly. But I was *there*, Colin. Liam

checked the ingredients with Kathleen before he accepted any cake, and he told her about his allergy. Kathleen confirmed she didn't use coconut of any description in the banana bread. She's so used to people asking her for the recipe that she keeps a few printed cards in her handbag. I can give you the one she gave me. In fact, let me do that now,' she said, going to her tin of recipe cards, riffling through the cake section and taking out the card Kathleen had given her.

'Thank you,' Colin said, accepting it and glancing quickly through the printed words. Sure enough, the oil mentioned was sunflower, not coconut. And coconut wasn't listed in the ingredients, not even as an optional extra. 'If Kathleen's telling the truth and she didn't use coconut oil, how did coconut oil get into the banana bread?'

'I have no idea,' Georgina said.

'Can you run me through what happened at the church, again? Not that I'm doubting what you said earlier,' he added. 'It's just sometimes helpful to go over things again in the light of new information. Something might be significant when it wasn't before.'

'Walter left the church hall first, then the vicar,' Georgina said. 'Kathleen wrapped Liam's cake in greaseproof paper – she, the vicar and I ate ours in the church hall with coffee. Kathleen came into the church with Liam and me. We talked about the window and I took some photographs of Liam, but then he wanted to get on with removing the window. Kathleen went into the church hall to tidy up, and I went outside to take some background photographs. Liam was alone in the church. I would have seen anyone going into St Edmund's, and I didn't see anyone in the vicinity of the churchyard until Alfie – the builder – pulled into the car park.'

Colin almost asked her if Doris had seen anything. But that was one tiny step too far for him, and besides, that particular form of evidence wouldn't be admissible in court.

When had the coconut oil been added to the cake, how much, by whom, and how? And there was something else bothering him.

'Dominic McGowan – Liam's partner – seemed adamant that someone called Aaron Flint was to blame.'

'Aaron?' Georgina's eyes widened.

'Do you happen to know this Aaron?' he asked.

'I've never met him, but I know who he is,' she said. She looked worried. 'He's Kathleen's nephew and he works – *worked*,' she corrected herself, 'with Liam at the glass studio. Kathleen says he's had a rough time over the last few years. He lost his mum to cancer in his last year at college, and went off the rails a bit. He was getting himself back together when his dad sold the family home and moved somewhere too far for Aaron to commute to work.'

'I'm going to interview Kathleen again shortly, but I'd like to know as much as possible beforehand,' Colin said. 'Did she say how Aaron got on with Liam?'

Georgina winced. 'She said he was upset that Liam had been given the project – obviously, Aaron had a family connection to the church through his aunt and uncle, and he'd wanted to work on the glass. Kathleen was planning to make friends with Liam and persuade him to let Aaron work on the restoration.'

'Hmm. Jealousy's quite a powerful motive,' Colin said.

'There's something else you need to know,' she said. 'Kathleen thinks Aaron isn't eating properly, so she makes sure she cooks a proper Sunday lunch for him.'

Colin made the connection instantly. 'Did she make the banana bread yesterday?'

'You'd need to ask her, but I think it's highly likely,' Georgina said.

'If Aaron had lunch at his aunt and uncle's house yesterday, he was probably there when she made the banana bread,' Colin said. 'And if that cake is her equivalent to Cesca's lemon cake, and Aaron knew she was intending to make friends with Liam, he would have known that she was going to welcome Liam to the church with a hot drink and offer him banana bread.'

'That's very plausible,' Georgina agreed.

'Could he somehow have managed to get coconut oil into the

cake batter?' Colin had worked on a recent case where someone had adulterated sausage rolls without the baker knowing. Was this the same kind of thing?

'But how could he have done that, when Kathleen says she was on her own in the kitchen?' Georgina asked.

'Maybe she's covering for him,' Colin said.

'And why would he put coconut oil into the cake, if he knew that Liam was allergic enough to coconut to need an injection of adrenaline if he consumed it?' Georgina asked. 'That's tantamount to...' Her voice tailed off and she looked anguished.

Colin knew what she wasn't saying. *Tantamount to murder*. 'If Liam always carried an auto-injector which would stop any anaphylactic reaction should he accidentally come into contact with coconut, and Aaron knew that, it wasn't necessarily intent to murder. It could be classified as intent to cause grievous bodily harm,' he said.

'Or maybe – if he *was* the one who added the coconut oil to the banana bread – he didn't realise the allergy was quite that serious,' Georgina suggested. 'Maybe he thought it would just make Liam too ill to work for a while, so he would have to take over. And even then that would have been a gamble, because the project still might have gone to someone else at the studio. Is that a risk he would have been prepared to take?'

Typical Georgina: seeing the best in people rather than the worst, Colin thought. Though sometimes after a rough day at work he really needed that sunny perspective.

'I'm no baker,' Colin said. 'If you add extra oil to a cake mix, what happens?'

'It depends how much extra you add,' Georgina said. 'If it was just a little, it probably wouldn't show. If it was a lot, then the cake batter would be too thin and runny. Kathleen has obviously made that cake regularly, over the years, so I think she would have noticed if something wasn't quite right with the mixture.'

'What would she have done about it?' Colin asked. 'Thrown it out, or would there be a way to fix it?'

'If it was me, and I thought I'd accidentally added too much liquid to a recipe I knew very well, I'd simply add more dry ingredients to balance it out,' Georgina said.

'Thank you,' Colin said. He frowned. 'You know I'm not a cook. I've never even bought coconut oil, let alone used it. Does it look very different from olive oil or sunflower oil?'

'Yes. For a start, it's solid, unless the weather's very warm or you've heated it,' Georgina said. 'It's white when it's solid, and clear when it's liquid.'

'Kathleen said she uses sunflower oil. Is it possible to add coconut oil to sunflower oil?'

'In theory,' Georgina said. 'But sunflower oil bottles tend to be clear. If the bottle's been kept in a cool place – below the melting point of coconut oil – you'd see the lumps of solid coconut oil in the sunflower oil. Actually, even in a dark green olive oil bottle, you can see if the olive oil has started to solidify when the weather has turned cold.'

'She wouldn't think that the sunflower oil had just started to solidify because it's cold?' Colin checked.

'No,' Georgina said. 'Actually, I don't think I've ever seen sunflower oil solidify.'

'Thank you.' Colin gave her another hug. 'I'd better go and have a chat to Kathleen.'

'For the record, I liked her,' Georgina said. 'I don't think she's the sort to lie. Sybbie likes her, too. And Bernard's on the PCC with Walter.'

'Noted,' Colin said. 'And thank you for letting me think out loud.'

'And what we just talked about isn't going anywhere,' Georgina said.

He smiled. 'I know that already. But I appreciate the reassurance.'

'Have you eaten today?' she checked.

'I had a sandwich for lunch,' he said. 'Don't wait for me to get back before you have dinner. I need to interview Aaron today as well as Kathleen.' He knew Georgina was aware that in the early stages of the investigation, it was important to gather as much evidence as possible and he'd have to work ridiculous hours.

'I'll make something I can heat through quickly when you get back,' Georgina said.

'You really don't have to. I can make myself beans on toast.'

She laid an affectionate hand on his arm. 'Would that be mushy beans and burned toast? I think I'll spare myself from having to flap a damp tea towel underneath the smoke detector,' she teased.

'Then thank you. Just as long as you know I'm not taking you for granted.' He'd been there and done that, with Marianne. Although he and his ex-wife were on civil terms now, he remembered how dark life had been in the days before his divorce, and he wasn't letting that happen ever again.

'I know,' Georgina said, and kissed him lightly. 'Stop worrying. You have work to do.'

And how grateful he was for her understanding.


Kathleen Reeves ushered Colin into the living room and offered him a cup of tea. Mindful that this was going to be a difficult conversation, and that Georgie always persuaded people to open up to her over a cup of tea, Colin accepted.

Walter, her husband, eyed Colin suspiciously. 'I hope you don't think Kathleen had anything to do with the death of that young man. She tried to save him.'

'I know she did,' Colin said. 'But I need to make further enquiries.'

'Hmm,' Walter said.

Much as Colin hated to namedrop, he really needed to dampen the hostility here. 'Georgina tells me you're on the PCC with my friend Bernard Walters.'

'Lord Wyatt,' Walter said, clearly wanting to make the point.

'Indeed,' Colin said with an inward sigh.

Thankfully, Kathleen came through with a tray of tea, and dispelled the awkwardness.

'How can we help you, Inspector?' she asked.

'I'm afraid it's not good news,' Colin said. 'The pathologist came back to me. Liam Jacobs died from anaphylaxis, caused by the ingestion of coconut. Coconut oil, to be precise.'

Kathleen gasped. 'But it can't have been my banana bread. I don't use coconut oil.'

'I'm afraid,' Colin said gently, 'the lab results show that the sample of cake you gave me also contained coconut oil.'

She put her hand to her mouth, clearly distressed. 'I don't understand. How could that have happened?'

'That,' Colin said dryly, 'is something I'm investigating.'

'That poor young man.' She shook her head. 'It's unbearable to think that I caused his death.'

'You didn't use any form of coconut in that cake,' Walter said. 'Your word should be enough.'

'But it isn't, Walter. Of course we need physical proof,' Kathleen said. 'Inspector Bradshaw, you can take away the containers of everything I used to make that cake yesterday – they're still in my kitchen. Get everything tested. Prove that I'm innocent.'

From her reaction to the news and the way she'd immediately offered everything for testing, Colin was pretty sure that Kathleen was innocent. There was a chance that somehow her ingredients had been accidentally contaminated with coconut oil. But how, and was Dominic right about Aaron's involvement?

'Thank you, Mrs Reeves. I'll do that, and I'll bring everything back to you myself,' he said.

'Come with me now,' Kathleen said. 'And I'd like you to watch me pack them all in a bag, so you can be satisfied that I haven't swapped anything over.'

Walter rolled his eyes, but didn't say anything else.

Colin set his cup and saucer on a coaster on the coffee table, and followed Kathleen into the kitchen.

True to her word, she took the containers of flour, sugar,

baking powder, sunflower oil and ground flaxseed from the cupboard and packed them in a jute shopping bag printed with puffins. 'Obviously I used ripe bananas, too. If you want the skins, they're in the food waste caddy, unless Walter has already emptied it and taken the contents to the allotment for his compost heap.'

It was possible that coconut oil had been injected into the bananas, Colin thought. Not hugely likely, but he needed to be thorough; if there were any traces in the banana skins, Sammy would be able to find them. 'I'll take them, too, please,' he said. 'And I don't mind getting them out of the bin, to save you having to do it. I always have gloves with me.'

Her eyes filled with tears, and she indicated the small duck-egg blue compost caddy next to the sink.

He snapped on the plastic gloves from his pocket and fished out the banana skins, then placed them in an evidence bag.

'I'm so sorry to be the bearer of difficult news, Mrs Reeves,' he said gently.

'I would never, ever kill anyone,' she said. 'I tried to save that young man's life, not take it.' Her voice was quiet, steady and full of pain.

'I know,' he said.

'This morning was only the second time I'd met him. And I didn't know about his allergy until he mentioned it today.' She looked anguished. 'I can't bear knowing that eating my cake killed him.' She shook her head. 'I just don't understand how coconut was in the banana bread.'

'Was anyone in the kitchen with you when you made it?' Colin asked.

'No. As I told you earlier, Walter's no cook. There was just me, yesterday morning before church. He'd gone in to open the doors, tidy up and welcome people in, while I made a batch of cookies for people to have with their coffee after the service and then the banana bread. I left the cake cooling when I went to church. The service was at ten.'

'Noted,' Colin said, and turned to the next subject he needed to discuss with her. 'Could you tell me about Aaron Flint?'

She was sharp enough to realise what lay behind the question. 'You think *Aaron* was involved?' she asked, looking shocked.

'It's just a line of questioning, for now,' he reassured her. 'We're looking at everything.'

'Aaron's my nephew,' she said. 'He works at the glass studio. Things haven't been easy for him, the last few years, but he's a good lad at heart.'

'Tell me about him,' Colin invited.

She told him exactly what Georgina had said: that Aaron's mum had died in his last year at university, his dad had moved away, and Aaron had been struggling to cope. Kathleen made him come to Little Wenborough for Sunday lunch so she knew her nephew had eaten at least one proper meal in the week.

'Aaron didn't bake with you?' Colin enquired.

'No. He doesn't come over until after we're back after the service, and I did all my baking before the service.'

'Did he go into the kitchen at all?'

She frowned. 'He did the washing up after lunch – he always insists on doing that because he says the cook shouldn't have to do the washing up. His mum taught him that. As I say, he's a good lad at heart.'

'Was he involved with the restoration project at the church?' Colin asked.

'No, and he was disappointed about it. He'd wanted to be involved because of me,' Kathleen said. 'But I told him I'd talk to Liam and see if I could persuade him to let Aaron be part of the project.' She frowned. 'I do hope you're not suggesting that Aaron did something to my cake, because I can tell you, he wouldn't do anything like that.'

But Aaron had a motive, Colin thought. Aaron also knew that Liam was allergic to coconut, and he knew his aunt was highly likely to make her famed banana bread as a welcome. What if Aaron had brought the coconut oil with him? Doing the washing up and being on his own in her kitchen would have given him the opportunity to adulterate the cake with the coconut oil. 'It's a line of enquiry,' Colin said, as kindly as he could.

'Aaron wouldn't do anything like that,' Kathleen repeated.

'I do need a chat with him, as well as with Liam's other colleagues,' Colin said. He wasn't going to mention Dominic McGowan's accusations. 'Obviously I could wait until the studio opens tomorrow, but I'd prefer to speak to him today. Could you let me have his phone number and address?'

Kathleen looked troubled. 'He's a good lad,' she said again, but finally gave Colin the information he'd asked for.

'Thank you, Mrs Reeves,' he said. 'I'll be in touch, and I'll make sure you get these back.' He indicated the jute bag.

'All right,' she said.

## EIGHT

Back at his car, Colin rang Aaron Flint and arranged to interview him at his house.

The young man who opened the front door was thin, pale and had shadows under eyes that were dark pools of unhappiness. He was the walking stereotype of a tortured artist, Colin thought. Was that his general demeanour, or was there a particular reason why he looked unhappy – a reason that involved Liam Jacobs? 'DI Colin Bradshaw,' he said, showing his warrant card. 'Aaron Flint?'

Aaron nodded. 'Come in,' he said, and ushered Colin into an untidy living room.

Colin sat down. 'I assume you've heard the news about Liam Jacobs?' he asked.

Aaron looked haunted. 'Yes.'

'I'm investigating his death,' Colin said. 'I need to ask you a few questions, if that's OK?'

Aaron grimaced. 'I don't think I'll be able to help you much, because I wasn't at the church. I was at the studio.'

'I know,' Colin said. 'Tell me about Liam Jacobs.'

'I work – *worked*,' Aaron corrected himself, 'with him at the glass studio. He joined us six months ago.'

'Were you friends with him?' Colin asked.

'We were colleagues,' Aaron said.

Colin noted the distinction. Was there active hostility between them? he wondered. 'Did you socialise outside work?'

'Yes, on team nights out. We all went for a pizza, once a month,' Aaron said.

'Were you aware of Liam having any allergies?'

Aaron concurred. 'Coconut. We couldn't bring anything into the office that had coconut – food or anything else. He had an EpiPen for if he accidentally ate anything with coconut, though.'

'Did you ever know him to use it?' Colin asked.

'No,' Aaron said.

'What can you tell me about the project he was working on?'

Aaron shrugged. 'Two roundels at St Edmund's church in Little Wenborough, both thirteenth century. One was a centaur with a viol, and one was St Edmund. The leading had crumbled and some of the glass was damaged. The studio was commissioned to restore it.'

'Your aunt lives in Little Wenborough,' Colin said. 'Did you not want to work on the glass?'

Aaron didn't meet his eyes. 'The boss decides who works on a project.'

'Wouldn't your family connection make you a good choice to work on it, though?'

'Liam has – *had*,' Aaron corrected himself, 'more experience than me.'

'Your aunt was going to talk to him and persuade him to let you work on it, too,' Colin said.

'If you already know that, why are you asking me now?' Aaron asked.

'It's a line of enquiry,' Colin said. 'I believe you had lunch with your aunt and uncle yesterday.'

'I have Sunday lunch with them every week,' Aaron said.

'Were you there when your aunt was baking?'

'No. She always bakes before church on a Sunday, so the cookies or whatever are still slightly warm when she makes coffee for the congregation after the service. I normally arrive just after she and Uncle Walter get back from church.'

So he knew his aunt's routine well, Colin thought. 'Do you have a key to her house?'

Aaron frowned. 'Of course not. I don't live there.'

And now for the unexpected question. 'Is there any coconut oil in your kitchen?'

His face flamed. 'What are you accusing me of?'

Interestingly, not a denial. 'I'm not accusing you of anything,' Colin said. 'It's a line of enquiry.'

'No. I'm not much of a cook. Aunty Kath tried to teach me, but I...' He grimaced. 'Sandwiches are just easier. Or putting a pizza or chips in the oven.'

No wonder Kathleen insisted on feeding him once a week, to get some vegetables into him, Colin thought. Though his own culinary skills were almost as poor as Aaron's. Maybe he should learn to cook properly and share the load with Georgina. She enjoyed cooking and was good at it, but there was still the mental load of planning meals in advance and making sure you had all the ingredients. Doing the washing up – his main contribution – was the easy bit of dinner. 'Can you prove it?' he asked.

Aaron blinked. 'You want to see my kitchen cupboards?'

'And those of your housemates.'

'I...' He blew out a breath. 'Is this legal?'

'I can get a search warrant, if you prefer,' Colin said mildly. 'Of course, I'd need to stay here until the warrant was granted.' To make sure that any incriminating oil – if it did exist – wasn't removed during his absence. 'Or we can do it the quick way and you can offer to show me your kitchen.'

Aaron took time to think about it and sighed. 'Come through.' He ushered Colin into the kitchen. A quick inspection showed Colin that there were seven different types of oil owned by Aaron and his housemates between them, but no coconut oil. One of the boxes of granola contained coconut flakes, but there was no sign of desiccated coconut. The fridge also held a container of coconut yogurt, which according to Aaron belonged to a flatmate.

'Thank you for your co-operation,' Colin said. He'd check with Sammy about whether the yogurt could be the source of the coconut oil, but he still couldn't see how the yogurt could have been added to an already-baked cake without it being very obvious.

Georgina couldn't help with that question, either, when he got back to Little Wenborough. 'The only thing I can think of is some form of icing.' She checked a couple of websites. 'Yes – if you mix coconut yogurt with lemon juice and icing sugar, it makes a cake topping. But you saw the banana bread yourself. There was no kind of topping.'

'Back to the drawing board,' Colin said. 'Or maybe I need a chat with Cesca about how to get oil into a cake.'

'Would that be a chat over her lemon cake?' Georgina asked, a teasing glint in her eyes.

'Actually, I was thinking a cuddle with the baby,' Colin countered.

She grinned. 'You're an old softie at heart, aren't you?' Her smile faded. 'Do you really think Kathleen's nephew is involved?'

'I'm thinking about it,' he prevaricated. Aaron had claimed innocence, but he'd seemed jumpy. 'I can't rule him out, yet.'

'Poor Kathleen. She's had a rough time, too,' Georgina said. 'She lost her sister, she's trying to keep her nephew from going off the rails again, she wasn't able to save Liam, and the cake she offers all visitors to the church seems to have been contaminated by the one thing that made Liam extremely ill.'

'It hasn't been easy for you, either,' Colin said, giving her a hug.

'No.' Georgina sighed.

'And I'm not the only one with a case to untangle. You said something earlier about a case of typhoid and an accident, and neither of them was straightforward. How's your research going?'

Georgina filled him in on what she, Sybbie and Francesca had learned about Bram Locke and Martha Plowright.

'So you're thinking the typhoid might be murder – like the Victorian cases of arsenic poisoning that Will said had been mistaken for cholera or gastroenteritis?' Colin asked.

'Potentially,' Georgina agreed. 'Bram's obituary in the local paper made it clear he was very well loved. We looked through Bernard's family papers, and Amelia's diary said that everyone was devastated by Bram's death. Martha was popular, too. There aren't any likely candidates for the murderer.'

'Could it be that they really were just accidental deaths – one from typhoid and one a riding accident?' Colin asked.

'Potentially,' Georgina said. 'There's nothing in the parish record to say that anyone suspected otherwise.' She winced. 'But...'

'You think it was murder.'

'Martha told Doris she thinks it was murder,' Georgina confirmed. 'And that's where things start to get mixed up with the present day. Martha Plowright was Kathleen Reeves's great-great-grandmother.'

'Which would make Bram Kathleen's great-great-uncle?'

'Three times great,' Georgina corrected. 'Yes.'

'Does Kathleen know you're investigating their deaths?' Colin asked.

'Not yet,' Georgina admitted. 'I wanted to get all my facts straight before I talked to her about them. Though she was the one who brought them up when we were talking in her kitchen. She said Bram caught typhoid from some parishioners when he was visiting with food, and Martha died in a riding accident when she was trying to carry on his work and bring food to the sick.'

'So Kathleen doesn't think it was murder.'

'No. But she also mentioned this story about the treasure from the priory hidden in the tunnel – the one I told you about earlier. Kathleen said that Bram was the kind of man who was interested in lots of things. She called him a scholar. She thinks if anyone had been able to find the tunnel, it would have been him.' Georgina paused. 'Like Sybbie and Bernard, Kathleen has a family archive of papers. Walter has apparently been going through them in detail, recently.'

Colin frowned. 'Hang on. So does this treasure actually exist?'

'It might do,' Georgina said. 'Bernard said he heard stories about the tunnel, when he was a boy, and he spent quite a lot of time trying to find it. But he never found a trace of it. There's nothing on any of his maps. He thinks it's just a story – there are lots of similar stories in the county, apparently. But he also thinks that Walter is very level-headed and if there's any truth in it, Walter will get to the bottom of it. As you know, Bernard's on the PCC with Walter,' she added.

'Hmm. Dominic McGowan's writing a book on folklore. He told me there are a lot of legends in the county about hidden tunnels,' Colin said. 'He was going to investigate St Edmund's.' He paused. 'Though he doesn't seem to think much of the guy who did the podcast.'

'I haven't listened to it yet,' Georgina said, 'but Bernard has, and he said it was quite entertaining.'

'That clears up something for me,' Colin said. 'Dominic was a bit snooty about his academic background. Obviously he doesn't like popular history.'

'You really didn't take to Dominic, did you?' Georgina asked.

'No.' He wrinkled his nose. 'Which makes me feel a bit mean. Or it might simply have been professional jealousy on his part. His book is probably covering similar topics to the podcast.' He paused. 'What did you make of Liam Jacobs?'

'He was a nice guy, actually. Definitely not an intellectual snob. He loved his subject and wanted to share it with the world. I think you would have liked him,' Georgina said. 'What was Aaron Flint like?'

'Nervous, I'd say, and a bit of a fish out of water,' Colin said. 'I felt sorry for him. But something feels off. I can't put my finger on it right now. I need to think about it.' He sighed. 'I'm going to inter-view the rest of Liam's colleagues tomorrow.'

'And I'm going to talk to Kathleen,' Georgina said. 'But right now I'm going to heat through the chili I made earlier for you.'

Colin thought of the chili that had given him a few more grey hairs, a couple of months previously. He decided not to ask whether she'd made it with chicken mince. 'Thank you,' he said. 'And I'll put the kettle on.' Funny how domesticity could be so calming. And he was really grateful for Georgina.

NINE

Colin was in his car on Tuesday morning, heading for the glass studio to interview Liam's colleagues, when his mobile rang. He answered it via the hands-free system on his car. 'DI Bradshaw.'

'I've got proof it was him,' the person on the other end of the line said, without preamble.

Colin thought he recognised the voice. 'Is that Mr McGowan?' he asked.

'Of course it is,' Dominic snapped.

Clearly Dominic believed that the police only dealt with one case at a time.

'I've got proof,' he said again. 'Cast-iron proof.'

Playing dim might be a good idea, Colin thought. 'Proof of what?'

'That Aaron Flint was behind Liam's death. I found a text from him on Liam's phone. It's a threat.'

Colin sighed inwardly. He had the feeling that Dominic McGowan was the kind of person who'd be loud and persistent until he had his say. It would be better to deal with this on the way to the glass studio, because then he'd be able to do his interviews without interruptions. 'I'm on my way,' he said. 'Are you at home?'

'Yes.'

'I'll be twenty minutes,' he said. He called the glass studio on the way. 'I'm sorry, I have an urgent call to make on the way to you. I'll be a bit late, I'm afraid,' he said, hoping he wouldn't have to spend too much time with Dominic McGowan.

The 'proof' turned out to be a single text. *I'll get my aunt to sort you out.*

'Mr McGowan, this text is in isolation. I need to see it in context,' Colin said, as kindly as he could.

'It's a threat,' Dominic said stubbornly. 'Look at it. It's from Aaron Flint. He said he'd get his aunt to sort Dominic out. And she did exactly that, didn't she? She poisoned him with that cake.'

How did Dominic know that Liam's death was from anaphylaxis caused by coconut oil in the banana bread? Colin hadn't told him, because he was waiting to hear back from Sammy about the tests she'd sent off.

'May I see the phone, please?' he asked.

Dominic frowned, but handed over the phone.

The message was the only one from Aaron on Liam's phone, and it didn't appear to be in reply to a message from Liam. Liam also didn't seem to have replied to it. In Colin's experience, arguments conducted via a text app tended to contain more than one message. A single message – dated almost a month previously – seemed odd. Was Dominic McGowan so desperate to make it look as if Aaron was to blame for Liam's death that he'd deleted all the other messages in the conversation? Did he think the police were too stupid to spot that, had he forgotten that Colin had arranged for a copy of all the data on the phone to be made so could check it quite easily, or was he simply unhinged by grief?

'You need to arrest Aaron Flint,' Dominic said, his eyes narrowing. 'He's the one behind all this.'

'I'll investigate,' Colin repeated, 'and I'll let you have the phone back as soon as I can. We're doing our best to find out what happened, Mr McGowan.'

'It's Aaron Flint's fault,' Dominic insisted again.

Back in the car, Colin messaged Larissa to ask her to check the conversation in the data from Liam's phone. He was going to the glass studio anyway, so he'd check Aaron's phone to see if he could find the rest of that text conversation.

Georgina was about to take Bert for a walk when there was a rap on her kitchen door, and Sybbie walked in, looking upset and cross. 'I need your help,' she said.

'What's happened?' Georgina asked.

'Kathleen called me just now in floods of tears. It seems that Liam's partner, Dominic, is sitting in the church, glowering at everyone. Someone told him that the cake Liam ate was the thing that killed him. And everyone knows that Kathleen makes the cakes for the church.'

'Oh, no.' Georgina had a nasty feeling that she knew where this was going.

'Dominic had a go at her when she went into St Edmund's before the ten o'clock service to set up the tea and coffee. He said if there was a god, he'd strike Kathleen down for being in cahoots with her nephew and murdering someone with banana bread. He said she'd added coconut to the cake on purpose.' Sybbie winced. 'It was quite a spectacular rant, apparently. And she rushed out in tears.'

'Was anyone else there to try and calm him down?' Georgina asked. The vicar would be the obvious person, but she didn't think that Craig Phillipson's social skills would be up to defusing a row of these proportions.

'Several of the parishioners were there for the service. Walter – who was absolutely spitting feathers about it – told Craig Phillipson he should ask Dominic to leave and stop causing trouble, or at the very least behave appropriately in church,' Sybbie said. 'And the vicar, of course, refused because he says Dominic needs the comfort of God in his bereavement.'

'The god that Dominic more or less said he didn't believe in, in front of the rest of the congregation?' Georgina asked wryly.

'Exactly.' Sybbie rolled her eyes. 'Why on earth did they appoint such a clueless, spineless buffoon as Craig Phillipson?'

'Maybe they thought that Little Wenborough would help to shape him,' Georgina suggested.

'I think he needs more than *shaping*,' Sybbie said, scowling. 'Kathleen says she feels she can't do anything in the church, because it would be rubbing Dominic's nose in Liam's death. She can't do the flowers, she can't welcome visitors, she can't make tea and coffee after a service, she can't bring in cake – all the things she usually does during the week. Plus she's convinced herself that she murdered Liam Jacobs, even though that's utterly ridiculous and of *course* she didn't murder the poor man! Walter's livid because he knows Kathleen's innocent and he thinks she's being pushed out of the place she loves by someone who's being utterly unfair to her.'

'Dominic's being more than unfair,' Doris chimed in.

'Sorry, Doris – how do you mean?' Georgina asked, and filled Sybbie in on what Doris had said.

'He's acting very oddly. He's been sitting in the church, in the pew next to where Liam died, and I heard him say to the vicar that it makes him feel close to Liam to be right there. Everyone thinks he's grieving for his partner and they're tiptoeing round him. But that's not the odd thing,' Doris continued. 'Now everyone's gone, he's not sitting in the pew with his head bowed and his hands covering his face, the way he was when everyone was still in the church to see him grieving. He seems to be searching the church systematically, taking photographs and making notes on his phone.'

'Searching the church? Maybe he's trying to solve Liam's death,' Sybbie said.

'It doesn't feel like that,' Doris said.

Georgina repeated her words for Sybbie's benefit.

'Why else would he be searching the church?' Sybbie asked.

'He told Colin he was writing a book about folklore. Maybe he's heard the stories about the alleged treasure in the tunnel and he's looking for evidence,' Georgina said.

'And he's using Liam's death as an excuse to make everyone

feel too awkward to go into the church, meaning that he can look around at his leisure without interruptions?' Sybbie asked. 'The more I hear about this man, the more obnoxious he sounds. And you said Liam was *nice*. What on earth was he doing, getting involved with someone so unpleasant?'

'You can't help who you fall in love with,' Georgina reminded her. 'And maybe Dominic was different with him.' She sighed. 'You're right – we need to boost Kathleen's spirits. I'll cut some tulips for her before we go and see her.'

'Way ahead of you, dear girl,' Sybbie said. 'I cut a few from my garden before I came here. They're in the car. You can't really take cake to cheer a baker up – even if it *is* Cesca's – but I think lovely red tulips would make anyone feel a bit brighter.'

'They would,' Georgina agreed. 'Let's go and see her now.' She bent down to make a fuss of the spaniel. 'Bert, my lovely, I still don't like leaving you, but I know I'm being paranoid and I need to stop being so twitchy. I have to go out for a bit, but I promise we'll go to the park when I'm back.'

'I turned the car round in your yard so we're ready to go,' Sybbie said when Georgina had settled Bert in his bed and was locking her kitchen door. She crunched over the gravel to the car. 'Hop in. You, too, Doris, if you don't mind continuing our conversation in the car.'

'Of course,' Doris said.

'I was going to ask you if what we found out yesterday helped Martha to remember any more,' Georgina said.

'It did,' Doris confirmed, sounding excited. 'Martha remembers that Bram used to smell of carbolic soap and oranges.'

'Oranges?' Georgina asked, surprised. 'Carbolic soap, I can understand – Lister used carbolic acid as an antiseptic in the 1860s and it was an ingredient in the first germicidal soap sold to the general public. It makes sense that Bram would use it. But why would he smell of oranges? Was it some sort of cologne, perhaps?'

'Citric acid's a mild disinfectant,' Sybbie suggested. 'It smells a bit better than carbolic soap, too. Normally, lemon is used, but maybe oranges were easier to get hold of than lemons back then.' She paused. 'I read through some more of Amelia's and Caroline's diaries. Amelia thought that Bram wore some kind of cologne that smelled like oranges. And so did Harvey, the doctor.'

'That would support your disinfectant theory, especially as Bram was visiting people who'd contracted typhoid,' Georgina said. 'But weren't oranges rare, in Victorian times?'

'I don't know.' Before she turned the key in the ignition, Sybbie did a quick search on her phone. 'No. According to Henry Mayhew's *London Labour and the London Poor*, in the 1850s nearly 62 million oranges were sold every year in London.' She looked up another reference. 'As opposed to about 15 million lemons. So maybe the disinfectant theory is correct.'

'It would make sense,' Georgina said. 'Doris, did Martha remember anything else?'

'She thought Bram might have talked to John Barton, the sexton, about the tunnel,' Doris said.

'I'm showing my ignorance here, but what does a sexton do?' Georgina asked.

'The sexton was in charge of digging graves, ringing bells and cleaning the church,' Sybbie said. 'He'd know the church and the churchyard like the back of his hand. He'd know where all the graves were. Maybe the tunnel – if it exists – led to an old grave. The sexton would know which one was the most likely.'

'Martha thinks Bram wanted to find the treasure to pay for building repairs to the church,' Doris added. 'Plus he would have money left over to do more for the villagers. He planned to set up a hospital with Harvey Plowright, and help the villagers with food and clothes.'

'He sounds like a thoroughly decent man,' Sybbie said, when Georgina relayed the information. 'I think our present-day incumbent could learn a lot from him.'

'Couldn't he just?' Georgina asked wryly.

When they arrived at the cottage, Walter opened the front door to them. 'Are you here to see Kathleen, Lady Wyatt?'

'Yes.' Sybbie rolled her eyes at him. 'And you've known me for enough years by now to use my first name, Walter.'

'It's a mark of respect,' he said.

'Hmm,' she said. 'In my view, it'd be more respectful if you used my first name.'

'Come in. I'll make the tea.' He ushered them through to the kitchen, where Kathleen was sitting at the table, her eyes red and swollen from crying.

Sybbie handed the tulips to Kathleen. 'I hope these might brighten your day a bit.'

'They're beautiful. Thank you, Sybbie,' Kathleen said. 'I feel terrible about what happened yesterday. I've hardly slept, and I've been racking my brains as to how my cake could have contained coconut oil. But I *know* I didn't use it. I'm not senile. I don't even have any in my kitchen!'

'We all know you didn't use coconut oil. Yes, I know the inspector said it showed up in the lab tests, but science isn't always right,' Walter said.

'But that young man this morning said...' Kathleen bit her lip. 'Everyone thinks I'm a murderer,' she whispered.

'No, they don't. They know you. He was totally in the wrong, the way he talked to you,' Walter said. 'Reverend Phillipson should have stood up for you, instead of being as much use as a chocolate teapot.' His mouth thinned. 'Please sit down, your ladyship and Mrs Drake.'

The mugs of tea he put in front of them were way too strong for Georgina's taste, but no way was she going to criticise the effort he'd made. She appreciated the way he was supporting Kathleen.

'I would offer you cake, but in the circumstances...' Kathleen shook her head. 'Right now, I don't think I'll ever be able to bake again.'

Sybbie squeezed her hand. 'Kathleen, anybody who's ever met you will know you've done nothing wrong. You didn't know Liam was severely allergic to coconut, and you didn't put coconut of any form in that banana bread. It was a tragic accident. Think of all the people who come to church because it means they actually get to talk to another human being – you welcome them after the service with tea, coffee and cake, bringing them a bit of happiness, and that's a gift that shouldn't be thrown away. Everyone knows you make the church the place it is. Without the warmth of your welcome, people might not have the courage to walk in.'

'Who told Dominic McGowan about the banana bread anyway?' Walter asked, narrowing his eyes at Georgina. 'The policeman?'

'I doubt it was Colin,' Georgina said. 'He was still waiting to hear about some more lab results. And he would have warned you before he said anything, because Dominic seems a bit volatile.'

'Volatile isn't the half of it. He's a troublemaker,' Walter said. 'He might be saying he wants to be at the church to be close to Liam, but I think he's got other motives for prowling around St Edmund's.'

As did Doris.

Sybbie and Georgina waited, but Walter didn't enlighten them. Instead, he said, 'I've got a pretty good idea who had loose lips. He doesn't have two bits of common sense to rub together. Whatever floats into his head comes straight out of his mouth.'

Georgina and Sybbie exchanged a glance, guessing exactly who Walter meant. The new vicar.

'We're stuck with him until he decides to move on, but I don't think anyone else would have him.' Walter scowled. 'When Reverend Martyn left, we were doing all right with the curate from St Mary's at Great Wenborough. She's lovely, a real woman of God who pays proper attention to her parish and its people.'

For someone who gave the impression of being a stickler for traditional views, Walter had a surprisingly modern outlook, Georgina thought.

'Right when it was first suggested that we appoint another vicar, I said we should be looking at a joint benefice with St Mary's instead,' Walter continued. 'The way things are nowadays, there simply aren't enough parishioners to support the costs of two churches in both villages. Group benefices are common around here; we should have done the same. And at least then we would have had someone decent as the vicar.'

'Why was Craig Phillipson appointed, Walter?' Sybbie asked.

'He's the bishop's nephew,' Walter said grimly. 'Apparently, he hadn't managed to stick to any career for more than a few months since university. Then, a couple of years ago, he decided to follow in his uncle's footsteps. Personally, I don't think he has a calling to the church. I think he believed that being a vicar would be a cushy little number and he could just float around, smiling beatifically and getting people to make him cups of tea – like the vicars you see on TV.'

'He couldn't have been ordained without going through ministry training, though,' Sybbie pointed out. 'You'd know better than I do, but I thought that means up to eighteen months being assessed and mentored, two years of full-time training, and then up to three years as an assistant curate.'

'Yes. Though that worked out as six months as an assistant curate, in his case,' Walter said. 'Apparently, he was fast-tracked. I wonder if that had anything to do with the fact that his sponsoring bishop was his uncle?'

'That's cynical, Walter,' Sybbie said.

'Realistic,' Walter countered. 'The man's hopeless. He would never have got through ordination on his own. I'll bet you anything he's the youngest son of the bishop's favourite sister, who said how worried she was about her son and she thought he needed a bit of help.'

'That's unkind, Walter,' Kathleen said.

'But it's also true. He's not a good vicar.' Walter sighed. 'And right now we could do with someone to pull the community together.'

At the glass studio, Colin talked to everyone in the company one by one in the meeting room. He discovered that Liam was well liked and good at his job, and nobody could think of anyone who would have wanted to harm him.

Aaron repeated what he'd said, the previous evening.

'Would you mind unlocking your phone and opening your messages app, please?' Colin asked.

Aaron looked surprised, but did so.

'And could you select the messages you exchanged with Liam Jacobs, please, and let me see them?'

Aaron shook his head. 'I'm afraid I don't have any.'

Colin frowned. 'But he's your colleague. Surely you sent each other some kind of messages about work?'

'You can look on my phone for yourself,' Aaron said. 'But my last girlfriend was a bit of a techie. She said my inbox was a mess and took up way too much space, so she set my phone up to auto-delete messages after a fortnight.'

Colin checked anyway. Frustratingly, there were no messages to or from Liam Jacobs in the main folder or the archive. That message Dominic had shown him had been dated more than two weeks ago, so if Aaron wasn't spinning a line about how long he kept messages, it would be impossible to check. And a quick look at Aaron's deleted messages folder showed him that the younger man had been telling the truth; the oldest message was only a fortnight old.

He just had to hope that Larissa would find something in the data back at the police station.

'Do you remember messaging anything to Liam over the last month?' Colin asked.

Aaron shrugged. 'Nothing in particular, no.'

The lack of messages to and from Liam looked suspicious, but Colin didn't have the impression that Aaron was good at dissembling. If Aaron had threatened Liam, it would have shown on his face. It looked as if Colin would need to get hold of the rest of the conversation through the phone provider's records.

'Am I in trouble?' Aaron asked.

That rather depended on what the rest of that text conversation said. 'I'm just checking a few things,' Colin said. 'I'll write up your statement and ask you to read through it, alter anything that isn't right, then sign it.'

Once that had been done, Ralph Kennedy, the head of the studio, called Aaron into his office. A couple of minutes later, the young man slammed the office door and stormed out of the building, looking angry and upset.

Colin went to see Ralph. 'Problems?' he asked.

Ralph winced. 'I've had to put Aaron on gardening leave for a while. Just until things calm down.'

'Calm down? Why? What's happened?' Colin asked.

'Liam's partner has been kicking up a storm on social media, hinting that Liam's death wasn't an accident and suggesting that Aaron was behind it.' Ralph looked grim. 'I've had a couple of clients call the office this morning. They're concerned that there's no smoke without fire, and they've said they don't want Aaron on the team for their projects.'

'That's a bit unfair. We don't have evidence to say for definite that Liam was murdered, let alone evidence to charge anyone with murder – and at the moment I don't have any kind of proof that Aaron was involved,' Colin said.

'I know it's unfair, but I need to nip things in the bud. Rumours can bring down a business very quickly,' Ralph said. 'I've worked hard to build up the studio. I need to take my customers' feelings into account. The last thing I want is for people to start cancelling projects, to the point where I have to start laying off some of my staff.'

'Do you think Aaron's capable of murder?' Colin asked quietly.

Ralph frowned while he thought about it. 'I think anyone's capable of murder, given the right circumstances. And Aaron's had a difficult few years.' He sighed. 'It was my wife who persuaded me to give him a chance. She felt sorry for him because he lost his mum so young. She thought once he was back on his feet he'd do well.'

'Has he lived up to her expectations?'

'In the main,' Ralph said. 'Though he can be a bit on the surly side. And he's been sulking about not getting the project at St Edmund's. But Liam was the obvious choice to lead the job because he had more experience.'

'I'm not telling you how to run your business,' Colin said mildly. 'But in my experience, loyalty works best when it goes both ways.'

Ralph had the grace to flush. 'Things will settle down again soon.'

Given the way Dominic had drawn his attention to some incriminating evidence, Colin didn't think it would be quite as easy as that. 'I hope so,' he said. 'I'll be in touch.'

Back in his car, he called Larissa, his DC. 'Can you get onto a couple of phone providers for me, please? We need a copy of the text messages between Liam Jacobs and Aaron Flint, for the last six weeks. I've got Liam's phone, but there's only one message, which feels out of place, and it turns out that Aaron's one of these people who deletes everything to save storage space – well, actually, I think he's a bit disorganised, and he claims his last girlfriend sorted it out for him.' He gave her the relevant phone numbers.

'On it, guv,' Larissa said.

'Thank you,' Colin said. 'I'm on my way back in.'

And hopefully soon Larissa would find some answers from the phone providers. Something that would shed a bit more light on how cordial or difficult the relationship between Liam and Aaron had really been, and whether Dominic McGowan was telling the truth about Aaron being behind Liam's death.

# TEN

Kathleen's mobile phone rang. 'I'll let it go to voicemail,' she said. 'It's probably someone about what happened in church this morning and I don't want to talk about it.'

But whoever was calling clearly didn't want to leave a message and her phone continued shrilling. She glanced at the screen and frowned. 'Oh. It's Aaron – my nephew. I'd better take this.'

'Let me talk to him, Kath,' Walter said. 'And don't worry. I'll be tactful.'

'All right.' Kathleen let him take her phone.

Walter came back, a few minutes later, looking grim. 'That McGowan chap really is a nightmare. It seems he's been kicking up a fuss, and Aaron's been put on gardening leave.'

Kathleen looked shocked. 'What? Why?'

'McGowan is claiming that Aaron is behind Liam's death.' Walter rolled his eyes. 'And he's put enough nonsense on social media that clients have been calling the studio and saying they don't want Aaron working on their jobs. Aaron's boss has put him on paid leave until it all settles down.'

'What? But that's ridiculous,' Kathleen said. 'And it's so unfair. Aaron's done nothing wrong.'

'Exactly,' Walter said. 'I'm going to have a little word with the vicar and make him do the right thing. We need to get that trouble-maker out of our church as soon as possible.'

'Walter, think of your heart,' Kathleen counselled. 'You're not supposed to get worked up. Maybe you should leave things be.'

'I'll get a lot more worked up if I do that,' Walter said. 'Dominic McGowan is up to something shady, you mark my words. There's a reason why he's sitting in the church, and it isn't grief. There's something about him I just don't trust.'

From what Doris had said earlier, Georgina was pretty sure Walter was right. Not that she could explain to him why she agreed with him. She exchanged a glance with Sybbie.

'The vicar probably won't take a blind bit of notice of me,' Sybbie said, 'but shall I call Bernard to come and back you up?'

'I don't want to bother his lordship,' Walter said. 'I won't be long. I'll get it sorted out.'

'There's no stopping him when he's got a bee in his bonnet,' Kathleen said gloomily when Walter had left. 'I can't believe poor Aaron's been dragged into this. And I'm beginning to wonder if my family's been cursed.' She sighed. 'Bram died from typhoid when he was trying to help the sick, Martha had that riding accident and died very young, my sister died before her time, it seems I've killed someone with my cake – even though I don't understand how it happened – and now Aaron's on gardening leave and might even lose his job.'

'It's just a run of bad luck,' Sybbie said. 'Life goes like that, sometimes.'

'This might be a weird question, Kathleen, but yesterday you told me a bit about Bram and how he'd died serving his parishioners. Are you absolutely sure that he died of typhoid?' Georgina asked.

Kathleen frowned. 'How odd that you should ask that. Actually, Martha wrote in her diary that she thought there was something not quite right about her brother's death, but she couldn't prove anything. After she died, there was nobody to chase it up –

and it all happened so long ago, I think it's too late to do anything now.'

'Sybbie and I have helped solve a few cold cases,' Georgina said. 'Maybe we can look into your uncle's case for you.'

Kathleen looked doubtful. 'There probably won't be anything to find after all this time.'

'You said you were the custodian of your family's papers,' Georgina reminded her. 'Perhaps Sybbie and I could borrow some of them for a couple of days, and go through them? Or, if it would be easier for you, perhaps I could photograph them? Then you'd have a digital copy to keep, too.'

'I guess it wouldn't hurt for you to borrow them,' Kathleen said. 'Though I can't let you have the things that Walter borrowed from the vicarage because they're not mine to lend.' She winced. 'Also, as I told you, I don't think Reverend Phillipson knows that Walter has borrowed them. I don't want to stir up any trouble.'

'We won't say a word,' Sybbie said.

'But maybe we could look at them here and take photographs?' Georgina suggested.

'Do you think that Martha was right, and Bram didn't die from typhoid?' Kathleen asked.

'There are a few things that don't add up. Martha's husband was the village doctor and saw the same people that Bram did, but he didn't catch typhoid. He was Bram's best friend, so surely Bram would have followed Harvey's advice on how to avoid catching typhoid?' Sybbie said. 'Amelia – Bernard's great-great-great-grand-mother – wrote about Bram in her diary and said he was very well liked in the village. She said he did a lot to help the parishioners, and he always smelled of oranges.' She smiled. 'I can get Georgie to take photographs of the relevant pages, if you like, so you have a copy. She also mentioned Martha, and said how tragic it was that Martha died in that riding accident when the baby was only four months old.'

'It was,' Kathleen agreed.

They were still talking about Bram and Martha when Walter came back, looking cross.

'Are you all right?' Kathleen asked. 'Your face is a bit red,' she added anxiously.

'I'm fine, love. You don't need to worry about me,' Walter reassured her.

'What happened?'

'The vicar did his mealy-mouthed thing, as usual,' Walter said. 'And then that guy from the podcast turned up at the church, looking for the abbot's hidden treasure. I told him that he's looking for completely the wrong thing. The treasure in the church is actually its people, and the love and kindness in their hearts.' He huffed. 'Though I can't say I feel very much love or kindness towards Dominic McGowan right now. And I noticed he was looking daggers at the podcast guy. It's obvious they don't get on.' He looked at the two slim leather-bound volumes on the table. 'Are those Bram's?'

'His last diary and his last notebook. I've said Sybbie and Georgie can borrow them for a few days,' Kathleen said.

'Looking for the abbot's hidden treasure, too, are you?' Walter asked, giving them a pointed look.

'The treasure might have been real at some point, but I'm not convinced it's still hidden, or that the tunnel even exists,' Georgina said. 'Bernard was telling me about the undercrofts in Norwich, and all the legends about secret tunnels across the county.'

'There are plenty of them, particularly the ones about Fiddler's Hill – there are a few of those,' Walter said, nodding. 'And I've no doubt those same stories were told elsewhere across the country. If you ask me, the tunnels were probably old mine-workings. In this part of the world, they'd be chalk workings, like the ones underneath Norwich. Or maybe flint mines, like the pits out at Grime's Graves. But it suited some vicars to use the stories to warn their flock about getting involved with itinerant musicians. And *those* sort of tales are worldwide – there's the one about the blues guitarist Robert Johnson being taught to play by the devil at the crossroads.'

'Very Faustian,' Georgina agreed.

'But if you don't think the treasure exists,' Walter said, 'what's your interest in Bram?'

'I heard the story, and I think it's a bit strange that he caught typhoid, considering he took precautions while ministering to the sick,' Georgina said. 'He used carbolic soap and oranges.'

'Oranges?' Walter asked, looking interested. 'What makes you say that?'

'Something we read in Bernard's great-great-great-grandmother's papers,' Sybbie said. 'Our theory is that he might have used citric acid – in the form of oranges – as a kind of disinfectant. Lister had just started using carbolic, but if Bram couldn't get hold of enough supplies, he might have used other alternatives.'

'We think there might have been a miscarriage of justice regarding Bram and the typhoid,' Georgina said. 'Our theory is that he was looking into the story of the treasure and the tunnel. Maybe somebody believed he'd actually found it and tried to beat him to it – that, or get Bram out of the way before he could find it.'

'Bram stops talking about the treasure in his diary, about a month before his death,' Walter said. 'And then he starts leaving bigger gaps between the lines when he writes. There are some blank pages, too. That struck me as a bit strange. Paper wasn't cheap, and he wasn't rich. Any money he had was spent on helping the poor, not on self-indulgence.'

Georgina thought of the diary she'd worked on a few months ago, the tiny writing and the use of every piece of space. And even Amelia, from a wealthy background, hadn't been profligate with her diary. 'My son shared a house with a historian, in his university years,' she said. 'His friend said that paper was very expensive and every scrap was used. In Regency times, as soon as they got to the end of the page when they were writing a personal letter, they used to turn it ninety degrees and treat it as if it were another sheet of paper.'

'I guess we're lucky Bram didn't do that with his diary,' Walter said. 'And you mentioned he smelled of oranges, which makes me think of the Gunpowder Plotters. They used orange juice for ink. The writing in juice faded as it dried and it was invisible until it was heated over a candle flame. Though apparently it stayed visible once it had been heated, and that's how the plotters knew whether their letters had been intercepted.'

'Do you think that might be the real reason why Bram smelled of oranges?' Georgina asked. 'Not because he used it as a kind of disinfectant, but because he used it as invisible ink?'

'Invisible ink could account for the gaps between the lines in his diary, and for the blank pages,' Walter said slowly. 'I'd been wondering about that. Though I haven't wanted to heat the paper to test my theory, because I don't want to risk damaging it. From what I've read, you have to almost singe the paper for the chemical reaction to work.'

'My daughter Bea is an actress. She works as a probate genealogist when she's resting. One of her former colleagues, Kirsty, has a job at the National Archives in Kew,' Georgina said. 'She's been working with multispectral imaging to look at documents that have faded. Apparently, the lighting and cameras help the archivists to see and interpret writing in ink that had been illegible before.' She looked at Walter. 'If Bram wrote his findings in orange juice to keep them secret, maybe Kirsty could help us read it.'

'Using the new technology, so it doesn't damage the original?' Sybbie asked. 'That's a really good idea.'

Walter looked at them, clearly thinking about it.

'Perhaps you can have a word with her and see if she can help.' He paused. 'If she can do something, how long would it be likely to take?'

'I don't know,' Georgina said honestly. 'So do you think the tunnel exists, and Bram found it?'

'I think he found *something*,' Walter said. 'His earlier diaries talk about looking through the records of previous incumbents. I borrowed some of the things he talked about from the archives at the vicarage, to see if I could find what he discovered.'

'Before the new vicar was installed?' Sybbie asked wryly.

'As the senior churchwarden, I needed to keep an eye on the vicarage and its contents,' Walter said. 'They belong to the church, not to the vicar. I've been thinking for a while that the two oldest parish registers really ought to be deposited with the county archives. In the meantime, I'm merely a servant of the church.'

'There's nothing "mere" about you, Walter Reeves,' Kathleen said.

Walter sighed. 'But, yes, you're right. I intended to tell the new vicar about it, but unfortunately I think I have Reverend Phillipson's measure. If I tell him about my theory, he's likely to say something that isn't accurate in front of the wrong people, and it might cause a tricky situation.'

'In other words, he'll hype it up and there will be people coming to the church at all hours, trying to find treasure and digging where they shouldn't be digging?' Sybbie asked.

Georgina thought back to Colin's case where nighthawks had been on the Manor's lands, looking for treasure and destroying the archaeological layers at the dig. People could get very single-minded when it came to treasure, not thinking about the damage they were doing to their surroundings. 'I don't blame you for not wanting that kind of publicity,' she said. 'I'd like to reassure you that you can rely on our discretion.'

'Absolutely, dear girl,' Sybbie agreed. 'What do you think Bram's working theory was, Walter?'

Walter was silent for a long, long moment. And then he sighed. 'I trust you, your ladyship.'

'Sybbie,' Sybbie reminded him.

'Your ladyship,' Walter repeated obstinately.

She gave him a rueful smile. 'You're two hundred or so years after your time, you know.'

'I was brought up with good manners,' Walter said. 'And

because you're her ladyship's friend, Mrs Drake, I believe I can trust you.'

'Good,' Georgina said. 'You can.'

'Let me make some more tea,' he said. 'And then I'll tell you what I know.'

Once they were all sitting round the scrubbed pine table with cups of tea, Walter took the floor. 'We know there was a priory in Little Wenborough. It was one of the smaller religious houses, with an income of less than £200 a year, so it was one of the first batch to be dissolved, in 1536. The land, money and silver plate belonging to the priory were confiscated by the king, and the estate was sold in the first place to John Howard, the third Duke of Norfolk – who bought rather a lot of monastic land locally. Eventually the Howards sold the site to the first Baron Wyatt, and I'd say at least some of the stone from the priory was used to build the manor.'

'But Bernard's family weren't Catholics, unlike the Bedingfields at Oxburgh,' Sybbie said, 'so there are no priest's holes or anything like that in the house. Bernard thinks the manor's cellars were used for storing wine and beer brewed on the premises, and he combed every inch of the cellars as a child, looking for the tunnel. He doesn't think it exists.'

'It doesn't exist *anymore*,' Walter said, 'but I think it might have existed when the priory was still there. Several abbeys are thought to have hidden at least some of their treasures and relics from Henry VIII. There's a story about Shaftesbury Abbey, where an elderly priest hid some treasure in a tunnel but died from a heart attack before he could tell the abbess where the secret chamber was, and the chamber and its contents has never been found. It's entirely possible that something similar happened here.'

'Do you think the other end of the tunnel is in the church? Or might the tunnel have led to one of the older graves in the churchyard, maybe someone with a connection to the priory?' Georgina asked.

'Not to an older grave. It's very rare to find gravestones in a churchyard dating before the seventeenth century,' Walter said. 'Churchyards tended to run out of room for burials, and I don't mean just during the plague years. So the older graves were opened up, the bones removed and stored in a charnel house, and then the grave was free to hold a new body.'

'Like in Donne's "The Relic",' Georgina said. '"When my grave is broke up again/Some second guest to entertain..." I remember being really shocked in a tutorial when our tutor told us that the graves in a churchyard were reused.'

'Because nowadays we expect our graves to last for ever and ever, even though there's a physical limit to how many bodies you can fit into a graveyard,' Walter said. 'Back in the Renaissance, they took a more practical view.'

'So where was the other end of the tunnel?' Sybbie asked.

'My theory is that Bram was looking at the crypt – which we always keep locked. Not because I'm a killjoy who wants to stop people looking for treasure,' Walter said, 'but because it's a health and safety nightmare and we simply can't afford for someone to fall down the stairs, hurt themselves and sue the church. The buildings insurance wouldn't cover it. Or if it did,' he added gloomily, 'the premium would skyrocket, and like many parish churches St Edmund's is struggling for money as it is.'

'I didn't realise there was a crypt in St Edmund's,' Sybbie said. 'Which makes me feel rather stupid, considering how many years I've lived in Little Wenborough.'

'I left it out of the church guidebook on purpose, to try to avoid issues,' Walter said. 'The crypt used to be the charnel house. It's beneath the chancel, and there's a medieval door from inside the church leading down to it. If anyone asks me about it, I say it's just storage, and they seem to assume it's a cupboard for vestments or what have you and don't ask any more. The stone steps are dangerous, the room itself is damp, and there's no actual light down there.'

'That definitely sounds like a health and safety nightmare,' Sybbie sympathised.

'Walter has this dream of restoring the room, making it safe and turning it into a museum,' Kathleen said.

'And then I'd revamp the church guidebook and talk about its history. But restoring the crypt and installing lights down there – even if we used battery-powered ones rather than electric – would cost money,' Walter said. 'Money that we don't have. Besides, the crypt restoration is way, way down in the list of priorities of things that the church needs. The most important issues right now are the roof and that damp patch with the moss.'

'If you found the tunnel and the treasure,' Sybbie said, 'you'd be able to pay for all of that *and* sorting out the crypt.' She paused. 'You said Bram was looking at the crypt as the potential site of the treasure. Did he want to restore the crypt, too?'

'No. He planned to use the money to fix the church roof. Some things never change,' Walter said wryly. 'And then he wanted to set up a hospital with Harvey Plowright.'

'What made him think that the tunnel might be in the crypt?' Georgina asked.

'Something he read in a former vicar's journal, and in the back of a parish register,' Walter said. 'Parish registers didn't have a standard form, in the early days. Some churches were already keeping records of marriages, baptisms and burials, but in 1538 Thomas Cromwell brought in a law that said all churches had to keep records. It was unpopular because people believed Cromwell was planning to use the records to start raising taxes.'

'Which sounds about right for Henry VIII and his government,' Sybbie said.

Walter gave a nod of agreement. 'Books were expensive and usually they were donated by someone of high standing in the area. In practice, they used the cheapest paper possible. Obviously the registers deteriorated quickly, so hardly any originals survive from the sixteenth century. Then in 1597, Elizabeth I ordered that copies of records from the beginning of her reign had to be written on parchment, and from the year after that the vicar had to send copies of the register to the bishop every year, within a month of Easter.'

'The bishop's transcripts,' Georgina said. 'I've come across those before.'

'Sometimes they survive where the originals haven't, which is very useful for family historians,' Walter said. 'But the early registers are a complete jumble. They weren't separated out into books for births, deaths and marriages, or even listed on separate pages; they were just written down as they happened during the year, and some of the vicars gave the barest minimum of details – you won't even see the age or occupation of the person who was buried or married. Some vicars were chatty and added little comments in the margins, but our registers at St Edmund's were quite basic until the 1700s.' He paused. 'At the back of St Edmund's registers, there are pages of memoranda. That's where the vicar might mention building work that needed doing, or if a donor gave something to the church – something like new kneelers, or a lectern, or perhaps even a stained-glass window. In one of the later registers, one of our vicars talks about a terrible storm in 1860 which caused the chimney of the vicarage to collapse and it needed to be rebuilt.' He looked at Sybbie and Georgina. 'But the entries that interest me most are from one of the earliest vicars, Gulielmus Nashe. He wrote his entries entirely in Latin – the memoranda as well as the registers themselves.'

'Gulielmus – that's William, isn't it?' Georgina asked.

'Yes,' Walter said.

'My Latin is a bit scrappy, nowadays,' Georgina admitted.

'Mine's still relatively OK, at least enough to do a rough translation,' Sybbie said. 'May I see?'

'Give me a moment. I've kept it in the safe.' Walter left the kitchen, and returned carrying something wrapped in what Georgina recognised as archive paper. He unwrapped it gently to reveal a slim leather-covered book.

'I feel as if I should be wearing cotton gloves before I touch this,' Sybbie said.

'Nowadays, the experts think cotton gloves will cause more damage than hands alone,' Walter said. 'But I need to ask you something for the sake of the parchment – are you wearing hand cream?'

'No,' Sybbie said. 'Bernard's just as careful with the early records in the Manor archives. I know that oils or creams on your hand can damage the records and you won't know until years later, when it's too late. I'll wash my hands and dry them properly before I look at the book.'

'The cloakroom's in the hall, next to the front door,' Kathleen said.

Sybbie went to wash her hands. When she returned, she looked at the page Walter had opened for her.

'I see what you mean about the handwriting,' she said, squinting at it. 'Let's see – oh, now that's interesting. William Nashe is writing here in 1599. He mentions that the charnel house wall needed repair yet again. Clearly the problem with damp has been going on for centuries.'

'Indeed. Now have a look at the year 1570,' Walter said. 'You're looking for a burial. Robert Fysshe.'

Sybbie gently turned the pages until she found the right one. 'That's a different hand – and it's even harder to read. Robert Fysshe *sepultus*... that's "buried"... *ultimo die mensis*... "the last day of"... *Septembris*... September.'

'Which, incidentally, was a Saturday,' Walter said. 'Now look at this.' He tapped into his phone and brought up a page. 'Scroll down until you see a name you recognise.'

'Priors of Little Wenborough. Robert Fysshe, elected 1522, last prior,' Sybbie read aloud. 'Is that entry for the same man?'

'I think so. The dates tally. Supposing that, like most abbots, he had to be at least thirty years of age before he could be elected as prior,' Walter said. 'That would make him around forty-six when the priory was dissolved, and seventy-eight when he died.'

'That was quite an age, in those days. And he'd lived through some seriously difficult times,' Sybbie said. 'Not just the Dissolution, but all the religious upheaval and uncertainty between Edward VI and Mary I after Henry VIII's death.'

'William Nashe's grandfather was an apothecary,' Walter said. 'He treated Robert Fysshe during his last illness. And he was close to his grandson. Just before he died, he confided to William that Robert Fysshe had told him he was warned about the arrival of Henry's commissioners coming to value the priory's belongings, and he hid some of the priory treasure in a tunnel which was then blocked up. William Nashe wrote down his grandfather's words, years later, in his journal. But Fysshe didn't say where the tunnel was and nobody ever found it.'

'Is that when the legend started, do you think?' Georgina asked.

'Perhaps. Fysshe was an elderly man nearing the end of his life, so he could simply have been rambling, confusing the past and the present,' Walter said. 'Like my father asking me to pay the coalman with a ten-bob note he'd put on the sideboard, a few days before he died – and that was decades past decimalisation and long after he'd moved to a flat with electric heating. Maybe Fysshe had heard tales of another former prior hiding treasure from the king's commissioners, and it was something he wished he'd done rather than something he'd actually done.'

'But the apothecary clearly thought it important enough to mention to his grandson, years later,' Sybbie said.

'I sometimes wonder if the treasure from the priory was the stained glass, hidden in plain sight. The commissioners wouldn't have cared about the glass itself, but they would probably have wanted the lead. Maybe our roundels were originally from the priory. Or our Angel Gabriel,' Kathleen suggested.

'Maybe,' Walter said. 'There's certainly no record of who made the glass, who paid for it or where it came from.'

'But you asked me to read the memorandum about the charnel house wall,' Sybbie said. 'Which suggests to me that *you* think that's where the tunnel is.'

'Charnel houses fell out of favour after Dissolution,' Walter said. 'Most of them were cleared and used for other purposes. The one at St Bartholomew's in Brisley was used to keep prisoners overnight on the way from the assizes at King's Lynn to the gallows at Norwich.'

Georgina shivered. 'That's horrible.'

'Practical, though. And I think Bram believed the tunnel entrance might be in the charnel house because, back in medieval and early modern times, it's somewhere people wouldn't even think of looking,' Walter said. 'When it was still a charnel house, nobody would have disturbed the bones, out of respect for the dead. After it was cleared... Well, memories live on longer than people. There would have been whispers about the bones that were once kept there, and people would worry about disturbing unquiet spirits. Remember, the stairs are uneven and the area is damp, so they're slippery. People who lost their footing on the stairs would be likely to blame it on ghosts.' He shrugged. 'Not that ghosts exist.'

Georgina and Sybbie exchanged a glance. Doris wasn't with them right at that moment, but they knew she definitely existed. It wasn't an argument that Georgina wanted to start.

'You mentioned that Bram had seen something in a former vicar's journal. Was it William Nashe's?' Georgina asked.

'Yes, though I've never seen the journal myself. I only know of its existence because Bram wrote about it,' Walter said. 'I've looked for it – but it's not at the vicarage, and it's not in Bram's papers, either. Bram wrote a history of the church, though it was never finished, let alone published. I used it as one of my sources when I wrote the guidebook for St Edmund's ten years ago, when I retired. He doesn't talk about the legend of the treasure in the book. But then I wondered, would there be something in his notes that he didn't include in the book, just like I avoided mentioning the crypt in the church guidebook? I looked through his working papers, and that's where he quoted verbatim from the journal of Gulielmus Nashe. In Latin, and then translated into English.'

'Have you checked the crypt yourself, to see if there's anything out of place?' Sybbie asked.

'Yes. And there is a damp patch in the wall – maybe even the same one that William Nashe talked about,' Walter said with a sigh. 'We need to keep an eye on it, and it's not a high priority right now. But before we can consider repairs, we'd have to talk to the Diocesan Advisory Committee to check that it's within the *de minimus* works provision. Depending on what the DAC says, we might get a faculty to approve the work, or we might have to jump through a few hoops and consult English Heritage, the Council for the Care of Churches, and the local planning authorities. There might need to be a public consultation. The wheels grind very slowly. Plus we have an overexcited vicar who can't quite grasp that things have to be done in a certain way or we'll end up in litigation – if we just take the wall down, we can be sued for trespass by the Consistory Court of the Diocese if we don't have permission to do the work.' He grimaced. 'I'm not sure I have the energy for that particular fight.'

'But if Bram's diary gives us proof that the tunnel is there, and that particular wall needs remedial work anyway, might that not sway the authorities into letting you look at what's actually there?' Georgina asked.

'Maybe,' Walter said.

'May I take photographs of the entries in the register, please?' Georgina asked. 'And perhaps the last pages of the diary and notebook, too, so we have a working copy of them and I can leave the originals with you.'

'Good idea,' Kathleen said.

Walter nodded. 'Sensible suggestion.'

'Thank you,' Georgina said. She took the small camera she carried around in her handbag and photographed the relevant pages methodically.

'Thank you both for trusting us,' Sybbie said. 'Bernard has experience with planning permission for work on a listed building. He'll be a useful ally for you on the PCC, Walter, though obviously he won't breathe a word to anyone without talking to you first. May I share this with him?'

'Of course, your ladyship,' Walter said.

'Good,' Sybbie said.

'I'll speak to Bea and ask her to have a chat with her friend – who will also obviously keep everything confidential,' Georgina said. 'May I share this with Colin? He's sensible and, given his job, he's used to confidentiality.'

Walter gave her a wry smile. 'Thank you for having the courtesy to ask. Yes.'

'I'll keep you posted on the situation, once Bea has talked to her friend,' Georgina promised.

## ELEVEN

Bea was delighted when Georgina rang her to tell her about the cold case and request help via Kirsty, Bea's former colleague. 'How exciting, Mum! Who knows, there might even be a treasure map in the diary or the notebook, with X marking the spot.'

'It might all be a red herring,' Georgina warned. 'There might not even be anything to find. At the moment, it's just a theory.'

'But it's a really interesting one. And I'm sure lots of people knew about using citrus juice as invisible ink. I'm only surprised nobody's already tried putting the diary on a warm radiator for a while to see if it produces any changes on the paper,' Bea said.

'Walter was worried about damaging the original,' Georgina said. 'He looked relieved to have potential help from an expert.'

'I'll have a word with Kirsty and ring you back,' Bea said. 'And if she says to bring the diary to Kew so she can look at it and maybe run some tests, I'll come and meet you for lunch. We can work it round the matinee performance. And now Will's back in London with his new job, maybe he can make it for lunch with us as well.'

Seeing both her children would make the day perfect, Georgina thought. 'Sybbie's helping me with the case, so she'll probably be with me. And Walter and Kathleen might want to come to Kew, given their connection to the diary and the church,' she warned.

'I don't mind sharing you, and neither does Will,' Bea said. 'The main thing is we get to see you. Love you.'

'Love you, too,' Georgina said, and she was smiling when she put the phone down.

It turned out there was a problem with the data copied from Liam's phone, so Colin had to call the phone providers in order to get copies of the messages. For once, the phone providers worked quickly and sent copies of the relevant messages to Colin.

The incriminating-looking message was there: *I'll get my aunt to sort you out.* But the other messages in the conversation made it very clear that it wasn't a threat at all. Liam had tried to contact the new vicar, and learned that he wasn't available for a couple of weeks, and he needed access to the church so he could survey the window properly. As Aaron had family contacts at the church, could he help?

Aaron had gone straight to the person he knew would help: his aunt. Aaron had been talking about sorting out access for the survey, not 'sorting out' a difficult person. Dominic McGowan either thought that the police were stupid and wouldn't know how to check the deleted messages, or he was so affected by grief that he was twisting the evidence so he had someone to blame. Possibly both, Colin thought. He was going to have to tread carefully here.

Later that afternoon, Georgina was just back from taking Bert for a walk when her phone rang with a number she didn't recognise. It might be a work commission, she thought, and answered. 'Georgina Drake.'

'Mrs Drake? It's Kirsty, Bea's friend, in the archives,' the woman on the other end of the line said.

'Thank you so much for calling me, Kirsty – and do call me Georgie,' Georgina said, smiling.

'Bea told me about the diary and the story behind it. It sounds so exciting. I'd actually booked a day off tomorrow, but I'd only planned to do chores. I'd be more than happy to meet you at the archives instead and have a look at the diary, if you're free,' Kirsty said.

Which also gave Kathleen an iron-clad reason not to be at the church tomorrow, so she'd be out of Dominic McGowan's orbit, Georgina thought. And that was a very good thing. 'I'm free,' Georgina said. 'That's very kind of you.'

'Not at all. It's not every day you get to help solve a centuries-old mystery,' Kirsty said.

'I know this is going to sound a bit cheeky, but would it be possible for me to bring the owners of the diary and my friend who's helping me with the case?' Georgina asked.

'Of course you can,' Kirsty said. 'If I have any questions, they're the most likely people to have the answers.'

'Wonderful,' Georgina said. 'And I'd love to take you out to lunch – with Bea, too – to say thank you for your help.'

'That would be lovely,' Kirsty said. 'But what I'd really like is to be able to use the story in a blog piece for the archives.'

'You'd really need to ask Kathleen, as she's the one who owns the diary,' Georgina said. 'But, given what you're going to do for us, I'm pretty sure she'll say yes.' She'd talk to Kathleen before tomorrow, to make sure of it.

'Thank you. I'll see you tomorrow at the archives,' Kirsty said. 'How early do you think you can be here?'

Georgina calculated it mentally. Two hours on the train, an hour across London... Maybe it would be easier to drive. 'Is there somewhere I can park reasonably close by?' Georgina asked.

'Yes. I'll arrange a parking space, if you can text me your registration number,' Kirsty said.

'Thank you. We'll aim to be with you for ten,' Georgina said. 'If we get stuck in traffic or held up somewhere, is this the best number to call to let you know?'

Kirsty confirmed it, they wrapped up the call, and Georgina texted Bea to let her know the arrangements, then called Sybbie and Kathleen. She arranged to pick everyone up early the next morning, and persuaded Kathleen to let Kirsty write a blog piece about the diary.

'It's the very least we can do, as she's giving up her own time to help us,' Kathleen said.

'As long as she doesn't publish it until after we've checked out the crypt,' Walter said.

'I'm sure that will be fine,' Georgina said.

'Normally I would make some cake to say thank you,' Kathleen said. 'Though, given what's happened this week, maybe that's a bad idea.'

'Actually, I think cake is an excellent idea,' Georgina said. 'Or maybe those choc-chip cookies you mentioned. I'll double-check with Bea in case Kirsty has any allergies.'

Bea came back almost straight away to say that Kirsty loved choc-chip cookies and had no allergies.

Baking again might help Kathleen to feel more normal again, Georgina thought, and passed the message on.

She'd just put the phone down when there was a knock on her kitchen door. She opened it to see Jodie, the young woman who helped her with the holiday let of Rookery Barn, and who was part of the team solving past cases. 'Come in, Jodie. I'll put the kettle on,' she said.

'Thanks for the offer, but I'll say no to the tea because I can't stay long – Mum's looking after Harry for me,' Jodie said, referring to her eight-year-old son. She bent down to make a fuss of Bert. 'I just wanted to check whether you need me on Friday for the barn, because if you don't, Mike' – her brother, and the owner of the Red Lion – 'says I can do the lunchtime shift there.'

'I can manage the barn, if Mike needs you,' Georgina said.

'Thanks. Mike was telling me about that poor bloke who died

yesterday. He said it's the first time anyone's asked him for the defibrillator.'

'We didn't use it, though, because the paramedics had already arrived when the builder came back from the Red Lion,' Georgina said. 'Kathleen Reeves and I had been doing CPR, but sadly between us we couldn't save him.'

'He wasn't much older than me, by the sound of it,' Jodie said, and shivered. 'Which is a bit scary. You never know how much time you're going to have, do you?'

'No,' Georgina agreed, thinking of Stephen and the retirement they hadn't had the chance to enjoy together.

'It must have been horrible for you. And for poor Mrs Reeves. She was my form teacher when I first went to high school,' Jodie confided. 'I was always hopeless at art – I couldn't even draw a straight line with a ruler – but she was always so kind. And she used to make us cookies on the last day of term. They were the best choc-chip cookies ever – even better than Cesca's, though don't tell her I said that!'

'I take it you've heard all the rumours?' Georgina asked.

'That the bloke died because of her cake? Yeah, and that's a load of rubbish. She's proper nice, Mrs Reeves,' Jodie said indignantly. 'She'd never hurt anyone, let alone kill them. If I hear anyone saying that, I'll set them straight.'

'That's kind,' Georgina said.

'Anyone who knows her will know the truth,' Jodie said. 'And it's a shame she's being driven out of the church by people who should know better. Churchy people are always running on about being kind and turning the other cheek, but they don't always practise what they preach, do they?'

'Some don't,' Georgina agreed. She smiled at Jodie. 'Actually, she won't have to face them tomorrow. Sybbie and I are taking her to London to meet up with an old colleague of Bea's who's offered to look at some documents.'

'Ooh – have you got another cold case?' Jodie asked.

Georgina nodded. 'Someone who allegedly died from typhoid, but that might not be what actually happened.'

'I don't think I'd be very good at reading really old handwriting,' Jodie said, 'but if I can do anything to help, just give me a yell. And if you think I can cheer Mrs Reeves up a bit, I'll pop in to see her on Thursday with some flowers or something.'

'I think she'd like that,' Georgina said.

'Give her my best,' Jodie said. 'And I'll see you at Pilates on Thursday.'

'It's Cesca's turn to drive,' Georgina said. 'We'll pick you up at the usual time.'

'Right you are.' Jodie made a last fuss of Bert. 'I'd better get back to Robbie. See you later!'

Colin arrived at Rookery Farm that evening, looking completely out of sorts.

'Tough day?' Georgina asked sympathetically.

'It's a horrible case,' Colin said, and grimaced. 'I shouldn't really—'

'—discuss it with me,' Georgina said, 'but we both know it helps you to think aloud talking to me, and you know whatever you say isn't going any further than me.'

'I do,' Colin said. 'And I appreciate it. And you.'

'Sit down and gather your thoughts,' Georgina said. 'I'll make us some tea.'

'No. You sit down and I'll make the tea,' he said. 'It isn't your job to wait on me hand and foot.'

Georgina had friends whose husbands expected them to wait on them hand and foot – even in this day and age – so she appreciated the sentiment.

Colin made them both a mug of tea, then joined her at the ancient oak table with its mismatched chairs.

'Tell me about it,' she said.

Colin sighed. 'All the evidence points to Liam Jacobs's death being a tragic accident. Kathleen didn't know about his allergy and the lab tests on everything from her kitchen came back clear. She didn't have a reason to want him dead, either – actually, nobody has a motive as far as I can see. I have no idea how the coconut oil got into the cake, but somehow it did. Dominic McGowan can't accept that it wasn't deliberate, and he's insistent that Aaron Flint is behind Liam's death. He even showed me a threatening text from Aaron to Liam as evidence.'

'A threatening text?' Georgina blinked in surprise.

'Except it wasn't. Out of context, yes, it did look suspicious – particularly as Aaron's phone is set up to auto-delete texts and messages after a fortnight and he didn't have a copy on his phone. But when I got the messages in from Liam's phone provider, it was clearly completely innocent, and it was actually Aaron offering to help him get the access to the church he needed.' Colin frowned. 'I know grief can hit people in unexpected ways, and people react differently, but Dominic McGowan has refused the help of a family liaison officer and nothing I can say to him will convince him that this isn't murder.'

'I know he's very angry. He caused quite a row at the church today,' Georgina said. 'Apparently he's been spending all his time sitting in the pew next to where Liam collapsed, saying it makes him feel close to Liam – and he told everyone in the congregation at morning service that Kathleen and Aaron murdered Liam.'

Colin winced. 'That's unfair – and it's also slander.'

'Kathleen fled the church in tears. Walter asked the vicar to make Dominic leave, but the vicar refused; he says Dominic needs the comfort of the church, even though Dominic was pretty clear that he doesn't believe in God,' Georgina said.

'So is the village grapevine red-hot right now?' Colin asked. 'Does everyone have a theory on what happened to Liam Jacobs?'

'Sort of,' Georgina said. 'Jodie dropped in to see me earlier. Apparently Kathleen was her form tutor at high school. Jodie says that Kathleen was really kind and she isn't the sort to hurt anyone, let alone kill them, so Jodie says if she hears anyone gossiping, she'll set them straight.'

'I like Jodie,' Colin said. 'She gets to the point.' He paused. 'Were you at the church this morning to see all the drama, then?'

'No. Kathleen rang Sybbie, who came to see me. We spent the morning at Kathleen's, trying to give her a bit of a boost,' Georgina explained. 'And that's how I also know that her nephew has been put on gardening leave. Aaron rang her to let her know while I was there.'

'I was conducting interviews at the studio when that happened,' Colin said. 'It's nasty all round.' He frowned. 'I know you have photos to take for your article, but is there any way you can avoid the church for a while – at least until Dominic has calmed down a bit?'

'Do you think he's that dangerous?' Georgina asked.

'I think he's volatile and needs careful handling,' Colin said. 'I know you're one of the people who'd do that best, but given what I've seen of him so far, I'd rather you weren't involved.'

'I'm working on the cold case,' Georgina reminded him. 'And, as Bram was Kathleen's great-great-great-uncle, I need to discuss it with her and Walter. Plus it involves the church itself.'

'I think I'd rather you talked to Doris,' Colin admitted.

'I've been doing that, too,' Georgina said. 'And things have taken a very interesting turn. I'm taking Walter, Kathleen and Sybbie to Kew tomorrow.' She filled him in on Walter's theory about Bram finding the location of the tunnel in the crypt, and Kirsty's offer to see if she could find any hidden writing in the diary and notebook. 'Will can't join us for lunch, but Bea can.' She grinned. 'She's dying to know if there's a treasure map in Bram's notebook, written in some kind of invisible ink with an X marking the spot.'

'That would be incredible,' Colin said. 'Russell Dawson from the podcast has obviously done a bit of research into the legend. Has Walter talked to him about it?'

'I don't think so. He definitely hasn't discussed it with Dominic

McGowan.' Georgina paused. 'When you said you'd rather I talk to Doris... I think perhaps you need to know some inadmissible evidence.'

Colin looked at her. 'Which I won't be able to use in court.'

'But if it points you in the right direction,' Georgina argued, 'it might help you to discover some evidence that you *can* use. Just like her advice points me in the right direction for finding documents in the cold cases.'

He took a deep breath. 'OK. I'm listening.'

'Dominic's clearly trying to blame Aaron for Liam's death,' Georgina said. 'He gave you that message out of context, and he was abusive to Kathleen before the service in St Edmund's this morning, making quite sure that she doesn't feel comfortable in the church. Walter tried to get the vicar to stand up for her, but it didn't work. While people are there to witness it, Dominic seems to be playing the grieving partner.' She winced. 'Actually, that might be unfair. He probably is grieving. But he's also hamming it up a bit.'

'Are you telling me you think he might be responsible for Liam's death?' Colin asked.

'No. But I do think he has another agenda,' Georgina said. 'When the church is empty again – and of course the congregation won't stay for coffee and cake afterwards, since Kathleen isn't there to welcome them and everyone feels awkward about the situation – then he stops the histrionics and he starts searching the church systematically. He's been pacing up and down and making notes. And I think that's a little bit suspicious.'

Colin looked surprised. 'You're telling me Doris saw him do that?'

'Yes,' Georgina said. 'I know you can't use that in court, but isn't it odd behaviour? Shifty, even.'

'Pacing up and down and making notes.' Colin thought about it. 'It might look odd, but remember what he does for a living. Maybe he paces and makes notes when he's developing a lecture – I mean, I think better sometimes when I'm walking Bert and muttering to myself.' He gave her a wry smile. 'Or to Bert. Yes, Dominic's being a bit dramatic about it, but maybe it's just the kind of person he is. Maybe he's telling the truth that he wants to be in the church to feel close to Liam.'

'That sounds as if you're on his side,' Georgina said.

'I'm on the side of truth and justice,' Colin reminded her. 'My job isn't about being on someone's side. It's about looking at the facts, seeing things from all angles, and finding out what really happened.' He paused. 'Do you – and Doris – think Dominic might be searching for the alleged hidden treasure?'

'Dominic lectures on folklore, so he would have heard about the tale associated with St Edmund's. It's been on a popular podcast quite recently, too, so he would have been aware of that, too.'

'He mentioned it to me,' Colin confirmed. 'That he knew about the legend, and about the podcast.'

'Given his job, he'll have access to sources that most people don't even know about. So yes, I do think he's looking for the treasure.' She paused. 'He doesn't like Russell Dawson, possibly because the TreasureChest podcast isn't aimed at academics, and you said yourself that Dominic is a bit of an intellectual snob.' She smiled. 'Bernard says the podcast is very entertaining.'

'I haven't spoken to Dawson yet,' Colin said. 'He wasn't there when it happened and he probably doesn't have a connection to the case, but I'll arrange to talk to him for background.'

'Plus I think Dominic is manipulative – look at the way he's behaved towards Kathleen,' Georgina said.

'Not to mention the way he tried to make me think that Aaron was threatening Liam. They're all fair points, though it could simply be a matter of his personality rather than anything suspicious,' Colin agreed. 'On the surface, Liam's death looks like an accident.'

'But?' she asked, because the word was almost written on his face.

'But my copper's hunch says otherwise,' he admitted awkwardly.

'You believe in hunches,' Georgina said, 'but not in Doris.'

'I'm *trying* to be more open-minded,' Colin said, clearly remembering her previous attempts to prove Doris's existence. He looked awkward. 'Um, Doris, if you're here, I'd like to say thank you for the information.'

He really *was* making an effort, and Georgina appreciated it, because she knew he found it hard to believe in the existence of something unprovable: a ghost. 'She isn't here, as it happens, but I'll pass the message on next time I talk to her.'

'It's still hard to get my head round,' Colin said.

'But at least you're not dismissing it completely out of hand anymore,' she said.

'So where do we go from here?' Colin asked.

'I don't know,' Georgina admitted. 'And I'm not sure if there's a connection with what happened to Liam and what happened to Bram Locke and Martha Plowright, other than that Kathleen is Bram and Martha's direct descendant.'

'I think I need to sleep on this,' Colin said. 'But maybe you'll learn something tomorrow that could spark off something that would help in Liam's case.'

'I'll keep you posted,' she said.

'And if there really is a treasure map,' Colin said, 'I think Bernard and I would both love to see it.'

'Whatever we find, there will be photographs,' Georgina promised.

## TWELVE

Georgina had checked on her satnav, and it would take a little over two and a half hours to drive from Little Wenborough to the archives at Kew. Allowing three-quarters of an hour for rush-hour traffic and delays, she'd arranged to pick Sybbie up at half past six on Wednesday morning. Bernard had offered to take Bert for the day, mindful of the fact that Georgina was still twitchy about leaving him alone after the case at the windmill in the next village. 'No extra snacks, and he'll get a good W-A-L-K with me and the boys,' he promised.

'Thank you, Bernard. I owe you,' she said.

'Just keep Sybbie out of the antique shops and well away from Staffordshire pottery dogs,' he said with a grin.

'We're not going anywhere near any antique shops,' Georgina reassured him. 'And with luck I'll bring back a map.'

With Sybbie in the front seat, she picked up Kathleen and Walter five minutes later, and drove them to London. It was a beautiful clear morning and the sun was just rising; the sky was all shades of peach, gold and pink. Georgina tuned the radio to Classic FM, so the music was soft and soothing.

'I made choc-chip cookies,' Kathleen said. 'I bought all the ingredients from the farm shop yesterday afternoon, and I have the receipt to prove it.'

'Dear girl,' Sybbie said, using her trademark phrase even though Kathleen was older than her, 'you do realise we all know you had nothing to do with Liam Jacobs's death and we're on your side?'

'This whole thing has really thrown me,' Kathleen admitted.

'If it makes you feel any better,' Georgina said, 'Jodie Fulcher, who works with me on the holiday cottage, dropped in to see me yesterday and said you're one of the nicest people she knows and no way would you be involved.'

'Jodie was in my form group,' Kathleen said. 'She must be, what, twenty-four or twenty-five, now?'

'Yes,' Georgina said. 'She has fond memories of your choc-chip cookies. Sybbie, close your ears, but she says they're even better than Cesca's.'

'They are,' Walter said. 'I tested this batch myself yesterday evening.'

Kathleen nudged him. 'Not that you're biased.'

Georgina was glad that Kathleen seemed to be relaxing, now they were away from Little Wenborough and Dominic's accusations. They were lucky with the traffic and no hold-ups, so they reached the car park by the archives a few minutes before ten o'clock. Walter had his archive box containing Bram's diaries and notebooks.

Together, they went to the reception desk and Georgina asked for Kirsty. A few moments later, a tall young woman with a mass of red curls came through to greet them. 'I think I would have known who you were even if I hadn't seen Bea's photos,' she said. 'You look so much like her!'

'Bea's joining us for lunch,' Georgina said.

'It'll be lovely to see her again and catch up properly,' Kirsty said. She ushered them through to the office where she worked. Kathleen gave her the box of cookies, which Kirsty accepted with alacrity, and Walter handed over the archive box with the documents. 'We appreciate your promise to keep this confidential,' he said.

'And we'll give you any help you need with your blog post when this is all settled,' Kathleen added. 'Including photographic copies of the documents and a transcription. Even if we've been barking up the wrong tree and there isn't anything to find.'

'Thank you,' Kirsty said. 'I have to admit I've been intrigued and excited about it. Not so much about finding gold or what have you, but being part of putting the clues together and solving a mystery – seeing information that's been hidden for years and years and years. Bea told me about the cold cases you've worked on,' she added to Georgina. 'If she's unavailable at any time in the future, please feel free to call on me for help.'

'That's very much appreciated,' Georgina said with a smile. 'Thank you.'

Kirsty opened the archive box, opened one of the books to check, and nodded approvingly. 'You've kept these properly – no plastic, acid-free paper and clearly at a stable temperature. That's always a good start. You know we have the Gunpowder Plotters' orange juice letters in the archives here?'

'I do,' Walter said. 'I was reading about them. That's when I started to wonder if the gaps in Bram's diaries and notebooks were because he was writing in some kind of invisible ink. And then her ladyship told me she has papers saying that Bram smelled of oranges.'

'Which we assumed at first might be some kind of cologne. Then, as he was visiting typhoid patients and taking them food, we thought Bram might have been using citric acid as a kind of disinfectant, perhaps if he'd run out of carbolic soap,' Sybbie said. 'But now we agree with Walter's theory: it might be because Bram had been using orange juice as invisible ink.'

'And you haven't tried warming the pages of the diary to check your theory?' Kirsty asked.

Walter grimaced. 'I was worried about damaging them. From what I've seen online, you have to use quite a bit of heat. There are videos of people using Bunsen burners and you can see scorch marks on the paper. I didn't want to destroy the diary by singeing it.' He looked at her. 'That's why we asked for help. With something like this, I always think it's better to talk to someone who knows what they're doing.'

'A warm iron, with the pages sandwiched between pieces of acid-free paper, would be my suggestion of a starting point,' Kirsty said. 'Though I should warn you now that it's an irreversible chemical reaction. If there really is invisible ink made from citric acid there, it will be visible permanently once we've applied heat to it. Are you sure you want to do this?'

Kathleen and Walter looked at each other for a long, long moment, their faces full of doubts.

'Yes,' Kathleen said. 'And Georgina took photographs of the pages yesterday, so we still have a working copy of how it looks now.'

'Good,' Kirsty said. 'We just so happen to have an iron in the office.'

'You've clearly done this before,' Sybbie said with a smile. 'How exciting.'

'Don't get your hopes up,' Kirsty warned. 'The last two or three I did turned out to be illegible, and even my box of tricks hasn't helped much.'

'It's this diary and this notebook,' Walter said, picking out the two slim leather books. 'The last ones. In the earlier books, and in the early pages of these ones, Bram uses all the space on the paper. Towards the end, he starts leaving gaps.'

'The Gunpowder Plotters did something similar,' Kirsty said. 'Though they wrote on the reverse of the paper and it was very hard to read the orange-juice writing because the ordinary ink bled through it.' She raised her eyebrows. 'Obviously once it's warmed, the writing stays dark enough to read – basically it's oxidisation of the carbon in the citric acid. As I said, it's an irreversible change. Seeing the orange-juice writing would have tipped off the conspirators that the letters had been intercepted and read. Henry

Garnett's keepers at the Tower of London needed a confession, so they tried to find out more information by copying his letters – including the sections in orange-juice ink – and making sure they reached the intended recipients.'

'That's devious,' Walter said. 'And they must have had someone who was good at copying handwriting.'

'Absolutely,' Kirsty said with a smile. 'I thought you might like to see one of the letters, so I booked one out of the archives to show you.' She produced the letter from her desk drawer, and they examined it.

'In between the lines. That's so clever. Is that how the writing might look in Bram's diary?' Kathleen asked.

'I hope so,' Kirsty said. 'And if it doesn't, that's when we can use my box of tricks to see if we can make it more legible.'

A few minutes with a warm iron and some acid-free paper netted the results they'd all been hoping for: Bram had indeed used orange juice as invisible ink in his diary, in between the ordinary ink lines in the last few pages. Even though there were blobs obscuring parts of some of the words, it was legible, because Bram's handwriting was very neat and clear.

'That's amazing,' Sybbie said when Kirsty showed them the first page.

'May I?' Kathleen reached out for the diary.

'He's your great-great-great-uncle,' Kirsty said. 'Of course.'

Kathleen took a deep breath and read the entry out loud.

'*I have been talking to John the sexton about the treasure. We think it best to keep it between ourselves until we are sure of the facts. We do not want to risk someone breaking into St Edmund's, going down to the crypt and breaking down the wall. If we are right and Robert Fysshe really did hide some of the priory's treasure, it could make such a difference to the village. We could repair the church roof. Harvey and I could set up a cottage hospital for Little Wenborough, so he could treat our patients locally instead of sending them to Norwich and fearing they will be turned away because they cannot pay. The voluntary hospitals do not help the destitute, and the workhouse hospitals are practically a gateway to death. Harvey showed me a letter in the* British Medical Journal *stating that that cottage hospitals draw away interesting cases from the general hospitals, harming the education of medical students. We disagree, because the general hospitals turn most of such cases away. We could make such a difference if we can find the treasure. And I truly think we can find the entrance to the prior's tunnel if we follow the clues.'*

'He sounds like a lovely man,' Kirsty said. 'He really does want to work for the greater good.'

'Bram was my great-great-great uncle,' Kathleen said. 'He had such plans for the village. We thought he died from typhoid.'

'Who's Harvey?' Kirsty asked. 'I assume he's a local doctor, if he has a copy of the BMJ.'

'He was. He was Bram's best friend, and also my great-great-grandfather,' Kathleen said. 'Harvey was treating the typhoid patients and Bram was taking them food and ministering to them.'

'Did Harvey catch typhoid, too?' Kirsty asked.

'No,' Kathleen said. 'And he spent as much time with the patients as Bram did.'

'That seems odd,' Kirsty said. 'Surely both of them would have caught it? Unless the doctor took extra precautions or Bram had a weaker constitution, perhaps?'

'They were planning the hospital together,' Kathleen said. 'Harvey would have made Bram take the same precautions that he did.'

'Our theory is that Bram's death wasn't actually from typhoid,' Georgina said.

'His little sister, Martha – my great-great-grandmother,' Kathleen said, 'thought there was something strange about his death and started asking questions, but she'd recently had a baby and everyone said she was sleep-deprived, seeing monsters where there weren't any.' She paused. 'Though Martha died in a riding accident shortly afterwards.'

Kirsty shivered. 'Put like that, it's either extreme bad luck, or someone was responsible for both deaths.'

'We think the latter. The killer might have been someone who wanted to get their hands on the treasure, which meant getting Bram out of the way before he could find it and silencing Martha,' Georgina said. 'We think it's unlikely the killer was Harvey, because he was Bram's best friend and he was married to Martha.'

'Harvey would have benefited from the hospital being set up,' Kathleen added, 'and he never remarried because nobody could ever replace Martha for him.'

'That's plausible,' Kirsty said. 'But if you look at it objectively, could it possibly have been his guilty conscience?'

'No,' Kathleen said. 'Doctors tended to be quite well off, in those days, because they charged for their services – sometimes by a chicken or some produce instead of actual money – but I know that Harvey treated the poor without charge as often as he could. He was a good man. Obviously he died years before I was born, but there are photos in the family albums of his daughter Grace holding me as a tiny baby when she was really old, and I remember my granny, Grace's daughter Florence. My mum was close to Grace, who always said her dad was the kindest, loveliest man. And my mum thought Harvey would really have approved of the National Health Service.'

'I think John the sexton is a more likely suspect,' Georgina said. Although she hadn't shared the information with Walter and Kathleen – particularly given Walter's views on ghosts, it would be too awkward to explain – Martha had told Doris that she'd planned to talk to John the sexton. And now they had documentary evidence that Bram had discussed his belief about the treasure's existence with John. Had the possibility of riches been too much for John?

'I'm not so sure about that. When I was researching the church guidebook, I came across mentions of John Barton, the sexton,' Walter said. 'I looked him up. He took over from his father, who in turn took over from *his* father. The third generation in the village. If he'd been working with Bram and killed him to get the treasure, would he not have disappeared with his ill-gotten gains, rather than staying in the village and serving the church for another twenty years?'

'Fair point,' Sybbie said.

'So where did the tunnel start and end?' Kirsty asked.

'Legend says one end was at the priory – which used to stand in the grounds of where Little Wenborough Manor is now, at the other end of the village – and one end was at the church,' Sybbie said. 'But my husband heard those stories when he was young and growing up at the Manor. He searched everywhere in the Manor's grounds, and he never found the slightest trace of a tunnel. He has a collection of maps relating to the local area, and none of them show a tunnel, either.'

'In the back of the first parish register – which I know *should* be kept in the local records office, and I intend to bring that up at the next PCC meeting and get it agreed,' Walter added, 'there's a note about a damp patch on the wall of the crypt. It used to be the charnel house. There's also a note in the 1570 register of the burial of Robert Fysshe, who I believe is the same Robert Fysshe as the man who was the last prior of Little Wenborough.'

'I took photographs of the relevant pages,' Georgina said, 'and downloaded them to my phone.' She took out her phone, flicked into the photographs app and handed it to Kirsty.

Kirsty stared at the photos, clearly mentally translating the text from the Latin as she read.

'That's amazing,' she said. 'And it really sounds as if you're onto something. Let me do the rest of the pages,' she said, and systematically slotted the archive paper back in place before applying the iron to the next page. 'Who else knows about these documents?'

'My partner, who happens to be a detective inspector and I'd trust him with anything,' Georgina said. 'Plus Bea – who as you know is used to confidentiality in the probate genealogy business.'

'And Bernard, my husband, who certainly won't be talking about it to anyone,' Sybbie said.

'And the four of us here – well, five, including you,' Walter said. 'If anyone wanted to go into the crypt, they would need to see me for the key. Or ask the vicar. But he's new and… is still finding his feet,' he added diplomatically, 'so I haven't mentioned the crypt or any of this to him. He might not even know his way round the whole set of church keys, yet.'

'What he's not saying is that the vicar's the sort who'd blurt everything out in the worst place at the worst possible time,' Sybbie said, 'and we don't need a stampede of treasure hunters taking a pickaxe or what have you to the church.'

'Absolutely,' Kirsty said. 'Why would Bram talk to the sexton about it?'

'The sexton was in charge of digging graves and maintaining the church,' Walter said. 'So he'd be the one with the pickaxe, if they were going to open up the wall.' He paused. 'There's still a damp spot on the crypt wall. I'm starting to think it might be because the wall is thinner in that part of the building.'

'And the tunnel is behind that?' Kirsty asked.

'It's a possibility,' Walter said.

Kirsty treated the rest of the pages, and when the first blank pages in the diary yielded nothing more, she handed the book back to Kathleen.

'He says that he and John checked the crypt and they're sure the tunnel entrance is there. He's drawn a plan and they're going to open it up later in the week. They're not going to tell Harvey just yet because the baby's had colic – oh, that's Grace he's talking about,' Kathleen said, sounding delighted to make the connection. 'And she's cutting her first teeth, so she's not sleeping and that means Martha and Harvey aren't sleeping much, either. Harvey can barely stay upright on his horse to visit his patients.' She smiled. 'Bram speaks of him so fondly, as if he's a blood brother rather than an in-law.' She turned to the next page. 'In the ordinary ink, he says here that Victoria Stebbings and her grandchildren John and Henry died from typhoid. He's upset that the care didn't work, and he's frustrated that some of the people in the village still have such poor sanitation. Oh, Sybbie, you'll like this – he says he wishes all the landlords in the area were as good as William Walters.'

'Bernard's great-great-great-grandfather,' Sybbie supplied for Kirsty's benefit. 'We've found a lot of information in his wife Amelia's diary. I'm glad he was one of the good guys.'

Kathleen read on. 'In orange juice: he really hopes that the treasure is still there, though of course there's a chance that someone else found it years ago, took it quietly and simply bricked up the entrance again. He hopes if the treasure does exist, when it's sold, there will be enough money to do something about the village sanitation as well as to fix the church roof and build the cottage hospital. If not, he hopes that maybe William Walters will help with the costs of the hospital, or help him persuade the local land-lords to do something about sanitation.'

She turned to the last page. 'Oh, no. Still in ordinary ink. He's not feeling well. He's got a headache and a fever.' She bit her lip. 'A bit later, the same day, he says his stomach hurts, too. He's been sick. He's terrified that he has the same symptoms as the Stebbings family. If he has typhoid, what if Harvey has been infected, too? Will Martha and baby Grace end up being infected? Grace is so tiny. Can she survive typhoid? He's going to send a message to Martha and Harvey via his housemaid Betsy, telling them not to come anywhere near and to watch themselves and the baby closely for symptoms. And then he's going to send his housekeeper and housemaid away, to make sure they're not infected by him. He's going to send a note to John the sexton to tell him to keep his distance, too. He hopes John will take the same view as he does: the tunnel's been there undisturbed for hundreds of years, so waiting a few more days to unbrick it won't hurt.' She blew out a breath. 'And that's the last entry. I know from the parish register and my family tree that he died the next day.'

Georgina reached across the table to squeeze her hand. 'That's so sad.'

Kathleen nodded. 'There's no more orange juice writing.'

'What about the map?' Walter asked. 'Maybe he didn't draw it in the diary because a blank page would draw attention to it and people might work out that he'd used orange juice as invisible ink. Maybe he drew the map in his notebook instead.'

Kirsty duly tested the blank pages in the notebook. The first ten remained stubbornly blank.

'I'm not giving up yet,' she said. 'Maybe he worked from the back of the book, if he wrote in juice.'

She turned to the last page, applied heat over the top of the acid-free paper, and then took the paper away.

There, on the last page of the notebook, was a very clear drawing of the crypt, along with measurements and a hatched area.

'The damp spot,' Walter said. 'From what I can see, it looks to be in the same place as the one I've noticed.'

'Then you have to open it up,' Kirsty said. 'For Bram, because he didn't get the chance to do it. Though I wonder why the sexton didn't open it up, seeing as he and Bram had worked together?'

'Maybe he felt it would be wrong to do it without Bram,' Sybbie suggested.

'It was a superstitious age,' Walter said. 'Perhaps there's a part of the legend that didn't make it down the years – say, that there was a curse on the treasure. Especially as it was hidden behind the wall of what was the charnel house.'

'We need to get that wall down and find out the truth, for Bram's sake,' Georgina said.

'That we do,' Walter agreed.

'But first,' Georgina said, 'I need to photograph the new pages.'


After a delectable lunch in a nearby riverside pub with Bea – including a whispered conversation to get her up to date with what they'd learned about the treasure in St Edmund's, followed by a much rowdier conversation where Georgina was relieved to see that the shadows were gone from Kathleen's eyes, at least for a little while – Georgina drove everyone back to Norfolk. This time, they were unlucky with a series of delays, and the journey home took more than an hour longer than the drive to London. On the plus side, Georgina thought, it gave them time to plan what happened next.

'So what do we do now?' Sybbie asked.

'I'll go into the crypt tomorrow,' Walter said, 'and confirm the damp patch really is in the same place. If it is, then at the next PCC meeting I'll suggest we get permission to check out what's behind the wall.'

'If the treasure really is there,' Georgina said, 'you'll have to report it to the finds liaison officer.'

'The law changed a couple of years ago,' Sybbie said. 'I remember Bernard looking it up. I have a feeling there are separate rules for churches. Let me check.' She tapped into her phone. 'Yes – the Treasure Act has a revised code of practice from 2023. It doesn't apply to shipwrecks or to things that fall under the Church of England's jurisdiction – which is apparently anything found in or on land, or in or under churches. So that would include the crypt or the part of the tunnel that lies within the boundaries of the church land.'

'Rowena Langham – the local finds liaison officer – happens to be a friend of mine,' Georgina said. 'She'd be able to help us.'

'Yes – it would count as a moveable object,' Sybbie said. 'And it says here that significant finds still have to be reported, and it has to be offered to museums before it can be sold.'

'We're getting ahead of ourselves,' Kathleen said. 'What if you get permission from the Diocese to open up the wall and there's nothing there?'

'Then we're no worse off than we are now,' Walter said. 'Tomorrow, I'm going to take a decent torch and a camera into the crypt, and see what I can find.' He paused. 'The only thing is, there's likely to be someone in the church.'

'*Someone* being Dominic McGowan,' Sybbie said.

'Exactly,' Walter said. 'I'd rather he didn't know about this.' He frowned. 'I know I'm biased because of the way he's behaved towards Kathleen, but I just don't trust him. There's something not quite sincere about him.'

'So how do we lure him out of the church?' Sybbie asked.

'Maybe he needs to have a conversation with a police officer,' Georgina said. 'Colin could perhaps update him on whatever he's found. And he might prefer to have that conversation somewhere other than the church.'

'Colin could send you a text to let you know that the church is empty,' Sybbie said. 'And then you could let Walter know.'

'I happen to know the vicar has meetings tomorrow afternoon,' Walter said. 'And none of our usual groups has booked the church hall. That would be a really useful time to check the crypt.'

'I'll talk to Colin,' Georgina promised.

THIRTEEN

Georgina dropped Kathleen and Walter home, then went back to the Manor with Sybbie to pick up Bert.

'He's been an angel,' Bernard said. 'Giles and I took him for a W-word with Max and Jet. He had a bit of ham when we made a sandwich at lunchtime, and he's been trying to convince me that he's a poor, starving hound – but I know that one from Max and Jet.'

Georgina chuckled. 'Well done for not falling for it.' She made a fuss of Bert. 'We've had an interesting day at the archives. It turns out we were right and Bram used orange juice as invisible ink.'

'Was there a map?' Bernard asked hopefully.

'Not as such,' Sybbie said. 'More a sketch of where Bram believed the tunnel entrance might be. Obviously we've left the originals with Kathleen and Walter, but Georgie took a photograph.'

Georgina took her camera from her handbag, switched the screen to playback mode, and showed Bernard the sketch she'd photographed.

'That's so interesting,' Bernard said. 'And it looks to be very near the damp spot in the crypt that Walter told me about some months ago.'

'He plans to investigate it properly tomorrow,' Sybbie said, 'but we need to get Colin involved to make sure Dominic is out of the church. The last thing we need is Dominic stirring up more trouble in St Edmund's.'

'It sounds as if the PCC is going to need an emergency meeting to discuss Walter's findings,' Bernard said, 'and we'll need to apply for a faculty if we want to open up the wall. If the damp spot in the crypt is caused by a tunnel, rather than just a drainage leak, it will be an incredible story and the publicity will benefit the church. And if the legend is true and the tunnel really *does* contain the prior's treasure, whatever's down there will belong to the church and Walter will finally be able to get the roof fixed properly, which he's been nagging about for years.'

'Here's hoping,' Georgina said.

Her phone beeped with a message, and she glanced at the screen. 'Colin's just about to head on his way home. He's suggesting dinner at the Feathers.' She wrinkled her nose. 'Given that I had lunch out today, I probably shouldn't go out for dinner as well.'

'Lunch was *hours* ago. Go to the Feathers, enjoy every mouthful, and walk it off tomorrow,' Sybbie advised.

'That,' Georgina said, 'sounds like a good plan. I'd better get this one home.' She scratched behind Bert's ears, and the spaniel closed his eyes in bliss. 'Thanks for looking after him, Bernard. And I'll keep you posted on any developments, Sybbie.'

Back at Rookery Farm, Georgina gave Bert his dinner, then downloaded the photographs she'd taken at the archives to her laptop and sent copies to Sybbie and Kathleen.

Colin arrived half an hour later, looking tired and fed up.

'Looks as if you've had a rubbish day,' Georgina said. 'The Feathers it is.'

'I hope your day has been better than mine,' Colin said.

'Very much so,' Georgina said, 'but I'll tell you all about it when we get back from dinner. It's not something I want people overhearing.'

'That sounds intriguing,' Colin said, brightening up. 'Was there a treasure map?'

'No, but there was a sketch,' Georgina said. 'I'll show you when we get back. And I also need to ask a favour.'

'Should I be worried?' Colin asked.

'No. We just need to make sure that Dominic McGowan isn't in the church when Walter goes to investigate. And I think you might be best placed to help with that,' Georgina explained.

After a light dinner at the Feathers – including Bert's customary sausage from Hannah, the chef – Georgina sat down with her laptop at the kitchen table and took Colin through what they'd learned with Kirsty's help, showing him the photographs.

'Walter needs to go into the crypt to check out the place where Bram thought the tunnel entrance might be. The vicar's in meetings tomorrow afternoon, so the church will be quiet. Except,' she added with a grimace, 'Dominic seems to have taken up residence. Kathleen texted me earlier this evening to say one of her friends had ventured into the church and Dominic had harangued her, saying that she couldn't call herself a Christian when she was friends with a murderer.'

'This isn't going away any time soon, is it?' Colin asked.

'I think Dominic's the sort who would argue with a coroner,' Georgina agreed. 'So even the official report won't stop him.'

Colin sighed. 'I'm not sure what I can do to get him out of the church tomorrow.'

'How about a repeat interview, just to check everything?' Georgina suggested.

'I'll do what I can,' Colin said. 'And if I can persuade him to leave the church, I'll let you know. Otherwise I assume Walter will have to lock up the church, last thing, and maybe he could check the crypt then.'

'Except the vicar is likely to be there and he'll ask what's in the crypt – I believe Walter's avoided talking about it to him so far –

and he'll get overexcited and probably call the TreasureChest guy, the local TV station, the radio station, the local paper and anyone else who'll listen. It'll be mayhem,' Georgina pointed out.

'It makes sense to keep something like this low-key until you're sure of the facts,' Colin said. 'OK. I'll do my best.'

On Thursday afternoon, Colin left his car in the little gravelled car park by St Edmund's and walked down to the church. As he twisted the heavy iron ring to lift the latch on the door, he could hear voices – and the conversation sounded heated.

He walked into the church to discover Dominic having what looked like an argument with a man of a similar age.

'Everything all right, lads?' he asked.

Dominic gave him a withering look.

Yeah, well. They were hardly lads, but Colin hadn't been able to think up another description that didn't sound even worse. 'Gents' would have sounded as if he was calling them both public toilets.

'I'm just leaving,' the man he didn't recognise said.

'And you are?' Colin asked.

The other man frowned. 'Who wants to know?'

Colin showed his warrant card. 'DI Colin Bradshaw.'

'Oh. I'm Russell Dawson.'

The podcaster, Colin remembered. 'Actually, I was hoping to have a word with you later today,' Colin said. 'For some background information. What's the best number to call you on?'

Russell Dawson fished a card out of his pocket and handed it over. 'If I don't answer, it means I'm recording. Leave a message and I'll get back to you.'

Like Georgina and her darkroom, Colin thought. 'Thank you.'

Dominic said nothing throughout the exchange, though there was a definite sneer on his expression. Given what he'd said to Colin the other day about Russell Dawson, Colin was pretty sure Dominic didn't like the man.

'What can I do for you, Inspector?' Dominic asked when Russell had closed the church door noisily behind him.

'I thought we could have a chat,' Colin said.

'You mean, you're finally going to arrest Aaron Flint?' Dominic asked.

'I'm still investigating,' Colin said. 'What were you arguing about with Russell Dawson, just now?'

'Nothing. He's poking his nose in where it's not wanted,' Dominic said.

'Always tricky,' Colin said. If Dominic was already this spiky and combative, it didn't bode well for his mission to persuade Dominic to vacate the church for a little while. He gestured to the pews. 'Shall we sit down?'

Dominic said nothing, but he did at least sit down.

'I know this has been a difficult week for you,' Colin said as gently as he could. 'I really do think a family liaison officer can help you. The offer's still open.'

Dominic shook his head. 'What's the point? It won't bring Liam back.'

'No,' Colin agreed. He looked at Dominic. The younger man might be difficult, verging on obnoxious, but he was clearly devastated by his partner's death. If Georgina was here, she'd give him a hug and a cup of tea and encourage him to talk. Colin wasn't going to hug the man, but he could offer tea. That would be a start. He took his flask out of his messenger bag. 'Let me pour you a cup of tea.'

Dominic looked shocked, as if he hadn't expected that.

Hopefully feeling wrong-footed might encourage Dominic to abandon his difficult stance, Colin thought. 'I know it sounds trite, but a cup of tea can sometimes help. This is English breakfast, medium strength with a dash of milk and no sugar. More importantly, it's hot – and this building's cold,' he added, pouring some into an enamel mug and handing it to the younger man.

'I...' Dominic stared at the mug.

'It's clean. I haven't used it yet today,' Colin reassured him.

Dominic still looked wary, but to Colin's relief he took the mug. 'Thank you. I brought food with me today, but I forgot a drink.'

Please let Georgie's way work, Colin begged inwardly, and poured tea into the lid of the flask, which doubled as a cup.

Dominic finally took a sip of tea, and sighed. 'I know I probably shouldn't still be hanging round here at the church, but I feel so *stuck*. I know Aaron Flint's behind Liam's death, but I can't work out how he did it.'

'It's hard to accept when someone dies,' Colin said. 'Sometimes it's easier to handle it if you can blame it on someone rather than it being an accident. And sometimes grief makes you see connections that aren't really there.' He paused. 'But so far I have no evidence against Aaron.'

Dominic's eyes widened with anger. 'I gave you evidence.'

'Yes, you did.' False evidence, though Colin didn't press the point. 'As I told you, I believe in being thorough and fair. I checked it against the phone provider's records.' He met Dominic's gaze head-on. 'That message reads rather differently in context of the message that Liam had previously sent to Aaron.'

'Are you going to charge me with wasting police time?' Dominic said, his face expressionless.

'I suppose I could,' Colin said, keeping his tone neutral. 'But that's not going to help anyone, is it?'

Dominic said nothing. But then he rummaged in his own messenger bag and brought out a box. 'Do you want some cake to go with that tea?'

Colin thought of his blood sugar levels and what the practice nurse would have to say about consumption of cake. Georgie, too, because she was a bit Food Police-y. But then again this wasn't just an offer of cake. It was an admission of guilt – because Dominic *had* wasted police time – and maybe also the nearest Dominic could come to making an apology. Accepting the cake might just help Dominic accept what else Colin had to say. 'Thank you,' he said.

'It's lemon drizzle. Liam's favourite,' Dominic said. 'I didn't make it. I bought it from the bakery round the corner from our house.'

'My favourite, too,' Colin said. 'Just for information, of course, I should tell you that the farm shop in Little Wenborough sells the best lemon drizzle I've ever tasted.'

Dominic said nothing.

OK. He'd shut up and try to bond with the man over cake. He took a bite – it was OK, though not a patch on Cesca's cake – and washed it down with a swig of tea.

'Grief counselling can help,' he said quietly. 'When you lose someone or something important to you, grief can be overwhelming. Sometimes it takes someone else, someone who's not involved in the situation, to help you process it.'

Still Dominic said nothing.

Sending a silent prayer for forgiveness to Georgie – and knowing that she might well have used this example to help Dominic, too – he said, 'My partner lost her husband three years ago. He died from a heart attack while she was working away. She blamed herself for not being there. It was her counsellor who taught her not to think that way.'

Dominic was silent.

'You don't have to go through this on your own,' he said. 'There are people who can help.'

'It doesn't feel as if anything's ever going to help,' Dominic said.

Even though he didn't particularly like the man, Colin couldn't help feeling sorry for him. 'Maybe being here is making it harder,' he said. This had stopped being about trying to get Dominic out of the church to help Walter and Georgina. It was about trying to shift things, to help Dominic come to terms with something incredibly difficult – something that Georgina herself would do. 'You're in the place where he died. Everywhere you look, you'll be wondering what could have happened differently, what could have saved him. You'll see the gorgeous stained glass, but you won't enjoy the art – you'll just see the loss of the man who could have talked you through it and shared his love of it with you. Maybe,' he said, 'you'd be better off getting out of these four walls. My partner says that walking really helps her when she's struggling. Hearing birdsong, seeing something green. There's actually a really nice walk through the village along the river. Maybe give yourself a break from this, just say half an hour, and see if it helps.'

Dominic stared at him. And then he gave a single nod. 'Maybe you're right. I'll do that. The river, you say.'

'Left out of the church, then cross the road and walk behind the Red Lion,' Colin said. 'Their beer garden is next to the riverside path.'

'All right. I'll do that,' Dominic said.

'I really am sorry for your loss,' Colin said quietly. 'As soon as all the lab tests are back, I'll be in a better position to tell you what happened. If someone's responsible for Liam's death, I'll make sure they're brought to justice. But if my findings say it was an accident, you'll need to find a way of accepting that.'

A muscle worked in Dominic's jaw and he said no more. But he drained his tea, handed the mug back to Colin with a nod of acknowledgement, and left the church.

Colin waited until he heard the heavy bang of the church door latch closing. Then he texted Georgina. *D gone for a walk by the river. C x*

The reply came back almost immediately. *Thank you. Will ring Walter now. G x*

Colin packed his flask and the enamel mug away, and went to his car, intending to head back to the station and arrange a meeting with Russell Dawson. But as he pulled out of the car park, there was a horrible metallic taste in his mouth and he could feel bile rising in his throat. His stomach hurt, too.

Rather than drive to work, he headed for Rookery Farm.

'Hello! This is a nice surprise,' Georgina said as he walked into the kitchen and Bert circled him, wagging his plumy tail in delight.

He didn't kiss her. He needed the bathroom. *Now.*

'Excuse me,' he managed, and made a dash for it.

. . .

When he came back into the kitchen, Colin looked ashen and drawn.

'You're not all right,' she said. 'What's happened?'

'I must have some kind of gastric bug,' he said. 'My stomach hurts. There's a horrible taste in my mouth, and not just because I threw up.' He gagged again. 'Give me a cloth and I'll clean up. And can I beg a glass of water? I'm really thirsty.'

'You're in no fit state to clean up. I'll do it,' she said, and filled a glass of water from the tap. 'There isn't a bug going round, as far as I know. Have you eaten something that disagreed with you?'

'No idea. I had hunter's chicken last night at the Feathers.' He paused. 'So did you. Are you feeling all right?'

'I'm fine,' she said, 'so I don't think it's that.'

'I'll be all right in a mi—' He broke off and dashed to the downstairs toilet again.

On his return, this time he was shivering. 'Can I have some more water, please?'

'Just sip it really slowly, this time,' she said. She refilled his glass and handed it to him, then sniffed. 'You smell really garlicky.' Which was odd, because there had been only the merest trace of garlic in the chicken dish they'd both eaten, the previous evening.

'Georgie, you need to get him to hospital. I think he's been poisoned,' Doris said into Georgina's hearing aid.

'Poisoned?' Georgina asked.

'Who are you talking to?' Colin asked.

She ignored the question, because the answer wasn't going to be helpful right now. 'Thinking aloud. What have you eaten today?'

'Granola with you for breakfast, a chicken salad wrap and an apple at lunch.'

'Anything else?' she asked.

'A piece of cake in the church,' he admitted.

'Something you bought?'

'No. Dominic McGowan gave it to me. Lemon drizzle cake.' His face had already lost all its colour, so he didn't pale further when the thought obviously hit him. 'Do you think I've been poisoned?'

She nodded.

'He was eating the cake, too. So he might be ill, too – and I persuaded him to go for a walk by the—' He rushed to the kitchen sink and nearly made it.

'Or he might be the poisoner,' Doris said. 'And there was someone else in the church when Colin got there, having an argument with Dominic.'

Georgina gave a brief nod of acknowledgement. 'I'm calling an ambulance.'

'You haven't got any proof that I—' Colin broke off and retched again.

'Oh, I think we do,' she said grimly. 'Who was the other person in the church?'

'Russell Dawson.' He looked at her in surprise. 'How did you know someone else was there?'

'I just do,' Georgina said, dialling nine-nine-nine.

'Neither of them has a motive to poison me.'

'Stop talking and sip water *slowly*,' Georgina said, 'and I need to take your pulse.'

He submitted a little too easily for her liking. And she really wasn't happy with how high his pulse rate was.

The emergency services answered her call.

'I need an ambulance,' she said, 'I think my partner has been poisoned. He's been vomiting, had stomach pains and—' She looked at Colin and mouthed *the runs?* At his nod, she continued, 'Diarrhoea. He's very thirsty, but can't keep water down. And his pulse is over a hundred.' She gave her name, number and address.

'The ambulance is going to be a while,' the call controller said.

She had no idea what kind of poison Colin had ingested or how quickly it would do serious damage. 'Would it be quicker for me to take him straight to A&E myself?' she asked.

'You can't—' Colin began.

'Yes, I can,' she told him. 'Can you let the hospital know I'm on my way and it's really serious?' she said to the call controller.

Much as she hated to leave Bert on his own, she knew he couldn't go to hospital with her. She settled him on his bed, then grabbed a couple of towels, filled her metal water bottle, took a large plastic container from the cupboard, ushered Colin outside, locked the door and supported Colin to the car.

'We've been here before,' she said to Colin, 'except usually it's me being sick and you rescuing me.'

'What if I'm ill in your car?' Colin protested.

It was the same argument she'd used to him. And she used his own argument back. 'I don't care about that. It's fixable. What I care about is you.' She got him settled in the front seat, draped him with the towel, made him hold the container on his lap in case he needed to be sick again – and at least it would be a sample for the hospital to test – and put his seatbelt on. 'Nothing matters except *you*,' she said fiercely.

## FOURTEEN

Georgina broke the speed limit several times on the way to the hospital, but she rather thought Colin's vomiting had more to do with the poison than her driving. At the hospital, she supported him into the emergency department and explained everything to the triage nurse. He was seen straight away. The ECG showed his heart rate was too fast, and one of the doctors said something about ST segment changes and a prolonged QT interval; she didn't understand, but kept a mental note. Colin's DC Larissa was married to a nurse, who might be able to translate everything into layman's terms for her.

Colin was sick again into the plastic container.

'The container was clean,' she said, 'so you should get a valid sample from the contents.' At the doctor's raised eyebrow, she said, 'Colin's a DI. I've learned some of the protocols.'

'I see. We're going to take him into Resus,' the doctor said gently, 'and I'm afraid you'll have to wait outside.'

'I think he's been poisoned,' she said. 'I'm sorry, I don't know with what, but he ate some cake at the church.'

'It just tasted of cake,' Colin said miserably, and retched again.

Georgina thought of Liam Jacobs. He'd died in St Edmund's after eating cake. But that had been an accident; she didn't believe that Kathleen had deliberately killed him. 'Where did Dominic get the cake?' she asked.

'From the bakery round the corner from his house, he said,' Colin muttered.

So not Kathleen's cake. Besides, Walter had said he was keeping her away from the church while Dominic McGowan was there. Georgina knew Walter was angry about the way Dominic had behaved towards Kathleen, but would he have taken poisoned cake to the church to get rid of Dominic?

No, of course not. He would know that anyone else who ate the cake would be poisoned, too, and he wouldn't poison the entire congregation just to get to Dominic. Besides, they'd agreed that Colin would help get Dominic out of the church.

Who else would want to poison Dominic? She didn't have a clue.

And then there was Dominic himself. Had he poisoned Colin? If so, what had he used? He couldn't have known that Colin would choose to talk to him in the church today, so had someone else been Dominic's real target and Colin was collateral damage?

Guilt flooded through her. She'd asked Colin to get Dominic out of the church so Walter could examine the crypt. If it hadn't been for that, he wouldn't have been at the church today and he wouldn't have eaten the cake – and he wouldn't be poorly now.

'You need to find Dominic. He ate the cake, too,' Colin said. 'He's somewhere by the river. If he's taken ill and falls in and drowns…'

'Then it won't be your fault. It'll be whoever put the poison in the cake,' Georgina said. 'Stop worrying and just concentrate on doing what the doctors say. I'll call Larissa and Mo to tell them what's happened, and they'll deal with everything until you're well again.' She squeezed his hand fiercely. 'And you *will* get better.' Provided they could find out what had poisoned him.

She was worried sick, but she knew she'd be no help to Colin if she gave in to the almost overwhelming urge to bawl her eyes out. She needed to concentrate – to be practical and try to find out what she could about the poison. She went back to the waiting area and asked the reception team to call her if she was needed because she was just going outside to call her partner's team at work.

Larissa answered the phone. 'Georgie. What can I do for you?'

'It's Colin,' Georgina said. 'I'm at the hospital. I've just driven him here. I think he's eaten poisoned cake, but I don't know what the poison is.' She dragged in a breath, forcing herself to push the panic back down. 'He was in St Edmund's church, talking to Dominic McGowan. The last two people he spoke to – obviously apart from me – were Dominic and Russell Dawson, the podcast guy. Dominic was the one who gave him the cake, and Colin's worried that he might have eaten some and is ill. Apparently he said he was going for a walk by the river at Little Wenborough.'

'I've got all that,' Larissa said. 'Did the doctors say he's going to be all right?'

'I don't know. He's in Resus and they asked me to go out of the treatment area. That's why I'm calling you now. Sorry. I should have called you on the way, but Colin was throwing up and I was concentrating on getting him to hospital as soon as possible. The nine-nine-nine team said the ambulance would be a while and I don't actually know what the poison is or how' – she swallowed hard – 'how quickly it works.'

'The guv's made of tough stuff,' Larissa said. 'And he's not going to want to leave you. I'll ring Alison' – Larissa's wife Alison was a nurse and worked at the hospital – 'and see if she can grab a moment to come over to see you. If nothing else, she can help to reassure you.'

It was oh-so tempting to accept. But that might get in the way of another patient being treated, and that wouldn't be fair. 'I can't interrupt Alison's work,' Georgina said.

'You're part of our team, Georgie,' Larissa said. 'I know how I'd feel in your shoes. You need some support.'

'I'll ring Sybbie,' Georgina said. 'Don't disturb Alison just for me.'

'If you're sure,' Larissa said. 'We'll get hold of Dominic

McGowan and Russell Dawson. Tell the guv not to worry. Me and Mo will handle it.'

'I already told him that – I knew that was what you'd say,' Georgina said. 'But I need to talk to someone about poison. My son knows a fair bit,' she added, 'because he's a chemist and his job used to be something he can't talk about, but he's hard to get hold of in office hours. Do you know someone?'

'Sammy Granger, the pathologist,' Larissa said immediately. 'Have you got her number?'

'No.'

'I'll text you,' Larissa promised, and a couple of moments later Georgina's phone beeped to signal an incoming message.

'Tell her the symptoms and the timings, and she'll work it out,' Larissa said. 'Ring me any time you need to. And give the guv our best. I know sometimes he feels like an outsider because he's from London and you have to live in Norfolk for about fifty years before you're accepted as a non-foreigner, but he's one of us.'

'I will,' Georgie said, just about managing to speak through the huge lump in her throat.

She called Sybbie next, and filled her in on what had happened to Colin.

'Oh, my God. I'll drive to the hospital now,' Sybbie said.

'You really don't have to do that,' Georgina said. 'Actually, if anything, I don't know how long I'll be here so I'd rather you grabbed Bert.'

'I'll get your keys from Jodie,' Sybbie said. 'Don't worry about Bert, and don't worry about how long you're at the hospital. Let me know if you need me to bring anything to you, and keep me posted.'

'Thank you,' Georgina said, grateful for her friend's kindness and practicality.

'Have they ruled out norovirus?' Sybbie asked.

'Yes. It's not ordinary food poisoning, either, because it came on so fast, though the symptoms are like those of a gastric bug and he's really thirsty,' Georgina said.

'It might still be a bug,' Sybbie said. 'It might not be intentional.'

'It feels it, though,' Georgina said with a sigh. 'Though I don't know who would want to poison Colin.'

'I don't want to worry you,' Sybbie said, 'but remember that case we worked on at Great Wenborough Mill?'

The case that had made her twitchy and overprotective of Bert. Right now, she was starting to feel twitchy and overprotective of Colin, too. 'Yes.'

'Will said that the symptoms of arsenic poisoning were similar to those of cholera, and it was often misdiagnosed as gastroenteritis,' Sybbie said slowly. 'Could it be that? Because I also remember Will saying that it's hard to get hold of arsenic nowadays, but it's still used by glass workers.'

Georgina went cold. 'We know three people who work with glass. Kathleen, her nephew, Aaron – and Liam Jacobs, who's dead.' Had they been wrong all along and Kathleen *was* a poisoner? But how had she got the poison into the lemon cake?

'Obviously it can't be Liam,' Sybbie said. 'And I really don't think it's Kathleen. But Aaron might be very protective of his aunt. If he's heard how Dominic behaved towards her in the church, he might have poisoned the cake intended for Dominic. Or maybe Walter did.'

'But Dominic told Colin he bought the cake from the bakery near his house. How would Walter or Aaron even know that he'd bought the cake, let alone manage to sneak into the church and poison it?' Georgina asked. She dragged in a breath. 'Or maybe Dominic is the one who poisoned the cake. If Liam worked on any glass at home and it involved the use of arsenic, then Dominic would have had access to the poison. Maybe Colin wasn't his intended victim. Maybe Dominic was either planning to get revenge on Kathleen, because she was the one who made the cake that Liam ate before he died, or on Walter, because Walter had stood up for Kathleen. He knows Walter is the churchwarden and would be at the church at some point today to lock up.' She paused.

'But Colin also said that Dominic ate some of the cake. I told Larissa he was worried in case Dominic had become ill, too, and fallen into the river.'

'Why would he fall into the river?' Sybbie asked.

'Colin persuaded him to go for a walk and get some fresh air, so Walter could slip into the church and check out the crypt,' Georgina explained.

'Then I suppose he wouldn't eat the cake if he knew it was poisoned. Unless,' Sybbie said thoughtfully, 'he only poisoned *some* of it, say by sprinkling the poison on top of it, and gave Colin the poisoned bit.'

'But why would he want to poison Colin?' Georgina asked.

'Good question. Would Will be able to tell you more about the symptoms of arsenic poisoning?' Sybbie asked.

'He'll be in the lab with his phone locked away. Larissa suggested ringing Sammy, the pathologist,' Georgina said.

'Do that,' Sybbie said. 'I'll go and get Bert, and in the meantime call me if you need me. And I mean that. Don't struggle alone because Bernard and I are here for you.'

'Thank you,' Georgina said gratefully.

Next, she called the number Larissa had given her.

'Dr Granger? It's Georgina Drake, Colin's partner. I'm sorry to bother you, but Larissa suggested you'd be the best person to help, and she gave me your number,' Georgina said.

'Call me Sammy, please,' Sammy said. 'How can I help?'

'Colin's in hospital and I think he's been poisoned,' Georgina said. 'But I don't know what the poison is, how much he ate – I think it was in some cake – and what a fatal dose is.' She dragged in a breath. 'This might sound mad, but what are the symptoms of arsenic poisoning? And I know I'm probably wasting your time and I should've done an internet search, but—'

'You're not wasting my time,' Sammy cut in. 'I'll do anything to help Colin. Arsenic poisoning isn't that common in this country. It's usually caused by contaminated water supplies. It tends to cause gastric symptoms.'

'Diarrhoea, nausea, vomiting, stomach cramps,' Georgina said. 'He has all of these. And he's really thirsty, said there's a horrible taste in his mouth. And he smells of garlic. In the Victorian cold case I was working on earlier this year, the lawyer threw flour containing arsenic on the fire, and it made the room smell of garlic. My son said that would have been arsine gas.'

'It would,' Sammy said. 'Right, well, that's pretty conclusive, to my mind. Tell the doctors that you've spoken to me, and give them my number if they want to talk to me. Tell them I think there's a very strong possibility it's arsenic poisoning, and they need to do blood and urine tests specifically looking for arsenic. Depending on how much he's taken, he might need chelation therapy – that's when they'll give him a medication that binds the arsenic and stops his body processing it. Go and tell them *now*,' she said. 'Can I text you on this number? Because I'll put it in medic-speak for them in case you get stuck with someone who's not very good at listening to anyone other than another doctor. And if they ignore *that*, ring me and I'll talk to them myself.'

'Thank you, and yes, please, a text on this number would be great,' Georgina said.

'I'll do it now. Please keep me posted. And give him my best.' Sammy gave a wry chuckle. 'Don't tell him this, but he's my favourite inspector. I enjoy working with him. I want him back on duty ASAP.'

'Thank you,' Georgina said, near to tears with relief. 'I promise I'll keep you in the loop.'

She ended the call, spoke to the reception team to explain that she had urgent information about Colin's case, then told one of the doctors who was treating him exactly what Sammy had said.

'Arsenic? Are you sure?' the doctor asked.

Sammy had sent the text almost immediately – including a digital signature that included her name, her qualifications and her job title. Georgina unlocked her phone, opened the message and showed him.

'Got it,' the doctor said. 'Sorry, we still can't let you see him.'

'I'll wait for as long as it takes,' Georgina said. 'Just please don't let him die.' She liked having Colin around, even when he was in grumpy middle-aged man mode.

'We're doing our best,' the doctor said gently.

She bit her lip. 'Sorry. Of course you are. It's just…'

'You're worried. I get that,' the doctor said. 'We'll come and get you as soon as you can see him.'

'Thank you,' Georgina said.

# FIFTEEN

Walter walked down the gravel path to the porch, and stood for a moment with his hand on the wrought-iron ring. How many people had walked through this porch over the centuries? he wondered. How many had been bowed down with worry, and then stepped into the gentle, inviting space on the other side of that door and felt lifted up?

He was still worried about lots of things. Kathleen had been his staunch partner for fifty years, yet now she seemed to be crumbling, thanks to Dominic McGowan and his unfair, baseless accusations. The death of the glass restorer in the church had shocked everyone, and Walter had noticed that several of the congregation had been reluctant to step inside the church since then. The new vicar was utterly hopeless and wouldn't know how to begin supporting his flock; there would be no lessening of the responsibilities for the churchwardens and the parish council. That patch of moss seemed to be gaining hold, and that dodgy bit of roof was getting frailer by the day. Meanwhile, donations to the church were lower; people in the village were struggling financially and couldn't afford to be generous. The same was true of the businesses. He couldn't keep asking them for more and more.

Without an influx of funds, the church would crumble and end up as yet another little redundant church. Norfolk had more medieval churches than any other county in England, thanks to the riches of the wool trade; it also had a substantial number of ruins, and he'd hate to see St Edmund's join that group.

Even the thought of it sent a pain through his heart. A pain he couldn't tell his wife about, because he knew how much Kathleen worried about his angina.

'Please, God, let that treasure be there in the crypt. Let us be able to sell it so we can fix the building, and keep supporting people with the food bank,' Walter whispered.

He twisted the handle to lift the heavy latch, and pushed the door. It creaked, as always, but the sound was comforting.

Please let Dominic McGowan really have gone, even if it was only a temporary respite. Please let the church go back to being the welcoming, calm place it had been for so many years. *Please.*

He'd printed out the sketch from Bram's diary, and had folded it and put it in his coat pocket with the church keys, along with a small but bright torch, a steel measuring tape and a pen.

Holding his breath, he walked into the church.

Sunlight filtered through the stained-glass windows, mottling the flag-stoned floor with colour, and he breathed out, relaxing into the familiar space. The Angel Gabriel seemed to be smiling down from his window, letting Walter know that all was well.

*All shall be well, and all shall be well, and all manner of things shall be well.* The words floated into his head, calming him. The first time he'd read Julian of Norwich's *Revelations of Divine Love*, those words had resonated deep inside him. They'd carried him through the sadness of Kathleen's miscarriages and the disappointment when the authorities had judged them too old to adopt. She'd thrown herself into her art and her teaching, and he'd thrown himself into accountancy and his duties in the church. He would so have liked a child's laughter filling the house. But he would never have abandoned Kathleen in pursuit of someone else who could have given him children. And he would lay down his life for her.

He still burned at the injustice of Dominic McGowan's hurled accusations. Could he not *see* that Kathleen was a gentle soul, one who projected love, not hate? And in this case Walter couldn't turn the other cheek. He wanted the man out of here for good.

Shaking himself, he walked into the church hall just to check. To his relief, nobody was there. No Dominic McGowan with his spiteful lies. The vicar was in a meeting at the vicarage, and Walter already knew that none of the groups who used the church hall had a session booked this afternoon.

He was alone here.

Perfect.

One of his hearing aids whistled, making him wince. Dratted thing. He turned off the battery and slipped the hearing aid out of his ear, then put it in his pocket before following suit with the other. He couldn't hear a thing without them, but he didn't need to hear anything down here. He concentrated better without the annoyance of the whistling, anyway, and he needed to concentrate now.

He took out the church keys and fitted the oldest one into the lock to open the medieval door that looked as if it led to a store cupboard – which was more or less how he'd glossed over it to Reverend Craig. It had been a white lie, told out of practicality rather than malice. Not quite a sin. With a last look over his shoulder to check that he was still alone, he opened the door and switched on the torch to illuminate his way down the uneven stone steps. The crypt smelled damp, as always, and there were patches of ancient plaster on the walls where repairs had been made over the centuries but had started to flake off.

In the room at the bottom, the floor was uneven terracotta paving stones, and the ceiling was low and heavily beamed. The narrow slit of a window wasn't enough to light the room, even on a sunny day like today. Back in its day as a charnel house, this place would have been gloom personified. Any light from a lantern would have reflected the dead light of bones: pitted, twisted, with shadowy gaps in skeletons where teeth had rotted out years before.

Walter shivered, and took Bram's sketch from his pocket. The tape measure followed, and he checked the measurements of the room against Bram's, noting them down on the paper. He'd just bent down to measure the damp patch he'd noticed a while back, intending to plot it against where Bram thought the tunnel was, when something heavy hit him over the head.

And everything went black.


'Mr Dawson?' Larissa asked.

'Yes,' the voice on the other end of the phone said. 'Who is this?'

'DC Larissa Foulkes,' she said. 'My colleague and I would like a chat with you.'

'Oh, would that be DI Bradshaw? He said he wanted a word.'

Larissa evaded the question. 'Could we talk to you now?'

'Now? I was about to get some documents from the archives in the city library,' Russell said. 'Can we make it later?'

'Now would be better, Mr Dawson,' Larissa said coolly.

'I'm not sure how much help I'll be – DI Bradshaw said it was background information – but all right,' Russell said. 'Shall I meet you here in the library?'

'We'll see you in ten minutes by the entrance on the ground floor,' Larissa said.

She'd already looked up Russell Dawson on the internet, so she recognised him from his photograph as the slender man with thinning fair hair, John-Lennon glasses, a vintage sweater and a long stripy hand-knitted scarf like that of a Dr Who from the 1970s.

'Mr Dawson?' she asked.

At his nod, she introduced herself and Mo, and they showed him their warrant cards.

A quick word with the librarian netted them a tiny room in a corridor with a glass door, but most importantly it had a table and four chairs and they wouldn't be overheard.

'Is this about the podcast and the Little Wenborough story?' Russell asked.

'Sort of,' Larissa said. 'What can you tell us about Dominic McGowan?'

Russell winced. 'He's a lecturer in folklore. We're pretty much in the same line of business, but we don't get on very well.'

'Why is that?' Mo asked.

'Because he's an intellectual snob,' Russell said. 'His degree is from Oxford, and mine's from a former poly – one of the newer universities. He thinks everyone else should defer to him, and he claims my research isn't good enough. Which isn't true,' he added, looking cross. 'The thing is, McGowan's books are as dry as dust and nobody buys them – whereas the TreasureChest podcast is popular and people pay to subscribe. He hates that. And, by extension, he hates me.' He shrugged. 'But that's his problem, not mine.'

'Can you tell me your movements this afternoon?' Larissa asked.

'Sure. I went to Little Wenborough this afternoon, just after lunch. I've done a podcast on the legend of the prior's hidden treasure, and I was hoping to talk to the vicar. I went to the vicarage, but unfortunately he was due to go into a meeting and couldn't see me. The churchwarden – Walter Reeves – wasn't about, so I was just having a look round the church. I didn't realise McGowan was there until he came out and told me I had no business being there.' He shook his head. 'It's a free country, and I wasn't doing any harm. But I wasn't in the mood for listening to yet another of his rants, so I was about to leave when a bloke walked in. He'd obviously heard McGowan having a go at me, because he asked if everything was all right and I told him I was just leaving. He asked my name and showed me his warrant card – DI Bradshaw – then said he wanted to talk to me, so I gave him my card.'

'And what time was this?' Larissa asked.

'About half past two.'

'And DI Bradshaw was fine when you left?' Mo asked.

Russell frowned. 'Yes. Why?'

'Just clarifying,' Larissa asked. 'What did you do then?'

'I drove into the city and came here to the library.' He rummaged in his pocket for his wallet, and brought out a car park ticket. 'I parked downstairs. You can see the time stamp on my ticket.'

'Interesting that you should have proof of timings,' Mo said. 'And that you didn't have to hunt for your ticket.'

'When you're self-employed, you make sure you keep your tickets and receipts safely because you need them for your tax return.' Russell gave them a boyish grin. 'Plus I learned what not to do from my dad. He can never remember where he's put his car park ticket and wastes ten minutes looking for it. Every single time. Whenever they're about to go out, he can never find his glasses or his keys or his wallet. It drives my mum and me bananas.'

Larissa found herself smiling back. Her mum was the same as his dad, chaos personified. That scattiness was one of the reasons why Larissa had a place for everything and kept everything in its place, at home.

'If you check with the librarians, they'll be able to tell you when I booked out some pieces from the local heritage section,' Russell said. 'I was working up there until you called me.'

It all checked out, Larissa thought. Despite his slightly scruffy appearance, Russell Dawson was organised and bright. And there was something endearing about him. She made a mental note to check out his podcast. She had a feeling it would be a good listen.

Colin had been moved from Resus to a ward and was currently asleep. Georgina was sitting in a hard plastic chair next to his bed. She was in the middle of composing a text to Larissa to update her on Colin's condition when her phone vibrated with an incoming call. Thankfully she'd put her phone on silent so it didn't wake Colin. The notification told her it was Kathleen calling.

Georgina thought about letting the call go to voicemail, then decided she'd better answer. It might be something important about the crypt – and if Kathleen was about to tell her they'd found the tunnel, it would be something to take Colin's mind off how awful he was feeling. She tiptoed out of the ward and into the corridor to take the call.

'Hi, Kathleen,' she said.

'Georgie, is Walter with you?' Kathleen asked.

'No. I'm not at home – I'm at the hospital,' Georgina said. 'Colin's been taken ill.'

'Oh, no! I'm so sorry. I, um, I'd better let you go.'

But Kathleen sounded worried. Rattled, even. Which wasn't like the calm, capable woman Georgina had come to know. 'Colin's asleep at the moment. I can talk for a little while.'

'What's wrong?' Kathleen asked.

'The doctors are still running tests,' Georgina said, not wanting to go into detail right now. 'Did Walter manage to get into the crypt?'

'I don't know,' Kathleen said. 'It's been a couple of hours, now. And I can't find him on that location tracker thing on my phone. He's vanished.'

Georgina had set up something similar on her own phone, in case she slipped and broke her ankle while out walking Bert, so Colin or the kids could direct rescuers to find her. 'Maybe he's in an area with a poor signal.' There were still little pockets like that in Norfolk, even in the middle of some of the villages. 'Or maybe the battery of his phone is flat.'

'Perhaps I should go and see if he's still in the church. He would have messaged me if he was going to the allotment.' Kathleen sounded worried. 'Walter doesn't like to admit to any weakness, but he has angina. He was quite poorly with it, last year, and it's been playing up a bit recently because he's been worrying about me and Aaron. Even though he's tried to keep it from me, I can tell when he's not well. I really hope it hasn't flared up and he's feeling too ill to grab his medication so he's lying somewhere, in pain, where nobody can see him.'

'Be careful, Kathleen. Dominic might be back in the church by now,' Georgina warned. 'It might be an idea to get someone to go with you.'

'This is ridiculous,' Kathleen said. 'I'm not going to let that man bully me or make me hide away like some little country mouse. If Walter's hurt and he needs me, then Dominic McGowan can say whatever he likes – he's not going to stop me helping my husband!'

Go, you, Georgina thought, but stopped herself saying it because it might come across as a bit rude and patronising. 'All right. Call me if you need me,' she said. 'And please let me know that Walter's OK.'

'I will. I hope that Colin's all right,' Kathleen said. 'I'll go and check the church now.'

When Kathleen walked into St Edmund's, she discovered that the church was empty. There was a service due at four-thirty, but nobody had turned up early to help with sorting out the church. There was no sign of the vicar, either.

More crucially, Dominic McGowan wasn't there. Despite her brave words earlier to Georgina, Kathleen hated confrontations and it was a relief not to have to deal with him. She headed for the door leading to the crypt. It was locked; she twisted the ring handle both ways, just in case it was simply stiff rather than locked, but she couldn't pull the door open.

'Oh, Walter. For pity's sake, where are you?' she muttered.

And then a nasty thought struck her. What if he'd locked himself in the crypt, to make sure nobody disturbed him while he was checking out Bram's diagram, and he'd had an angina attack?

'Walter? Are you here?' she called, her voice ringing clearly in the ancient building.

She was rewarded with the sound of a groan.

'Walter?' she called again.

The groan wasn't repeated and she hadn't quite been able to work out where it had come from. She hurried down the aisles, checking each of the pews in case Walter had keeled over in one of them and was lying on the floor, out of sight, but there was no sign of him.

Then she went through to the church hall. On the floor, just outside the kitchen, lay Dominic McGowan. Collapsed, and with a pile of watery vomit just in front of his face.

'Oh, no,' she said, and rushed over to him. 'Mr McGowan?' She shook his shoulder, and he didn't respond.

One death in the church had been bad enough. The thought of a second – especially so soon – was just too much to bear. She checked his pulse; to her relief, it was there, albeit thready.

She put him in the recovery position, grabbed her phone and called nine-nine-nine, telling the call controller her name and location, that a young man had collapsed and vomited and appeared to be unconscious, although he was still breathing and she'd put him in the recovery position. The controller promised to get an ambulance out immediately.

Then she called Georgina again.


Georgina's phone vibrated, and Georgina saw Kathleen's name on the screen again. She was already leaving Colin's bedside for a second time and on the way to the corridor when she answered the call. 'Hello, Kathleen. Did you find Walter?'

'No. But I found Dominic McGowan in the church hall, by the kitchen. He's unconscious and he's been sick, and I've got an ambulance on the way,' Kathleen said.

Oh, no. This was just what Colin had been worried about: that Dominic had eaten the same poisoned cake and been affected. Thankfully he hadn't collapsed into the river, as Colin had feared. And Georgina felt slightly guilty that Dominic McGowan's potential predicament had completely slipped her mind in her worry about Colin.

'Be careful,' Georgina said. 'Colin was sick a few times between my house and the hospital.'

'Is it a bug?' Kathleen asked.

'No. Poison,' Georgina said. 'Tell the paramedics that this is the second case, and they need to liaise with the team who's treating Colin Bradshaw. The cases are linked, and it's very likely they ate the same poisoned cake.'

'*Cake?*' Kathleen asked, sounding horrified.

'Cake,' Georgina repeated grimly. 'And there's no sign of Walter?' Surely, surely the poisoned cake had nothing to do with him? Or – a shiver of unease ran down her spine – with Kathleen? She'd liked both of them, but could her instincts be way off beam? Could either of them be murderers?

'No,' Kathleen said. 'And his location still isn't coming up on my phone.'

'Maybe he's still in the crypt,' Georgina suggested.

'That's what I thought, at first,' Kathleen said. 'But the door to the crypt is locked. I'm sure Walter wouldn't have been stupid enough to lock himself in. Not when the only other key is with the vicar, who probably doesn't know what all the church keys are for yet.'

And that was worrying. Walter wasn't the sort who took risks. He was *careful*.

Georgina really didn't want to leave Colin. But right now he was asleep and she knew there was nothing practical she could do to help him, whereas if she went back to Little Wenborough, she could at least help Kathleen to find Walter. Plus she needed to let Larissa know what had happened to Dominic, and the link to Colin. 'I'm on my way,' Georgina said.

She checked on Colin before she left the ward – he was still asleep – and had a quick word with the nurse in charge of his care, who promised to let her know when he woke and to tell him that Georgina would be back as soon as she could. She also passed on the information about the link to Dominic McGowan's collapse and the need to test him for arsenic poisoning, on the basis that it was better to hear something twice than for vital and possibly life-saving information to fall between the cracks.

On the way to Little Wenborough, she called Larissa.

'How's Colin?' was Larissa's first question.

'Right now, he's asleep, and they've admitted him for observation and chelation treatment. Thank you for putting me in touch with Sammy. She was brilliant,' Georgina said. 'But there's been a development. Kathleen Reeves – the one Dominic accused of killing Liam, because her cake was the last thing he ate – found Dominic in the church, collapsed in a puddle of vomit. Colin said Dominic gave him the cake; clearly Dominic ate it, too, but luckily he hadn't been taken ill when he walked by the river. *If* he walked by the river, that is. Maybe he went back to the church because he was starting to feel ill. Anyway, the ambulance is on its way to pick him up, and I've told the medics here about the case coming in so they can check him for the same poison as Colin.'

'Do you know what the poison was?' Larissa asked.

'Arsenic.'

'Arsenic?' Larissa sounded shocked. 'I thought that was a restricted substance?'

'It's used in glassmaking,' Georgina said. 'Sybbie and I were discussing it earlier. Liam would have had access to it, and that means Dominic would, too. But he wouldn't poison himself, would he? So that leaves Aaron Flint – the other person Dominic accused of being involved in Liam's death – or anyone else at the glass studio.' Feeling disloyal, even as she said it, 'And Kathleen's hobby is stained glass. But Dominic told Colin that the lemon cake came from the bakery round the corner from his house. Kathleen couldn't have known that he'd have cake with him, let alone poison it without him noticing.'

'I think I need to talk to Kathleen and Aaron, as well as Dominic – when he's conscious again,' Larissa said.

'And there's another complication,' Georgina said. 'Kathleen's husband has gone missing. That's why I'm going back to Little Wenborough, to help her find him. He was going to check out the crypt. The thing is, he has a heart condition, and she's worried he might have collapsed. And she can't see his location on her phone. He's disappeared into thin air.'

'Let us sort it out, Georgie,' Larissa said. 'Colin would kill me for letting you get involved in this.'

'Colin's in a hospital bed because I asked him to help me get Dominic out of the church and leave it free for Walter to go into the crypt without any arguments. I'm in this up to my neck,' Georgina said. 'I'll be careful, Larissa, I promise. But sitting around waiting for him to wake up again... it's making me twitchy. I'm better off doing something practical to help.'

'Don't take *any* risks,' Larissa said. 'And keep me posted. I'm in the middle of an interview, but what you've just told me might have a bearing on the case.'

'I'll keep you posted,' Georgina promised.

Larissa ended the call, and went back into their temporary interview room. 'There's been a development,' she said. 'What do you know about arsenic, Mr Dawson?'

'Arsenic?' Russell thought about it. 'It's a metallic element, poisonous, used in the production of green dye in Victorian times and thought to be part of the cause of Napoleon's death because it was in his wallpaper.'

'And where would you buy arsenic?' she asked.

'I have no idea. I imagine you'd have to get it from a specialist supplier – maybe one of the chemical suppliers that university labs use?' he suggested. 'Why?'

'Dominic McGowan is currently on his way to hospital with suspected arsenic poisoning,' Larissa said. 'And the last two people who saw him before his collapse, as far as we know, are DI Bradshaw and yourself.'

Russell blinked. 'Hang on. I admit, I don't get on with Dominic McGowan, but I wouldn't want to actually *kill* him.'

'Do you know Walter Reeves?' Larissa asked.

'Yes. He's the churchwarden at St Edmund's. Very old school, no nonsense. I had a bit of a run-in with him over the podcast,' Russell said. 'I wanted to talk to him about the treasure, but he told me it was a fairy tale and the treasure of any church is its people, love and kindness. I guess he has a point.'

'Tell me about the treasure,' Larissa said; she'd learned the basics over the course of the case, but she hoped Russell Dawson might say something to shed a bit more light on things.

'I covered it in my podcast. It's an old legend. Allegedly, the prior in Little Wenborough hid some treasure in a tunnel leading to the church, before Henry VIII's commissioners came to dissolve the priory and confiscate all its treasures,' Russell explained. 'Nobody's ever found it.'

'And that's what you want? To find the treasure?' Larissa asked.

Russell smiled. 'Yes, but it's not about how much it's worth. Apart from anything else, under the Treasure Act, anything found in land belonging to a church will remain with the church. It's the actual *finding* bit that interests me. Uncovering something that hasn't seen the light of day for decades or even centuries.'

'So, what, you go around with a metal detector?' Mo asked.

'Not very often, no, though I do have a metal-detecting friend who helps me out sometimes. I look mainly at the historical evidence. Maps, diaries, letters – that sort of thing,' Russell said. 'This particular story has circulated for decades. And it's got a lot in common with stories about other religious foundations which allegedly hid their treasure from Henry VIII.'

'So what did Dominic McGowan think of the story?' Larissa said.

'He scoffed about it,' Russell said. 'He said my research wasn't thorough enough. But why is he hanging round the church, if not to try and find the treasure himself?'

'Because his partner died there, earlier this week,' Mo said quietly. 'He's grieving.'

Russell winced. 'I apologise. But I've known McGowan for several years – we work in the same kind of area. He always has an eye on the main chance. And he's clever. I wouldn't be surprised if he's in the church and working out where the treasure might be hidden. And I think he's the sort who'd take it for himself.' His smile disappeared. 'I think you need to be asking *him* these questions, not me.'

Larissa ignored the comment. 'The whereabouts of Walter Reeves is currently unknown. Would you know anything about that?'

Russell frowned. 'No, I wouldn't.'

'Would you know something about lemon cake?' Mo asked. 'Specifically, lemon cake eaten by both Dominic McGowan and Colin Bradshaw, not long after you saw them both in the church today?'

'No. What are you accusing me of?' Russell's frown deepened. 'What's happened?'

'They've both been poisoned,' Larissa said.

'What? But how? Who'd do something like that?' Russell asked.

'I think,' Larissa said, 'we need to interview you a bit more formally, at the station.'

'Hang on. You don't think *I'm* responsible, surely?' Russell asked.

'You don't seem to have an alibi, Mr Dawson,' Mo said. 'And the last person both of them saw was you.'

SIXTEEN

On the way back to Little Wenborough, Georgina passed an ambulance heading towards Norwich.

'I'm guessing that's Dominic McGowan,' Doris said. 'Are you all right, Georgie?'

'Yes. Or I will be, when I know that Colin's going to come through this unscathed,' Georgina admitted. 'I need to tell his family what's happened, but they're all at least two hours away and I don't want to worry them silly, so I'm holding off for a couple more hours until I can give them better information.' She paused. 'Do you happen to know where Walter is?'

'No, but I can check the church quicker than you can,' Doris said.

'The last thing I knew, he was going to check the crypt. But he hasn't reported back to anyone, the door to the crypt is locked – and he wouldn't have locked himself in, surely? Kathleen's so worried because of his angina.' Georgina sighed. 'We should've insisted that someone else went with him.'

'Men,' Doris said, 'often seem to have tunnel vision and insist on things being done their way.'

'Tell me about it,' Georgina said wryly. 'I'd better warn Sybbie about all this.' She used the hands-free system on her car to call her friend and update her on Colin's hospitalisation and the new developments.

'Dear God. You must be worried sick, and Kathleen must be frantic,' Sybbie said. 'I'll come and meet you at the church to help look for Walter. Bert's happily settled here and Bernard will keep an eye on him.'

'Thank you,' Georgina said.

When she turned into the church car park, Sybbie was just walking up the path to the church. Georgina called her name; Sybbie turned round, waved and waited for her to catch up.

'Are you all right?' Sybbie asked.

'Yes,' Georgina fibbed. She was as worried about Colin as Kathleen must be about Walter, but she'd have to put her fears aside for now.

Sybbie gave her a brief hug. 'He's made of tough stuff, dear girl. And he's in the best place.'

'I know.' Georgina blew out a breath. 'Let's go and find Kathleen.'

The heavy oak door gave its usual creak when they lifted the latch and opened it, and they could see Kathleen sitting in one of the pews, her head bowed.

'Kathleen?' Georgina said gently.

'I'll check the crypt,' Doris whispered.

Kathleen stood up, and Georgina gave her a hug. 'I passed an ambulance on the way in,' she said. 'I assume it was from here?'

'Yes,' Kathleen said. 'I told the paramedics what you told me. Hopefully I found him in time.'

'They'll know which tests to run,' Sybbie reassured her, 'which will help. He's in the right hands, and so is Colin, so let's focus on Walter. You're quite sure he's not at the allotment, Kathleen?'

'I haven't actually checked there,' Kathleen admitted. 'But he said he was going to the crypt, and I haven't heard a thing from him since. He would have told me if he was going to the allotment. If nothing else, he would have called me to let me know that either he'd found something in the crypt, or it was all a wild goose chase.'

She shook her head, worry etched into her face. 'I really hope he hasn't had another angina attack. He always has his medication with him, but what if he felt too ill to get it out of his pocket?'

'We need to check the crypt,' Georgina said. 'Who else has a key?'

'The vicar,' Kathleen said. 'Though Walter didn't tell him what all the keys were for.'

'You need to get the key,' Doris whispered urgently. 'Walter's down there. And he's not moving.'

Georgina inclined her head slightly in acknowledgement of Doris's information. She couldn't tell Kathleen what she knew, but she needed to speed things up right now. 'If he's in the crypt and he's been taken ill, we can't afford to waste any more time. It's cold down there. Let's see the vicar and ask to borrow his keys. Is he likely to be at the vicarage?'

'Unless he's gone out somewhere after his meeting,' Kathleen said.

'In which case we'll call him,' Sybbie said.

The vicarage turned out to be a small modern house rather than the rambling Victorian pile Georgina had expected. To her relief, Craig was there. He looked nonplussed at the sight of three middle-aged women standing on his doorstep.

'Why would you want to borrow my keys to the church?' Craig asked. 'Walter has his own set.'

'Walter is missing,' Kathleen said.

Craig frowned. 'But why do you need my keys?'

'Because we think he's in the crypt,' Sybbie said.

'The church doesn't have a crypt,' Craig said.

'Yes, it does,' Kathleen said.

'What do you mean? Why don't I know about it?' The vicar's lower lip stuck out petulantly.

'Reverend Phillipson, we think Walter might be ill and need our help – rather urgently,' Georgina put in gently. 'Can we perhaps argue about this later?'

'Oh – oh, yes,' Craig said, looking awkward.

Even though Georgina had pointed out the urgency, Craig didn't seem to hurry. But at last they were in the church, standing in front of the medieval door to the crypt.

'Walter told me this was a storage cupboard that wasn't used because it's damp,' Craig said.

'It's a storage *area* that isn't used because it's damp,' Kathleen said. 'Please, Reverend Phillipson, could you just give me the keys so I can open the door?' As a former high school teacher, Kathleen was obviously used to dealing with recalcitrant and awkward teenagers, but it looked to Georgina as if Kathleen was on the cusp of losing her patience with the vicar entirely and yelling at him.

Looking slightly nettled, Craig handed over the bunch of keys. 'Who would have locked him in a cupboard?'

Kathleen didn't answer, concentrating on slotting the ancient iron key into the lock.

'We have no idea,' Sybbie said, clearly trying to engage him so he didn't annoy Kathleen any further.

The lock turned stiffly, but thankfully it turned and Kathleen twisted the ring handle.

'Oh, my word! There really *is* a crypt,' Craig said when Kathleen pulled the door open. 'I had no idea! There are stairs going down.'

His face became suddenly animated, and Georgina wondered whether he'd read the Narnia books as a child and had always hoped to find a secret way behind a door. This must seem like a dream come true to him; whereas in reality she had a nasty feeling it was going to be more of a nightmare.

'The stairs are uneven, and they're slippery because it's damp and they're stone,' Kathleen said. 'Please be very, very careful. And the roof's quite low, so mind your head.'

The vicar gave her an obstinate look.

Kathleen turned away. 'Walter! Are you down there?' she called. 'Are you all right?'

There was no answer.

She took out her phone and opened the torch app. 'There's no light down there, either,' she said to Craig. 'And no handrail on the stairs, so watch your footing. This is why Walter keeps the door locked – the last thing we need is someone deciding to explore, falling down the steps, hurting themselves and suing the church for damages.'

'Right,' Craig said.

Gingerly, the four of them made their way down the uneven, slippery steps, pressing a hand for balance against the wall. At the bottom of the steps, Kathleen shone the light from her phone around the crypt, and they saw a body at the far end, crumpled up next to the wall, with a torch and a metal tape measure on the floor next to him as if he'd dropped them when he fell.

'Walter!' Kathleen said, hurrying over to him. She knelt down and checked his pulse. 'He's still alive, but his pulse is thready and his breathing's shallow,' she said, her first-aider training clearly kicking in. 'Oh, my poor Walter.' She stroked his hair, then gave a sharp intake of breath. 'My hand feels sticky – oh, it's blood! But he *knows* the roof is low. How could he have hit his head? And hard enough to draw blood?'

'Reverend Phillipson, can you please call nine-nine-nine?' Georgina asked, shrugging off her coat. 'Kathleen, we'd better not move Walter, but he'll be cold from lying down here. Put my coat over him.'

'And mine,' Sybbie said, removing her coat.

'And mine,' Craig said gallantly, shrugging off his own coat. He took his phone from his pocket and hit the emergency call. 'Oh. There's no signal. I can't call them.'

'There's a signal upstairs,' Georgina said, as gently as she could.

'I'd better go upstairs, then,' Craig said, and started to straighten up.

Just as Kathleen warned, 'Mind your head,' they all heard him say, 'Ow!'

Craig rubbed his head. 'That beam's quite hard. I'm going upstairs to call an ambulance, now.'

It could be that Walter had had an angina attack, banged his head on the low roof, and fell forward. But apart from the fact that Walter was rather shorter than the vicar, Georgina had a nasty feeling about this. 'Before you put the coats on him, Kathleen, I want to take a couple of photos. Just so the police can see where Walter fell and how he was lying.'

'In case he dies, you mean?' Kathleen asked, her voice shaking.

'No. In case it helps them work out what happened to him – on the chance he didn't fall because he was ill,' Georgina said.

'You think someone did this to him? But who? And why?' Kathleen asked.

'It's just a funny feeling I have,' Georgina said. 'I think it comes from knowing Colin and hearing about his job. I don't take anything at face value, anymore.'

Kathleen stood aside and let Georgina take a couple of snaps, then piled the four coats on top of Walter. 'He's a grumpy, stubborn old man,' she said. 'But he's *my* grumpy, stubborn old man. He's a good man and he's been my rock for all these years. I'm not ready to lose him yet. Don't you dare die on me, Walter Reeves,' she said fiercely to the unconscious man. She sat down next to him, holding his hand and stroking his hair. 'And he hasn't got his hearing aids in. He hates them. I bet he took them out almost as soon as he left the house.'

'How deaf is he?' Georgina asked.

'As the proverbial post,' Kathleen said. 'If he's not wearing his hearing aids, I have to raise my voice almost to a shout.'

So if Walter had been concentrating on examining the wall, he wouldn't have heard anyone come down the stairs, creep up behind him and hit him over the head, Georgina thought.

'That's the third ambulance we've called to the church, this week,' Kathleen said. 'The second one today. Maybe, if this treasure actually exists, there's some kind of curse on it.'

'Pure coincidence,' Sybbie said briskly. 'But someone obviously didn't want Walter to look too closely at the crypt.' She paused. 'I would have said maybe Dominic McGowan, but he's in hospital himself. The podcast guy, perhaps?'

'And was whoever attacked Walter the same person who poisoned Colin and Dominic?' Georgina asked.

'I don't know. All I know is that I don't want Walter to die,' Kathleen said. 'I'd better get his hearing aids out of his pocket – that's where he always puts them when he's not wearing them. They nearly ended up going through the washing machine, last month,' she added ruefully, 'except I learned long ago to check his pockets.' She checked the first pocket. 'They must be in the other one,' she said. 'Ah, yes, here they are.' Then she frowned. 'That's odd. His keys weren't in either of his pockets.'

'They must be, if he locked himself in,' Sybbie said.

'Let me check in case they fell on the floor,' Georgina said, shining her phone light around. 'No. No sign of them. There's his torch, a measuring tape – oh, here's Bram's drawing, and a pen. But no keys.'

'Walter's always careful with his keys. And his wallet and specs: years ago, he used to be terrible about mislaying them in the house, but eventually I'd had enough of all the wasted time and the muttering. I bought him a little basket to put his keys, wallet and specs in so he'd know exactly where they were. It stopped him getting grumpy about not being able to find wherever he'd put them, and he's been meticulous about using it ever since,' Kathleen said.

It was starting to look more likely that someone *had* attacked Walter, Georgina thought, and taken his keys. But who? And why?

At last, the ambulance arrived. The paramedics strapped a spinal support around Walter's head and took him up the stairs on a stretcher. Craig made a point of asking Kathleen for his keys and locked the crypt door ostentatiously.

'Don't even think of going back in that crypt on your own,' Sybbie warned. 'Wait for one of us to go with you, or ask Bernard.'

'I'm thirty-nine years old, not a child,' Craig said huffily.

The three women exchanged a glance; and Georgina was the only one who could hear Doris voice their shared thought. 'But he acts like one.'

'Walter went down there on his own, and look what happened to him,' Kathleen said.

'I hit my head on the roof. Maybe Walter did the same, only a bit harder,' Craig said.

'Or maybe someone hit him over the head, left him there, and locked the door behind him,' Sybbie said, a sharp note in her voice.

'Or maybe he locked himself in, seeing as he was keeping the crypt secret.' The sulkiness in Craig's tone was more apparent.

'It's a bit hard to lock yourself in if your keys go missing,' Kathleen retorted.

This was starting to get out of hand, Georgina thought. She needed to change the subject before tempers really frayed and things were said that couldn't be retracted. 'Kathleen, go with the ambulance. I'll follow you in the car,' she said. 'And then I can give you a lift home, once Walter's settled.'

'I can't put you out like that,' Kathleen said.

'You're not putting me out at all. I'm going to the hospital anyway to see how Colin is,' Georgina said, 'before I ring his family.'

'And I'm coming, too,' Sybbie said, 'for support.'


Once Kathleen had left in the ambulance with Walter, Sybbie looked at Craig. 'I think we need a little chat,' she said. She gestured to the pews. 'Rather appropriate here to say, "take a pew", I think.'

Craig's eyes widened in seeming annoyance, but he sat down in one of the pews, and Sybbie gestured to Georgina to join her in the pew in front of Craig.

'We haven't been introduced properly yet,' Sybbie said. 'Sybbie Walters. I believe you know Bernard, my husband. Lord Wyatt,' she added, holding her hand out to shake his.

Sybbie was the last person to insist on using her title, Georgina thought, but she clearly had the measure of the new vicar and how he'd respond. She obviously thought he would be more prepared to listen to Lady Wyatt than to middle-aged gardener Sybbie.

'Oh, er, Lady Wyatt,' Craig said, and his cheeks turned pink.

'Now, dear boy, I know you're new and you've barely had time to settle in properly yet,' Sybbie said. 'What's happened at St Edmund's over the last week has been dreadful – that poor young man keeling over and dying, Dominic McGowan bullying Kathleen at Morning Service, DI Bradshaw being poisoned, Dominic being poisoned, and now Walter being hit over the head and left in the locked and very cold crypt, which is not exactly good for an elderly man with a dicky ticker.'

Craig winced. 'Er, yes,' he mumbled.

'And I'm sure,' Sybbie said, 'you're bright enough not to tell your parishioners what to do, but instead look at how you can work *with* the parish.'

He said nothing, but gave a nod of acknowledgement.

'Kathleen Reeves gets the flower arrangers to work in harmony instead of bickering. She welcomes people with tea and coffee and a listening ear after services, and she brings cakes and cookies she's baked out of kindness and at her own expense to make people feel brighter,' Sybbie added. 'I'm sure you've enjoyed her cakes yourself.'

'Indeed.' This time, there were two nods, a bit more enthusiastic.

Then Sybbie got to the point. 'It might be nice if you stood up for her when people are bullying her.'

'If you mean Dominic McGowan, he was distraught and needed the comfort of the church,' Craig blustered.

'Dominic McGowan practically told you he was an atheist, so do you really think he would be looking to the church for comfort?' Sybbie asked.

Craig winced again, clearly taking her point.

'He *bullied* Kathleen – who we all know wouldn't hurt a fly and who tried to save his partner, not kill him,' Sybbie said. 'And there's Walter. Yes, he can be a bit crusty. He's over seventy. Men of his generation are like that. But he's looked after this building for years, he sorts the accounts and he's done a lot to keep the finances of the benefice on an even keel. I think he deserves a little respect rather than being grumbled about, don't you?'

Craig's cheeks turned even pinker. 'I... Yes.'

'You're going to be without two real pillars of your church for the foreseeable future,' Sybbie said. 'It might be helpful if you can think about taking some of the strain off them. Find some more volunteers to help cover what they usually do until Kathleen and Walter are able to come back to the church. But don't make the pair of them feel as if you've replaced them and don't want them anymore. Make it clear it's *temporary* help and you value them. And perhaps taking them some spring flowers cut from your garden would be nice. Nothing flashy. Just some daffodils or some tulips.'

Craig flinched. 'I see.'

'I hope you do, dear boy,' Sybbie said. 'This is a lovely place to live. You've had a difficult week in the church, but on the whole people in Little Wenborough get on together. They support each other. And I rather think that's something to be encouraged.'

'I quite agree, your ladyship,' Craig said.

'Good,' Sybbie said. 'Oh, and give my best to your uncle Charlie when you next see him. I gather he's been missing Cocoa since he lost her, so you might let him know that Peanut – that's Max's mother,' she added for Georgina's benefit, 'is due to have her final litter next month. I can put in a word with the breeder, should he be interested in reserving a chocolate Lab pup.'

'You know my uncle Charlie?' Craig almost squeaked.

'I know rather a lot of people, dear boy,' Sybbie said with a smile. 'Now. Remember what I said, and for pity's sake don't go into that wretched crypt on your own. Walter has a very sound reason for not making it open to the public. If someone slips on those stairs, the church will be liable for damages – which could be substantial, and there are more important things to spend that money on around here.'

'Yes, your ladyship,' Craig said.

Sybbie patted his arm. 'Good man. Georgie and I will head for the hospital now. I assume Kathleen has your number?'

'Yes.'

'Good. We'll call you to let you know how Walter's doing,' she said.

Georgina didn't say a word until they'd left the church and were in the car.

'Remind me never to get on your wrong side,' she said.

'Dear girl, you could never be on my wrong side,' Sybbie said with a grin.

'And you really know the bishop?'

'I've met a lot of bishops over the years. Charlie isn't our bishop, by the way – he's a couple of bishoprics away from Norfolk, actually,' Sybbie said. 'But we bonded over our respective chocolate Labradors at a very dull party, some years back.'

'I think Reverend Phillipson is going to be too scared of you to go into that crypt on his own,' Georgina said.

'Scared, indeed.' Sybbie chuckled. 'I'm a pussycat.'

'Hmm,' Georgina said, but she patted her friend's arm affectionately. And then she frowned. 'It's Thursday. I'd better call Jodie and let her know I can't do Pilates tonight.'

'I'll do it while you drive – and I'll let Cesca know, too,' Sybbie said. 'Because I'm staying with you.'

'Thank you,' Georgina said.

'Does she know Colin's in hospital?' Sybbie asked.

'Not yet,' Georgina said. 'The day's just whizzed by, and I didn't even think about Pilates until just now.'

'Leave it with me,' Sybbie said, and fished her phone from her bag. 'Jodie? It's Sybbie. I'm with Georgie and we're on our way to the hospital. No, she's fine, don't worry. But – look, I know I can trust you to keep this to yourself. Colin's been poisoned, and Walter's been bashed over the head and left in the crypt. We're not going to make Pilates, though I'm fairly sure Cesca will and she'll pick you up. I'll get her to ring you if anything's different. Yes, all right, I'll tell them. Speak soon.'

She called Francesca next and Georgina heard a similar conversation.

'Right. That's all settled. They both send their love and say to let them know if you need anything. Jodie says not to even think of doing the barn tomorrow because she can do it herself and she'll tell Mike to call in one of the others to do her shift. And Cesca says to tell Colin there's a lemon drizzle cake with his name on when he comes out of hospital.'

Colin's favourite. Though it might not be anymore, after what had just happened to him. 'It was lemon drizzle cake that poisoned him,' Georgina said wryly.

'Ah. Cesca might have to develop a new cake especially for him, then,' Sybbie said with a shudder.

'That crypt was grim,' Doris said. 'Poor Walter.'

Georgina remembered how Doris had died: hitting her head after falling down the stairs at Rookery Farm. Or, rather, after being pushed. 'I'm sorry, Doris,' she said. 'If I'd known that Walter was lying there with a gash on his head, I would never have asked you to look in the crypt.'

'You couldn't do it, without the key, and you had to be sure before you asked the vicar for his keys. I was the only one who could check the crypt,' Doris said. 'Is he going to be all right?'

'I hope so,' Georgina said. 'Are you coming to hospital with us?'

'No,' Doris said. 'But I wanted to let you know that Martha remembered something. That last trip she took – she'd just left her house and was on the way to see John Barton, the sexton, at his cottage on the other side of the village. But she's also convinced that she saw him just before her horse reared and threw her off.'

'Oh, no,' Georgina said, and repeated Doris's words to Sybbie.

'So Martha saw him near her house, where she didn't expect to see him. Does that mean she thinks that the sexton frightened the horse deliberately?' Sybbie asked.

'I'm not sure,' Doris said.

'John Barton is definitely a person of interest when it comes to Bram's death,' Sybbie said. 'He was the one Bram talked to about the tunnel's existence. And he was the one Bram asked to accompany him to the crypt to check that damp patch – the one he sketched in orange juice.'

'Which reminds me,' Georgina said, 'I picked up that printout Walter did of Bram's sketch. He'd written something on it. It's in my handbag, if you want to fish it out.'

Sybbie did so. 'It looks as if he was checking Bram's measurements. And that's interesting. Walter records the length of the crypt as being slightly shorter than Bram did.'

'It could be a mismeasurement,' Georgina said.

'I very much doubt it on Walter's part. Plus, the width is identical,' Sybbie said. 'Hmm. If the length of the crypt is shorter than Bram said it was, does that mean there's slightly more plaster on that wall now than there was when Bram measured it?'

'Which, in turn, would suggest that someone might have opened the entrance to the tunnel, then closed it again and added a bit more plaster to cover up the opening,' Georgina said.

'It's a definite possibility,' Sybbie said. She paused. 'Was that someone John Barton?'

'But didn't Walter say he stayed on here as sexton for another twenty years? Surely he wouldn't have done that if he'd just uncovered huge riches?' Georgina asked.

'Maybe he had trouble liquidating the treasure,' Sybbie said. 'He would have known that if he'd offered to sell it to the wrong person, he would have been hauled up before the magistrates.'

'Why did Martha want to talk to him? Was it simply because she knew Bram had discussed the treasure with him? Or did she think he was the one who killed Bram?' Georgina asked.

'We need to do more digging,' Sybbie said. 'Though quite where, I don't know. And I can't think of what else Doris could ask Martha.' She sighed. 'We're a bit stuck, Georgie.'

'Colin's investigation is stuck, too,' Georgina said. 'Not helped by the fact he's one of the victims, now.'

'Is it the same person behind everything, though?' Sybbie asked. 'We need to find someone with a motivation to kill Liam Jacobs, to poison both Colin and Dominic McGowan, and to whack Walter over the back of the head and abandon him while he was unconscious – worse, too, to try and cover it up by taking Walter's keys and locking the crypt door.' She paused. 'That's a point. Doris, did you happen to see who went into the crypt?'

'No,' Doris said. 'I left the church when Colin started talking to Dominic McGowan. I didn't come back until you did.'

Georgina relayed the information to Sybbie.

'I guess it would have been too easy if Doris had been able to solve it for us,' Sybbie said with a sigh.

'Let's look at our potential perpetrators,' Georgina suggested. 'According to Dominic, whoever killed Liam is either Aaron with the aid of Kathleen, or Kathleen on behalf of Aaron. Colin is investigating the case, so Aaron and Kathleen would both also have the motive to want to stop him; and, if Dominic's right about the identity of the murderer, they would both have the motivation to shut him up, too.' She paused. 'But then there's Walter, and that's where it falls apart.'

'Even if we say that Kathleen went temporarily insane while trying to fix things for her nephew and killed Liam, and then poisoned Colin and Dominic – which I don't believe in any case,' Sybbie said, 'as you say, then there's Walter. Kathleen adores him. They've been married for fifty years. Even though there are times when I could cheerfully throttle Bernard – and I'm sure you felt that way about Stephen, too, and Colin – I'd never actually hurt him. Kathleen wouldn't try to kill Walter, either.'

'I don't know her as well as you do, but I agree. That still leaves Aaron,' Georgina said. 'He wanted to do the glass restoration here, so that's his motive for getting Liam out of the way. There's a motive for stopping Colin investigating and shutting Dominic up. But if Aaron was close to his aunt, he'd know that she'd be devastated if anything happened to Walter. He wouldn't want to hurt her. So that puts a question mark against him.'

'What about the podcast guy?' Doris suggested.

'Good point, Doris,' Georgina said. 'There's the podcast guy. Russell Dawson.'

'He's all about the legend of the priory and the treasure. I can't see his motive for killing Liam,' Sybbie said.

'But Colin said he was arguing with Dominic,' Georgina said.

'And he had a run-in with Walter. If he's behind Dominic being poisoned, either he wanted to stop Colin investigating too closely, or Colin was just collateral damage and the poisoned cake was really intended only for Dominic. Bashing Walter – well, if he was after the treasure and followed him into the crypt, he would have wanted to stop Walter finding it first.'

'That's plausible. And then there's Dominic,' Georgina said. 'As for his possible motive for killing Liam: let's go sideways, here. Supposing it had nothing to do with the glass? I met Liam and he was lovely. I can't imagine his life partner being someone as unpleasant as Dominic McGowan. Supposing Liam had decided to split up with Dominic, and Dominic couldn't stand being rejected and killed him? And then Dominic was so vociferous about blaming Kathleen and her nephew as a way of trying to hide his own guilt. We know from Doris that he was searching the church, so he was presumably after the treasure, and that's why he attacked Walter – because he didn't want Walter to find it first. He poisoned Colin to stop the investigation, and then he poisoned himself to make it look as if he was the victim – a kind of double bluff. Actually,' Georgina added, 'it's just occurred to me. Dominic offered the cake to Colin. He didn't know he'd see Colin that day. What if he'd actually planned to give the cake to Walter, rather than bashing him over the head?'

'And Colin was collateral damage? That all fits,' Sybbie said.

'So let's look at means. Anyone could have put coconut oil in Kathleen's banana bread. She would have left it on the counter in the church hall kitchen. All anyone had to do was get the oil into the cake. Inject it in places, perhaps?'

'Which assumes the killer knew about Liam's allergy. That's a no for Kathleen, a question mark for Russell, and a yes for Aaron and Dominic,' Georgina said.

'The killer would also need access to arsenic, for poisoning Colin and Dominic. That's another question mark for Russell, a yes for Kathleen and Aaron, and a yes for Dominic because he would have had access through Liam,' Sybbie said.

'The killer would also need to have known about the crypt – and that Walter doesn't wear his hearing aids when he's concentrating. Well, that or they moved quietly,' Georgina said. 'To be fair, even with my hearing aids in, I wouldn't necessarily hear someone walking behind me.'

'Kathleen knew about the crypt. If Kathleen and Walter had discussed it with Aaron, he would have known – that's a question mark, really. If Russell and Dominic had investigated the right archive material – which I think is likely – they would have known about it,' Sybbie said. 'And they would have had to be in the church to watch for Walter opening the crypt.'

'Colin said that Russell Dawson left the church while he was starting to talk to Dominic,' Georgina said. 'How likely is it that Russell Dawson hid somewhere in the churchyard and just waited for Walter to go into the crypt?'

'Not very,' Sybbie admitted. 'Excluding you, me and Colin, the only person who knew that Walter was going into the crypt – and roughly what time, too – was Kathleen.'

'It worries me a bit that Kathleen seems to have a lot of ticks against her,' Georgina said.

'I've known her for years. I can't see her as a cold-blooded killer. In fact, I really can't see her as any kind of killer,' Sybbie said.

'She was Jodie's form teacher, and Jodie really liked her. You know Jodie would have said if there was anything not quite right about her,' Georgina pointed out.

'So we're back to Aaron, Russell and Dominic. Who all have possible motives, means and opportunities. In other words, we're stuck,' Sybbie said with a sigh.

SEVENTEEN

Colin was awake, and looking marginally brighter when Georgina and Sybbie arrived to visit him. 'I'll recover, but I'm going to be stuck here for a few days while they do the chelation therapy,' he said.

'So you're going to be bored and grumpy. I thought as much, so I have something for you.' Sybbie produced the puzzle book she'd bought in the hospital shop, and a pen.

'Thank you. And I hope I have more success in doing these than I'm having at puzzling out my current case,' he said. 'I'd love to know who had it in for me. Arsenic. That's nasty.'

'There are some nasty people about,' Sybbie said sanguinely, 'who might want to poison you.'

'Hmm,' Colin said.

'Jodie and Cesca send their love,' Georgina said.

'Cesca did mention making something for you,' Sybbie said, 'but, given why you're in here, that might not be such a treat.'

'It wasn't anywhere near as good as Cesca's lemon cake,' Colin said. 'Though I admit, the idea of lemon cake – even Cesca's – isn't very appealing right now.'

'I was thinking,' Georgina said. 'Now we've got a better idea of how you're doing and your treatment, I really need to let your family know what's happened to you. Would you mind if I ring your sister and Marianne? And I can tell them they can get in touch with you so they can hear you for themselves if they need more reassurance.'

'Given that I've called Bea and Will in the past to let them know that you've been poisoned, I can hardly object to you doing the same for me,' Colin said ruefully. 'Though I can do it, because you're busy.'

'You're in a hospital bed, and Georgie can't do anything to make you better. It might be kind to let Georgie feel that she's doing something useful,' Sybbie pointed out.

'There was a bit of an edge to your voice there, Lady Wyatt,' Colin said.

'A necessary one,' Sybbie said.

'I think we should make Sybbie the leader of the entire world,' Georgina said. 'There might be a lot more common sense and kindness in the world if she sorted everyone out.'

Sybbie smiled. 'I'm taking that as a compliment.'

'If you're both at a loose end, you can always solve my case for me,' Colin said.

'I know you're teasing,' Sybbie said, 'but actually, Georgie and I discussed it on the way in. We have theories.'

'You have a captive audience,' he said dryly, gesturing to his hospital bed and the drip in his arm.

'We went through motivations, means and opportunity,' Sybbie said.

'But first, you're missing two developments,' Georgina said. 'You were right about Dominic being poisoned – Kathleen found him in the church hall and called an ambulance. And then Walter went missing. We think someone hit him over the head, and they left him unconscious on the crypt floor and locked the door with his own set of keys. He's being treated in hospital right now.'

'If you hadn't found him in time, that could have become murder rather than actual bodily harm.' Colin paused. 'I assume you knew about the crypt from something that's not admissible in court.'

'Stop pussyfooting around the subject – and you can also stop being so narrow-minded,' Sybbie said. 'Our Doris is a good woman, I'll have you know.'

'I know, even though it's hard to get my head round,' Colin said. 'All right. Tell me your theories.'

'We have four suspects. Aaron Flint, Kathleen Reeves, Dominic McGowan and Russell Dawson,' Georgina said. 'We also have four victims: Liam Jacobs, you, Dominic McGowan and Walter Reeves. But none of the suspects has a motive to want all the victims either dead or indisposed.' She talked him through the theories she and Sybbie had discussed in the car.

'So either the killer wanted me to stop investigating, or they didn't mean to kill me with the arsenic and I was collateral damage?' Colin said when she'd finished. 'Hmm.'

'I honestly don't think Kathleen's involved,' Sybbie said. 'Georgie and I think Dominic is the most likely perpetrator. Supposing Liam had tried to break up with him, and Dominic was angry at being rejected. Then he would have a motive for all four murders and attempted murders.'

'Including the attempt on his own life?' Colin pointed out. 'If someone knew how to get hold of arsenic and also knew how it works and what it does to the victim, why would they take it themselves?'

'As a double bluff,' Georgina said. 'And they'd know to give themselves just enough to make them ill, not a fatal dose.'

'What if they misjudged the dose and took too much?' Colin asked.

'You pays your money and you takes your choice,' Sybbie quipped. 'And that's not *Huckleberry Finn*, by the way. It's an older edition of *Punch*.'

'Trust *you* to know that,' Colin said, but he was smiling. 'Have you told Larissa your theories?'

'She did tell us not to investigate,' Georgina said. 'Though I promise we have no intention of interfering in your case.'

'Good, because then I'd have to arrest you,' Colin said.

'You can *try*, dear boy,' Sybbie said, chuckling.

'Seriously. Tell Larissa what you're thinking,' Colin said. 'Have you got any further on in the cold case?'

'Walter didn't get a chance to look at the crypt properly before he was hit on the head,' Georgina said. 'Though he did check Bram's measurements. There's a discrepancy. And we have a theory about that, too.'

'I think,' Colin said, clearly trying hard to stifle a yawn, 'my arsenic-befuddled brain isn't really going to take any of this in.'

'We'll talk to Larissa,' Georgina promised. 'And we'll let you rest, now. We need to see how Walter's doing. I'll ring your family and Larissa, and I'll come back and let you know what's happening.'

'You,' Colin said, 'are the best thing that's ever happened to me, Georgina Drake. I hope you know that.'

'If you're being that sentimental, you're definitely still under the weather,' Georgina said, but the compliment made her feel all warm and gooey inside. 'And I need the phone numbers for your sister and Marianne.' She paused, remembering that Colin had a strained relationship with his parents. But in their shoes she'd want to know. 'Shall I ring your parents?'

'Maybe it's better to let Caroline deal with them,' Colin said. 'The numbers are in my phone.'

Georgina took it from his bedside table and handed it to him; he unlocked the phone, went into his contacts file and sent two numbers to her.

'I'll go and sort some coffee,' Sybbie said, 'while you make your phone calls. I'll be in the hospital café when you're ready.'


Calling Colin's sister to introduce herself and tell her that Colin was in hospital was a strange experience. But once Georgina had reassured her that Colin was going to make a full recovery, Caroline Bradshaw was warm and friendly, and promised to come down to Norfolk to visit her brother while he was convalescing.

Marianne, Colin's ex, was also friendly, once she was over the initial worry of Georgina's news and had asked a dozen questions about what had happened and who could have poisoned Colin and why. 'I'm so pleased to finally speak to you. You've made a huge difference to Colin,' she said. 'He's more relaxed and happier than he's been for a very long time. And he's become closer to Cathy, too.'

'Don't speak too soon. I think he's going to be grumpy and absolutely impossible, by the end of his hospital stay,' Georgina admitted, and Marianne laughed.

'Won't he just? I don't envy you trying to contain him if they say he has to be on bed rest.' She paused. 'He's a dreadful patient. Did you know he was shot in the line of duty, a couple of times?'

'No, I didn't,' Georgina said. She knew his job could be dangerous, but this news brought it shockingly home to her just how perilous it could be. And why hadn't Colin told her himself? She'd noticed a couple of scars, but when she'd asked him about them, he'd brushed them off as 'scratches'. She'd assumed that he wasn't comfortable talking about whatever had happened and hadn't pushed him, not wanting to bring up bad memories for him.

'That was what I hated most about his job. The fact he had to take risks,' Marianne said. 'And as for the case that broke him...'

'I know about that one,' Georgina said quietly. And she was glad to realise he hadn't kept *everything* from her.

'He's talked to you about it?' Marianne sounded surprised.

'It came up in connection with a case he had here,' Georgina explained.

'I'm glad – that he told you, I mean, not that he had a case that brought it all back. That's a really good sign,' Marianne said. 'I know Cathy's looking forward to meeting you, when you and Colin are ready. And you'd have a very warm welcome here if you're ever this way.'

'Likewise, if you and Cathy ever come to Norfolk,' Georgina said. 'Though I should warn you that I have a rather lively spaniel.'

'Bert. We've seen the photos. Cathy loves dogs,' Marianne said. 'So do I.'

'When Colin's out of hospital,' Georgina said, 'then maybe you'd all like to come for Sunday lunch and see him? Your partner, too?'

'I'd love that,' Marianne said. 'And I really appreciate you calling, Georgina. You could have left it to Caroline to contact us.'

'No, I couldn't. You needed to ask questions,' Georgina said. 'And in your shoes I would have wanted you to call me so I could ask things. It's fine.'

'Colin's told us quite a bit about you. And I hope,' Marianne said, 'we'll become friends.'

'I hope so, too,' Georgina said, heartened.

'May I give Cathy your number? She might want to text you about her dad,' Marianne said.

'Of course,' Georgina said. 'Better still, make us a WhatsApp group and I can send some photos to reassure you.'

'That would be wonderful,' Marianne said. 'Thank you. I will.'

'Everything all right?' Sybbie asked when Georgina joined her in the café.

'Yes. I liked Colin's sister – she's very practical and no-nonsense. She reminds me of you. And Marianne was lovely.'

'Good,' Sybbie said, and squeezed her hand. 'It's a shame it's taken something so drastic to get you in contact with each other.'

'I know. But it's going to be all right, now,' Georgina said.

When they'd finished their coffee, they went in search of Walter. They discovered that he'd regained consciousness and had been admitted to a ward with concussion. Given his angina, the hospital wanted to keep a close eye on him. When they went to the ward, he was asleep.

Kathleen's face had lost that pinched look, but she still had a worried expression.

'This is my nephew, Aaron,' she said, gesturing to a thin, sad-faced young man with dark shadows under his eyes. 'Aaron, these are my friends, Sybbie and Georgina.'

'Pleased to meet you,' Aaron said politely. But Georgina noticed how his knee was jiggling, and he was fiddling with his fingers. Was he simply upset that his uncle had been hurt? Was the hospital setting bringing back painful memories of his mother's last illness and he was trying to suppress them while supporting his aunt? Or was there something more to it?

She glanced at Sybbie, who gave the smallest of nods to let Georgina know that she'd noticed, too.

They needed to have a quiet word with Aaron, but not in front of Kathleen and Walter. And maybe only one of them should tackle him, so he didn't feel completely intimidated.

'Kathleen, have you eaten anything?' Georgina asked.

Kathleen shook her head. 'I couldn't.'

'I know you're worried sick, but you need to eat to keep your strength up. You can't support Walter if you're ill, too,' Georgina said. 'Aaron, will you come with me to the café and help me find something to tempt your aunt? And you, of course. Plus I could do with a hand bringing four coffees back to the ward.'

'I...' Aaron gave a helpless shrug. 'All right.'

'I'll stay here and keep Kathleen company,' Sybbie said.

'Good idea,' Georgina said, smiling.

She waited until they were in the corridor. 'I'm sorry for dragging you out with me, but you looked a bit overwhelmed, and I know if my son was in your shoes, I'd want someone to rescue him. You must be worried sick about your aunt and uncle.'

'I am,' Aaron admitted.

'Kathleen told me about your mum. I'm sorry. It's so tough when you lose someone so young.'

'Aunty Kath's been so good to me,' Aaron said.

And then he cracked.

'It's my fault that Uncle Walter got hurt,' Aaron said.

Georgina bit back the question, knowing it would be easier if she kept this open and let him tell her in his own words rather than being interrogated. 'Tell you what – let's get some coffee and have a chat at a quiet table in the café. I know I'm a stranger to you, but I'm a friend of your aunt's, and it's obvious to me that you don't want to worry her and it's hard to know who to talk to. Why don't you tell me about it, instead?' she suggested quietly.

Aaron nodded, and allowed her to buy him cake and a mug of coffee.

They sat in silence for a little while; Georgina didn't want to pressure him and make him bolt. He crumbled a corner of the cake, and then looked at her.

'It's because of Liam,' he said miserably. 'I knew Aunty Kath was going to make her banana bread to welcome him to St Edmund's, and I knew he was allergic to coconut. I thought maybe if I put some coconut oil onto the cake, it would make him ill enough not to be able to work on the glass, and I'd be called in to do it instead. It – it didn't occur to me that he'd *die*,' Aaron said, looking haunted. 'I thought he'd just have a stomach ache, the runs or an itchy rash. So I bought a jar of coconut oil, took it with me to Aunty Kath's and brushed it over the top of the banana cake when I did the washing up. I didn't use very much. It sank in straight away, so the cake didn't look any different. You couldn't smell it, either. I threw the rest of the jar of oil away when I got back to Norwich.' He dragged in a breath. 'I've felt terrible about it.'

But not terrible enough to admit to what he did sooner, Georgina thought. She knew Colin had talked to him and hadn't found any coconut oil in his house, but Colin had also sensed that something was off. Now she knew exactly what.

And it was tragic. She'd liked the young stained-glass restorer. How awful that Aaron had deliberately spiked the cake to make him ill, with something that had actually killed him. Yet, at the same time, she could see that Aaron's mental health was really shaky; had he been in his right mind, she was sure he wouldn't have taken that risk with his colleague's life. This wasn't a simple case of right and wrong, black and white.

'Go on,' she encouraged.

'Dominic guessed it was me. Of course he did.' Aaron's eyes were filled with anguish. 'But I never thought he'd go on at Aunty Kath the way he did. Or that he'd bash Uncle Walter over the head and leave him to die in the church, in revenge for Liam dying. So it's all my fault. If I hadn't tried to make Liam ill, Dominic wouldn't have tried to kill my uncle.'

'How do you know Dominic was the one who hit Walter over the head?' Sybbie asked.

'It's the sort of thing he'd do. He doesn't like people getting in his way,' Aaron said. 'I heard Liam talking to someone at the studio, saying that Dominic doesn't like to be crossed. He can be quite ruthless.' He paused. 'And Liam sometimes had bruises on his arms. He said he was clumsy and he'd walked into a door, but I don't think that was true.'

This was starting to get a bit more tangled than Georgina had expected. Was Dominic McGowan also guilty of domestic violence, if his partner did something that he didn't like? It also increased her suspicions about Dominic's behaviour in the church. Had he perhaps planned to poison Walter before the 4 p.m. service, but Colin had got in his way? And then Walter, thinking that the church was empty, had gone into the crypt and Dominic had crept down the stairs, hit him over the head, taken his keys and locked him in?

'I know you've already talked to Colin Bradshaw,' Georgina said quietly. 'He's my partner. And I promise you he's a fair man. He's in hospital at the moment, but I think you need to talk to his team. I've known them for a couple of years and they're lovely.'

'They'll lock me up and throw away the key,' Aaron said miserably.

'I'm not a legal expert, so I can't tell you what will happen. But I do think you'd be wise to talk to Mo and Larissa, Colin's colleagues,' Georgina said, keeping her tone gentle. 'They'll help you.'

'I can't,' Aaron said, panic flickering over his expression.

'The longer you leave it, the worse you'll feel,' Georgina said. And the worse it would be for him, though she judged it sensible not to pressure him that way.

'I...' Anxiety shone out of Aaron's face. 'I didn't mean to...'

He might not have meant to kill Liam, but by the sound of it, that was exactly what he'd done. For someone with a severe allergy, it only took a tiny amount of the allergen to cause a huge reaction, and an adrenalin injection could be the only thing to save them. 'Did you know Liam had an EpiPen?' Georgina asked.

'Yes. He kept one in his desk at the studio. Though he didn't always have it with him. One of the times when he had bruises on his arms, he was meant to go out on a job, but he didn't have his pen on him. He had to go back to his house to pick it up, and Bridget – she's the secretary at the studio – had to ring the client and make up an excuse,' Liam said.

Had Liam forgotten it, or had Dominic used the pen as a way of controlling him? Georgina wondered. 'It might be useful if you told that to Larissa and Mo, too,' she said.

'I...' He blew out a breath. 'I don't know how to tell Aunty Kath what I did. She's going to hate me.'

'She loves you,' Georgina said. 'You're precious to her. Right now, you're in a muddle, and I think she'll be on your side.'

'Even though it's my fault Uncle Walter's in hospital now?'

'You weren't the one who hit him over the head and left him on a cold stone floor,' Georgina reminded him. 'Let's get her a sandwich and some coffee, and then I can talk to Larissa and ask her to help you.'

'It's been a nightmare,' Aaron whispered. 'I haven't slept since Liam died. I thought Dominic would go after me. I never thought he'd go after...'

'I know, love,' Georgina said, suddenly aware of how young and how vulnerable Aaron was. He'd lost his mum at a difficult age, felt abandoned by his dad, and this had all got too much for him. 'It'll work out.'

They collected some sandwiches for Kathleen and some coffee.

'Do you mind staying with Kathleen and Aaron while I have a quick word with Larissa?' Georgina asked Sybbie.

Her friend clearly guessed that Aaron had opened up to her, because she smiled. 'Of course. I know you'll have to go and find a signal, with your phone playing up. I'll look after Aaron and Kathleen.'

Georgina went further down the corridor and called Larissa, who was fortunately still at the station. 'Colin's fine, before you start worrying,' she said. 'But there have been a couple of other developments since I spoke to you. We found Walter – he was in the crypt, and someone bashed him over the head and left him unconscious on the floor. Whoever did it also took his keys, and locked him in. He's in hospital right now, too.'

'Do you have thoughts on who did it?' Larissa asked.

'At the moment, either the podcast guy or Dominic McGowan, though my gut feeling is that it's Dominic,' Georgina said. 'Hear me out.' She took Larissa through the theories she and Sybbie had run past Colin.

'It's plausible,' Larissa said. 'A bit mad – I mean, why would you poison *yourself*? But there's logic behind that. Russell Dawson is here in custody and we're keeping him for further questioning. We'll have another chat to Mr McGowan. I assume he's still at the hospital?'

'I haven't actually thought to check,' Georgina said, feeling guilty. 'Because something else has happened. Kathleen's nephew has confessed to putting the coconut oil on the cake – the one that killed Liam Jacobs.' She told Larissa what Aaron had told her. 'I don't think he had anything to do with the missing EpiPen. I think that was purely an accident and Liam left it in his desk at the studio – obviously you'd need to look into that for yourself. Though Aaron also suggested that Liam's home life was a bit difficult, so it might be worth checking again with Dominic McGowan.'

'Well, I wasn't expecting *that*,' Larissa said. 'Do you know where he is now?'

'At the hospital – with his aunt Kathleen, Sybbie, and me,' Georgina said.

'Can you keep him there until Mo and I get there?' Larissa asked.

'Of course,' Georgina said, and told her the name of the ward. 'I'll find out where Dominic McGowan is and let you know about that, too.'

'Thank you, Georgie,' Larissa said. 'Tell his aunt he can have a duty solicitor with him or he can have his own solicitor, so if she wants to call someone, it'll save a bit of time.'

'I will,' Georgina promised.


Walter was still sleeping while Larissa and Mo read Aaron his rights, arrested him and took him in for questioning. Larissa also arranged to question Dominic McGowan in his hospital bed. Kathleen absolutely refused to leave Walter's side, so Sybbie arranged to call her neighbour and ask her to feed Kathleen's tabby cat, Boo.

'I'm still here?' Walter croaked, waking groggily as Georgina and Sybbie were about to leave.

'Yes, and Kathleen's staying with you,' Georgina said.

'What happened?' Walter asked.

'We think someone whacked you over the head. If you'd been wearing your hearing aids like you're supposed to,' Kathleen said, 'then you might have heard them.'

'They might have hit me over the head anyway,' Walter said. 'What about the treasure?'

'That can wait until you're better,' Sybbie said. 'You need to be there when we check out the crypt properly.'

'No, it can't wait,' Walter said.

'It'll have to,' Georgina said, 'because whoever walloped you also took your keys and locked you in the crypt. We had to borrow the vicar's keys to find you, and he locked the door again when the paramedics got you out.'

'Even more reason why you should borrow the keys again,' Walter argued. 'Otherwise whoever hurt me could let themselves into the church in the middle of the night, knock down the wall in the crypt and take whatever's behind it – and we'll never know what it was.'

'The person we think did it definitely won't be able to do that tonight,' Georgina said. Dominic McGowan would be either in hospital or at the police station.

Unless their theories were wrong and it really was Russell Dawson, and Larissa hadn't been able to hold him any longer...

'Go and borrow the keys,' Walter said. 'And make sure the vicar doesn't shoot his mouth off. Bram's measurements are off when it comes to that wall, so I think someone replastered it and there's something behind that wall. Take a pickaxe.'

'What about the faculty?' Sybbie asked.

'Whoever hit me isn't going to wait for the church's permission to knock a hole in the wall,' Walter said grimly. 'Besides, if you're coming down the last couple of stairs and you just so happen to slip, while holding a pickaxe, and you thrust the pickaxe at the far wall to help you get your balance... Well, I'd say that's an accident.'

'Now I know you definitely have concussion,' Kathleen said, 'because you always do everything by the book.'

'And maybe it's time I didn't,' Walter said. 'Don't the pair of you go on your own. Take Bernard. And that's not because I think women are feeble,' he added, 'because you're not. It's because whoever attacked me is probably physically stronger than you and I don't want you to be hurt.'

EIGHTEEN

Sybbie called Bernard on the way back to Little Wenborough, and he agreed to meet them at the church.

'Another deputation?' Craig asked.

'We came to let you know that Walter has concussion and they're keeping him in overnight, just to be on the safe side because of his angina. Lying on a damp stone floor in low temperatures won't have been helpful,' Sybbie said.

'Oh! Well, thank you. I had been worrying about him,' Craig said. 'And Kathleen?'

'She's staying with him,' Georgina said.

'Good, good,' Craig said vaguely.

'While we're here,' Sybbie said, 'perhaps we could borrow your keys again?'

Craig's eyes narrowed. 'What's this about?'

'Something that belongs to the church,' Sybbie said, 'and we need to keep it strictly confidential for now.'

'I can keep confidences,' Craig said.

Sybbie and Georgina exchanged a glance that said they weren't so sure.

'We really do need to keep this to ourselves,' Georgina said.

'You're going into the crypt again, aren't you?' he asked. Before Sybbie could protest, he added, 'You did tell me not to go there on my own. I can't possibly let you go on your own.'

'Hoist with our own petards,' Georgina murmured.

'Don't start Shakespearing me,' Sybbie murmured back.

'No, I can't possibly let you go on your own,' Craig repeated, completely ignoring the exchange in front of him. 'It's about the—' He paused. 'The T-word.'

'If this is his idea of keeping things confidential, you're toast,' Doris said in Georgina's ear.

Georgina rolled her eyes in acknowledgement.

Craig made a big show of locking up the vicarage, then shepherded Georgina and Sybbie over to the church, to discover Bernard waiting for them in the porch.

'Oh! Lord Wyatt,' Craig said. 'I didn't expect to see you here.'

'Reverend Phillipson,' Bernard said with a smile. 'Joining us in our confidential endeavours, are you?'

'Er – yes,' Craig said. 'It *is* my church.'

'It's Little Wenborough's church,' Sybbie said crisply.

The church, to everyone's relief, was empty.

'I think we should lock the doors,' Bernard said. 'I know Walter usually leaves the church open until nine, but as Walter's in hospital right now, I think we should take the precaution.'

'I suppose so,' Craig said, sounding reluctant, but he locked the door.

Bernard had brought three strong torches with him, and a bag of tools.

'As the vicar, I think I should go down first,' Craig said. 'Opening this door – it's like Narnia,' he added, and Georgina had to suppress a smile. Just as she'd guessed, Craig had reverted back to being a schoolboy.

By night, the crypt was pitch black. Even the narrow slit window didn't admit any light. But the torches gave the illumination they needed.

'According to Bram's map, the entrance of the tunnel is on this wall,' Bernard said, shining the light on the wall next to where they'd found Walter. 'And according to Walter's measurements, Bram's are slightly out. It looks to me as if someone's put an extra layer of plaster on here. It might have been to cover up the damp patch I can see coming through, so it could have been done at any time.'

'Or it might be the tunnel that leads to the old priory!' Craig said enthusiastically.

'The priory doesn't actually exist anymore,' Bernard reminded him. 'But yes.' He swept his fingertips over the wall. 'And this section that Bram marked on his drawing – it definitely feels damp. I think he might have found the tunnel's entrance.'

'Then we should open it,' Craig said.

Bernard winced. 'Strictly speaking, we can't do this without permission. We need a faculty.'

'It's easier to ask forgiveness than it is to ask permission,' Craig said. 'And my uncle's a bishop. He'll smooth it over.'

'How can you be so sure?' Sybbie asked.

'Because he always does,' Craig said blithely.

Which explained a lot, Georgina thought. Walter had said he thought Craig's mother was the bishop's favourite sister and had asked him to help. He hadn't been far off the mark.

'I feel bad that we're doing this without Walter and Kathleen,' she said. 'After all, Bram was Kathleen's great-great-great-uncle, and Walter was the one who worked out where Bram had left the clues.'

'Walter told us to do it now, before whoever hit him over the head gets the chance to knock down the wall and take whatever's behind it,' Sybbie reminded her.

'It might have been the podcast guy,' Craig said. 'I hear he's been taken in for questioning. He wanted to find the treasure, didn't he?'

'Let's just get on with it,' Bernard said dryly. He drew a chisel and a mallet from his bag.

'Oh! You came prepared,' Craig said. 'I was going to suggest using my penknife.'

'I think there are bricks behind the plaster,' Bernard said. 'Any mortar in this damp patch will have crumbled, so it'll be easy to take out.' He spread a couple of thick bin bags on the floor to protect it. 'Let's go.'

The plaster came away quickly, revealing the bricks. As Bernard had predicted, the mortar between them was loose and came out easily. Between them, he and Craig soon dismantled the brickwork, revealing a hole behind it.

'Well, that explains the damp patch,' Bernard said. 'Water seeping through the earth and into the wall.'

'A tunnel,' Craig said, his voice filled with excitement. 'So the story was true, after all!'

'It doesn't necessarily mean that the treasure was hidden there,' Bernard warned.

'But what if it really was hidden?' Craig asked.

'Nearly five hundred years ago? There's a good chance that someone found it decades ago, even centuries, and took it,' Sybbie said.

'Georgie, can you document this on your phone, so we have dated evidence?' Bernard asked.

'Of course,' she said. 'Though I think you two need to be out of the shot.' She photographed the hole in the wall.

Bernard shone his torch into the hole. 'Oh. That's not good.'

'What?' Sybbie asked.

'There's a skeleton,' Bernard said heavily.

Craig shone one of the torches into the hole. 'It looks as if its neck is broken, poor thing. But there are other things there in front of it.' He reached into the hole, and Bernard said, 'Wait. We need to document this.'

'Oh. Yes,' Craig said, his cheeks pinkening.

Georgina stepped up to the hole and took photographs. 'I wasn't expecting that,' she said, passing the phone to Sybbie so she could see it.

'A skeleton, an envelope, and something that looks as if it's wrapped in a cloth. The treasure?' Sybbie asked. 'But if someone bricked up what I hope was a dead body behind the wall, surely they would have taken the treasure?'

'There's only one way to find out,' Craig said, and reached into the hole to take out the envelope and the bundle. He laid them carefully on the floor so Georgina could photograph them.

'Unwrap it, and let's see,' Bernard said.

Carefully, Craig unwrapped the bundle. 'Oh. A book.'

'To me, that's treasure,' Sybbie said.

Craig opened it. 'Ah. It's written in Latin,' he said. 'I *think*.' He looked slightly shamefaced. 'I know vicars are supposed to know Latin, but I mean, you can't be good at everything.'

Georgina caught herself wondering what exactly Craig Phillipson was good at, and mentally chastised herself for being mean.

'May I see?' Sybbie asked.

'I'm not sure it *is* Latin. It might be in code,' Craig said. 'It's very hard to read.' But he duly handed over the book.

'It's Latin,' Sybbie confirmed. 'This is what's called secretary hand, Craig. And I agree, it's very hard to read unless someone's taught you. But I think what you've found is the diary of Gulielmus Nashe.' At Craig's blank look, she said, 'William Nashe. He was the vicar here back when Elizabeth I was on the throne. Bram Locke – Kathleen's great-great-great-uncle, and the vicar here in Victorian times – read this diary, and he thought it was proof that the legend of the treasure was true.'

'The last prior of Little Wenborough Priory was a man called Robert Fysshe,' Georgina continued. 'During his final illness, he was treated by an apothecary who happened to be William Nashe's grandfather. Fysshe told the apothecary that he'd had warning of the commissioners coming to seize the priory's belongings, so he hid some of the treasure. The apothecary told his grandson, who wrote everything down.'

'But Fysshe didn't say where the entrance to the tunnel was in the church. Nashe worked out that it must have been the charnel house – this room,' Sybbie said. 'And Bram agreed. He'd talked to the sexton about it, and they planned to try and find the entrance. Bram was worried that someone might get wind of what he was doing, so he wrote it down in his diary in invisible ink – in orange juice, just like the Gunpowder Plotters did.'

'Good heavens!' Craig said.

'But Bram died from typhoid before he could unblock the tunnel,' Georgina said. 'Except his sister thought it was all a bit fishy.'

'Do you think Bram is the skeleton behind the wall?' Craig asked.

'No. His doctor – who was also his brother-in-law and his best friend – certified the death,' Sybbie said. 'But that's as far as we've got in unravelling the mystery.'

'Poor man,' Craig said.

'He planned to sell the treasure and use the money to fix the church roof, and then to build a hospital for the village,' Georgina said.

'Poor man,' Craig said again. 'And the poor soul behind the wall. Perhaps the treasure *was* cursed. You know, like Tutankhamun's treasure, and everyone involved in opening the tomb died.'

'What's in the envelope?' Bernard asked.

'I think you should open it, your ladyship,' Craig said.

'We'll do it together,' Sybbie said, glancing at Georgina.

Carefully, they opened the envelope. Sybbie withdrew the single sheet of paper and unfolded it. 'It's signed by John Barton,' she said. 'Dated 15 March 1871.'

'Two days after Bram died,' Georgina said. She blew out a breath. 'I've got a nasty feeling about this.'

'So have I,' Sybbie said.

'Me, too,' Doris agreed.

'You read it, Georgie,' Sybbie said.

Georgina stared at the cramped script.

*May God forgive me for what I have done.*

*I did not love my son, Jesse Barton. He was always lazy and sly, more like his uncle than myself and his dear mother. He grew worse after she died when he was fifteen. He drank and gambled away whatever money he had and lost job after job because his employer could not rely on him.*

*Then he fell in love with Betsy. Betsy's mother was my dear friend Bram's housekeeper, and Betsy herself was the housemaid. I feared at first that Jesse might have compromised her, but he asked her mother's permission to marry her. I thought maybe love had changed him.*

*Alas, I was wrong. I had no idea that the blackness in his soul would corrupt Betsy, too.*

*Until today, when I came to open up the church as usual. Even though Bram had died from typhoid, the church had to be open for the parishioners in need. I saw the crypt door was open. I made my way down the stairs and found my son Jesse at the bottom, his neck at a strange angle and a spade lying some distance away from him. The candle he took to light his way had thankfully extinguished on the damp stone floor. But Jesse was dead. I wondered what he had been doing there – surely he could not have been searching for the treasure? Bram had kept it secret, and I was his only confidant. Perhaps he had seen a light in the church at a time no light should have been there, and went to investigate, taking the spade as a weapon in case somebody was up to no* good. Clearly he had slipped on the stairs and fallen to his death.

When I went to tell poor Betsy that she had been widowed, she broke down and confessed the plot to me. Jesse had overheard Bram talking to me about the legend of the prior's tunnel, his belief that he had found the end of the tunnel at St Edmund's and that the treasure was behind the wall of the charnel house. Jesse formulated a plan to find the treasure himself and sell it, so he could live a life of luxury without having to work for the money. He told Betsy they had to get rid of Bram before he found the tunnel. And he told Betsy to put poison in the cake she made for Bram.

My poor friend wrote to me when he was dying, warning me to keep away because he had caught typhoid – his symptoms were the same as those of Victoria Stebbings and her grandsons. Yet all along he had been poisoned, by his housemaid at the urging of my son.

Jesse had planned to break the wall down and take the treasure. When he did not come home that night, Betsy thought maybe Jesse had double-crossed her and had left her to take any blame. She panicked, not knowing what to do.

When I told her he was dead, she panicked that she would be blamed for his death as well as Bram's.

I was horrified. How could my son and my daughter-in-law murder such a good man?

I knew I should tell the constable and the magistrate. But then I thought some more. Everybody, myself and the doctor included, believed Bram had died from typhoid. If they knew the truth, my family name would be stained for ever. And Betsy also told me that she was pregnant. She would be kept in jail until the baby had been born, and then she would be hanged. I would be left to look after the babe.

But I had failed with his father. Without my wife to guide me, I would fail my grandchild as badly. And what if the baby had inherited the same blackness of soul as its father?

I said to her I would bury Jesse's body in secret. We would tell everyone he had gone to America to seek his fortune, and that he would send for Betsy when he was settled. I would pay for Betsy's passage to America in a month's time. She and her unborn child could make a new life there, where nobody knew her.

I plan to leave Jesse's body here in the tunnel that caused all the trouble in the first place, brick up the entrance and hide it behind fresh plaster so nobody will know it was there.

My punishment is to live with the knowledge that I can never atone for my son's sins. I have lost my only child, and I will never see my grandchild. And I know I will burn in hell alongside my son, when I die. Until then, I will try to live as godly a life as I can.

I leave this here as a record of events, should anybody find the body in years to come.

May God forgive me for what I have done.

John Barton, sexton of St Edmund's Church, Little Wenborough

'What a sad, sad story,' Bernard said. 'That's tragic. Bram

wanted the treasure to build a hospital, but Jesse Barton wanted it out of greed – so he killed Bram.'

'I should say a prayer,' Craig said, and did so.

'Now we know why John Barton remained as sexton until he could no longer lift a shovel,' Sybbie said. 'Trying to atone for his son's crime. I wonder if Betsy made it to America?'

'We can look in the records. Maybe Kirsty or Bea can help us,' Georgina said. 'I don't think we'll ever get to the bottom of Martha's accident, though. John would never have told her his secret. But I also don't think he would have wanted to add her murder to the guilt he was already carrying.'

'What about the treasure?' Craig asked. 'Did anyone find it? How far does that tunnel go back?'

'He has a point,' Bernard said. 'We still don't know who smashed Walter over the head and took his keys. If the treasure really is here, I'd prefer we found it and used it for good, the way Bram Locke planned, rather than someone who's clearly out for themselves finding it and taking it.'

'I agree,' Georgina said.

'We need to take Jesse Barton's remains out of the tunnel, before we start scrambling about in there,' Sybbie said. 'Bernard, do you have a sheet or something in your bag?'

'A towel,' Bernard said. 'Will that do?'

Sybbie nodded. She and Georgina spread the towel on the floor, and between them Bernard and Craig took Jesse's skeleton from behind the walls and laid them gently on the towel. Grimly, Georgina photographed the bones.

'Which of us is going in, then?' Craig asked.

'Whoever goes in needs to take photographs to document what they find,' Georgina said.

'I'm happy to do that,' Craig said.

The others exchanged a glance. Clearly the vicar was very, very keen to have his adventure. And who were they to spoil it?

'Go on, then,' Sybbie said. 'Talk us through what you can see, and take photos.'

'Rightio,' Craig said, and climbed into the hole. 'It's very dark in here. It smells damp.'

'Torch,' Bernard said, and leaned into the hole, holding out one of the torches.

'That's better. It's – well, all I can see is earth. Roots of some plants. It doesn't go back very far,' Craig said. 'I think the tunnel's blocked.'

'Colin found some smugglers' tunnels when he was investigating a case, last year,' Georgina said. 'He said they smelled dank, like a church crypt. And they were blocked in places.'

'How exciting,' Craig said. 'Oh! I think I've found something.'

'Be careful,' Bernard said.

'Yes, yes,' Craig said, and his voice had the exact tone of an eye-rolling teenager saying 'Yeah, yeah' to a parent spoiling their fun.

'Photos first,' Georgina reminded him.

'Got it,' he said, and fired off some snaps. 'It looks like a bundle of cloth. Ooh, but it's heavy. I'll bring it out and unwrap it with you,' he said.

'It *is* heavy,' Bernard said, sounding surprised, when he took the bundle from Craig.

The vicar hopped nimbly out of the hole.

'That cloth looks very much as if it's been nibbled by rodents,' Sybbie said.

Bernard set the bundle on the ground, and together he and Craig unwrapped it while Sybbie train her torch on the contents and Georgina took photographs on her phone.

The material fell apart under their fingers, and then they all saw a flash of gold.

'I think I know how Howard Carter felt when he broke through to Tutankhamun's tomb,' Craig said. He removed the last fold of material to reveal an ornate gold cross. 'Well. The legend was true, after all.'

'The prior's hidden treasure,' Georgina said, and took a final photo. 'I think we need to call the police. We've messed up the scene quite a bit with our DNA, but if there's any evidence of either Dominic McGowan's or Russell Dawson's DNA in the crypt – because we know they haven't been in here with permission – that might contribute to the evidence of who assaulted Walter and left him here.' She gave a wry smile. 'Between us, we might have solved Colin's case as well as most of the cold case.'

'And when I tell Martha what you found,' Doris added, 'she'll be upset, but she'll also be able to rest because we know now what happened to her brother.'

# NINETEEN

'You found *treasure*? Oh, my God. Colin will be spitting tacks that he's stuck in a hospital bed and missed this,' Larissa said when Georgina rang her to fill her in on the latest developments. 'Actually, I'm a bit upset that *I* missed it.'

'We couldn't risk waiting, in case whoever hurt Walter came back to knock the wall down,' Georgina said. 'I'm sorry, we've rather messed up the crime scene for Walter's assault, but we'll all give you DNA samples so your team can exclude us. And if you find DNA from Dominic McGowan or Russell Dawson in the crypt, you'll know who committed the assault, because neither of them has ever been in the crypt. The only people who have keys are the vicar and Walter, and the vicar didn't know about the crypt until this evening, so he couldn't possibly have opened it to let anyone down there.'

'Thank you, Georgie,' Larissa said. 'I'll need to speak to Dominic McGowan's doctors and ask them to assess him for fitness to be interviewed, to make sure there isn't a potential miscarriage of justice. But I'll send someone out to the church to check for prints and forensic evidence.'

'We'll wait here for them. Warn them the crypt's dark and there's no electricity down there, plus the stairs are damp and slippery,' Georgina said. 'We've also found a skeleton. There was a letter with it that supports what we know from contemporary sources, so I'm pretty sure it's from 1871 so it'll count as historical remains rather than of bones interest to the police, but you probably need to get Rowena Langham' – the county's finds liaison officer, who had worked with Colin before when Bert had found bones, and had become friends with Georgina – 'to come and take a look. Bernard and Sybbie Walters are going to keep the cross in their safe for tonight, because their security is a bit better than that of the vicarage.'

'Got you,' Larissa said. 'I'll stay in touch.'

Georgina made them all a mug of tea in the church hall kitchen while they waited for the forensics team to come and check the cellar.

But it was Colin rather than Larissa who rang her, later that evening.

'I can't believe I missed the finding of the treasure,' he said.

'You're not well enough for Sybbie and me to have sprung you from hospital,' Georgina said lightly.

'Hmm. And you solved my case into the bargain,' he said. 'Larissa and Mo questioned Dominic this evening. They casually mentioned that they were picking up forensic evidence from the crypt and expected to know before midnight exactly who whacked Walter over the head. And that was when he broke down and admitted it was him. Liam had arsenic back at their house, for glassmaking purposes. Dominic took some and sprinkled it on the cake – only a little bit, he said, and he intended to give it to Walter. The aim was to make him keel over and be sick rather than die, so Dominic could get the keys and check out the crypt. He'd worked out where it was from studying the inside of the church and looking at really old church guides in the archives.'

'So why did he give *you* the cake instead?' Georgina asked.

'Because I was asking questions. It made him nervous and he wanted to shut me up. Obviously it worked. He came back from his walk and the crypt door was open, so he went down, saw

Walter, and knocked him out. He didn't plan to kill him, just stop him getting to the treasure,' Colin said. 'Then he realised he wouldn't have time to open up the tunnel before someone came into the church and realised something was going on. So he took Walter's keys, locked the crypt, and hid the keys in the church. He realised several people had seen him in the church and he'd be a suspect for bashing Walter, so he panicked and thought if he ate some of the poisoned cake, he'd be ill and it would shift suspicion from him – and hopefully onto Russell Dawson.'

'So he ate the cake, and that's why Kathleen found him in a pool of vomit. He could've choked on his own vomit and died,' Georgina said. 'And part of me thinks that would be his just deserts. Walter could have died in the crypt.'

'He realises that now. And I think he also realises how serious the charges against him are going to be,' Colin said.

'Rowena Langham is coming to Little Wenborough tomorrow,' Georgina said. 'She's going to take a look at the cross at Sybbie's, then come to the church to confirm whether the skeleton we found is classed as bones of antiquity. Though I think she's most excited about getting the chance to handle a sixteenth-century diary – it's the one Walter couldn't find in the vicarage archives. Thankfully John the sexton had wrapped it up in oilcloth, so it wasn't damaged by the damp.'

'So you found out what happened to Bram.'

'Mostly.' She talked him through John Barton's letter. 'Sybbie and I are going to have a look at the records tomorrow and see if we can trace what happened to Betsy Barton and her baby. We might ask Kirsty and Bea to help.'

'Good idea,' Colin said. 'What's going to happen to the cross?'

'The church will decide, but I think Craig's uncle will go in to bat and persuade the head honchos to let St Edmund's sell it and use the money to fix the church roof and open up the crypt to the public,' Georgina said. 'Craig's keen to have a replica of the cross made and the story told in the church to encourage visitors. He rather enjoyed his Narnia moment.'

'Hmm,' Colin said. 'What next? Appearing on Russell Dawson's podcast?'

'He'll probably want to do a follow-up piece. Larissa said when she interviewed him, he's not bothered about financial gain. What interested him was the puzzle, and the actual finding of the treasure.'

'I can understand that,' Colin said. 'It's kind of what you, Sybbie and the gang do – find the evidence and tell the story. Giving closure. It's been a privilege helping you, from time to time.'

'It's a privilege to find out the truth,' Georgina said. 'Anyway, you're supposed to be resting.'

He groaned. 'I hate resting.'

'Marianne says you're a dreadful patient.'

'You're going to gang up with her, aren't you?' Colin asked.

'And Larissa and Mo,' Georgina said. 'And your sister.'

'I think,' Colin said, 'I might just give in gracefully...'

# TWENTY

## THREE WEEKS LATER

'It's been quite a month,' Colin said, sitting in Georgina's back garden with a glass of sparkling elderflower on the table in front of him, Bert at his feet, and birdsong filling the air. 'And I'm very glad to be out of hospital.' He grimaced. 'Though I've got weekly check-ups for the foreseeable, in case any complications develop from the arsenic poisoning.'

'Better to check and find it early, so it can be treated,' Georgina said.

'I guess. And at least I'm allowed back to work next week. Though I think Larissa is going to be bossy with me.'

Georgina chuckled. 'Good. That's what you need.'

'It was nice of you to invite Caroline, Marianne, Cathy and Ed' – Marianne's new partner – 'over for Easter Sunday,' he said.

'It was about time we met,' she said. 'They needed to see you for themselves, too.' Though Colin had baulked at inviting his parents, saying he wasn't quite ready for that. 'And I liked them all.'

'They liked you, too. And your kids. And Bert. And the rest of the gang.'

What started as a small family lunch had extended into after-noon tea, and Francesca had outdone herself on the cake front as the Walters family contribution with carrot cake, chocolate cake and sticky toffee cake – though in deference to Colin's brush with arsenic she hadn't brought his favourite. It was too soon for him to face lemon drizzle cake again.

Georgina had thoroughly enjoyed having a houseful. Doris and Harrison had turned up, too, though Georgina was the only one who knew they were there.

'I can't believe how quickly everything wrapped up, once Aaron and Dominic confessed,' Colin said. Aaron was to be indicted for murder, and Dominic on two counts of attempted murder and actual bodily harm. The mystery of the missing EpiPen was solved as simply as Aaron had suggested: it was found in Liam's desk at the studio.

'And the cold case,' Georgina said. Rowena had confirmed that the skeleton from the crypt belonged to a man in his mid-twenties, and the body had obviously been moved not long after his death as well as the skeleton being brought out from the tunnel by Bernard and Craig. The small traces of fabric around the bones had all fitted the profile of Victorian textiles.

With a little help from Kirsty, the archives revealed that Betsy had boarded a sailing packet in Liverpool, bound for New York, a month after Jesse Barton's alleged crossing to America; but she'd died on the ship, together with the baby, and John Barton's family faded from history after his death.

Kirsty wrote up the story of the orange juice diary for the archives blog; and the glass studio persuaded Kathleen to come and work with them on the restoration of the roundels. Craig and Walter – recovered from his ordeal – starred together on Russell Dawson's updated podcast about the treasure. Craig's uncle smoothed over the issue of not having a faculty when they'd dismantled part of the wall in the crypt, and helped with the decision to declare the cross treasure trove. The money raised by a local museum was enough to pay for fixing the roof and the damp patch in the crypt, and Craig was organising a wooden gilded replica of the cross and a display case to tell the story of the prior's treasure.

'It's worked out very well,' Colin agreed. 'Though there is just one more thing.'

'What's that?'

'I had a chat with Bea and Will at the weekend,' he said. 'So this isn't going to be quite out of the blue.'

'What isn't?' Georgina said, having no clue was he was rambling about.

'That arsenic poisoning was a little too close for comfort. It made me realise that we really never know how much time we have. *Carpe diem*,' he said.

And then he truly shocked her by standing up, and dropping on one knee in front of her. 'I wanted to propose to you using a Shakespeare quote, and I spent hours looking up something suitable, but I didn't want you to feel I'm trying to take Stephen's place. Besides, none of the declarations I looked up felt quite right to me. So I'm just going to do it plainly and simply. I love you, Georgina Drake. Will you do me the honour of marrying me?'

Georgina stared at him. 'You're asking me to marry you.'

'To be my equal partner. I want to support you the way you support me. I want to be a full part of your family, and I want you to be a full part of mine. I love you,' he said.

She looked into his grey eyes and saw the sincerity as well as the love.

And he had a point.

They didn't know how much time they would have.

They *should* seize the day.

'I love you, too,' she said. 'Yes.'

# A LETTER FROM THE AUTHOR

Huge thanks for reading *The Body at St Edmund's*; I hope you enjoyed Georgina, Doris and Colin's journey. If you want to join other readers in hearing all about my new releases and bonus content, you can sign up for my newsletter.

www.stormpublishing.co/kate-hardy

If you enjoyed this book and could spare a few moments to leave a review, that would be hugely appreciated. Even a short review can make all the difference in encouraging a reader to discover my books for the first time. Thank you so much!

This series was hugely influenced by three things. Firstly, I grew up in a haunted house in a small market town in Norfolk, so I've always been drawn to slightly spooky stories. (I did research it when I wrote a book on researching house history, but I couldn't find any documentary evidence for the tale of the jealous miller who murdered his wife. However, I also don't have explanations for various spooky things that happened at the house – including the anecdote about Sybbie's dogs in *The Body at Rookery Barn*, which happened in real life with our Labradors and a tennis ball.) Secondly, I read Daphne du Maurier's short story 'The Blue Lenses' while I was a student, and... I can't explain this properly without giving spoilers, so I'll say it's to do with how you see people. Thirdly, I'm deaf; after I had my first hearing aid fitted, once I'd got over the thrill of hearing birdsong for the first time in years, my author brain started ticking. The du Maurier story gave me a 'what if' moment: what if you heard something through your hearing aids that wasn't what you were supposed to hear? (The obvious one would be someone's thoughts; but that's where my childhood home came in.) It took a few years for the idea to come to the top of my head and refuse to go away, but what if you could hear what my heroine Georgina ends up hearing?

And so Georgina Drake ends up living in a haunted house in a small market town in Norfolk...

In Norfolk, we have nearly a thousand medieval churches. It's an absolute joy to visit these quiet spaces and see the stained-glass windows, wood carvings (whether they're bench ends or angel roofs) and ancient brasses. I borrowed various items for Little Wenborough from churches not far from me: the centaur roundel and the Angel Gabriel from St Peter's church at Ringland, the St Edmund roundel from St Mary the Virgin's church at Saxlingham Nethergate, and the ironwork on the door from St Edmund's church at Taverham.

There are also various legends in Norfolk about the Dissolution and treasure hidden by priories in tunnels, so I couldn't resist making one up for Little Wenborough. The crypt owes a little to St Bartholomew's church in Brisley, whose crypt was used in the nineteenth century as a place for condemned prisoners to spend the night on the way from King's Lynn to Norwich. As for the orange juice 'invisible ink' – that really was used by the Jesuit priest Henry Garnett, who was involved in the Gunpowder Plot, and his letters are in the National Archives at Kew. (Kirsty is a product of my imagination, though!)

Little Wenborough isn't a real place, but the name is a mashup of Attleborough, the market town where I grew up, and the River Wensum, which flows through my village and curves round the city of Norwich. Several of the places I mention are real, and I'd definitely recommend a visit to both Blickling Hall and Foxley Wood for the bluebells. Norfolk is an amazing place to live. Huge skies (with incredible sunrises and sunsets), wide beaches (aka my best place to think, and the Editpawial Assistants are always up for a trip to Wells-next-the-Sea), and more ancient churches than anywhere else in the country.

Thanks again for being part of this amazing journey with me and I hope you'll stay in touch – I have so many more stories and ideas to entertain you with!

All best,

Kate Hardy

http://www.katehardy.com

 instagram.com/katehardyauthor

 facebook.com/authorkatehardy

 x.com/katehardyauthor

# ACKNOWLEDGMENTS

I'd like to thank Oliver Rhodes and Kathryn Taussig for taking a chance on my slightly unusual take on a crime series; Emily Gowers for being an absolute dream of an editor – incisive, thoughtful and a wonderful collaborator as well as being great fun; and Shirley Khan and Catherine Lenderi for picking up the bits I missed! I've loved every second of working on this book with you.

Gerard, as always, has been a particular star with location research on this book.

Special thanks to my family and friends who cheer-led the first Georgina Drake book, made useful suggestions about cake for this one, and are there through the highs and lows of publishing. You know who you are, and I appreciate you all.

Extra-special thanks to Phil Gell for talking me through how the PCCs and lay volunteer systems work; to Gerard, Chris and Chloë Brooks, who've always been my greatest supporters; to Chrissy and Rich Camp, for always believing in me and being the best uncle and aunt ever; and to Archie and Dexter, my beloved Editpawial Assistants, for keeping my feet warm, reminding me when it's time for walkies and lunch, and putting up with me photographing them to keep my social media ticking over while I'm on deadline.

And, last but very much not least, thank *you*, dear reader, for choosing my book. I hope you enjoy reading it as much as I enjoyed writing it.